# The Dropouts

By

Gary Sprague

# The Dropouts

1

I joined my first band when I was fifteen, about a month after getting my first guitar. It was a birthday gift from my dad, who grew up listening to the Beatles and the Stones and hoped his son might grow up to be the next George Harrison, without all the weird Hare Krishna hippie shit. I quickly found I had a knack for playing guitar and after a couple of lessons from an older kid down the street who taught me the basic chords and riffs to "Smoke on the Water" and "Strutter", I was ready to rock.

The band was called the Dropouts. Maybe you've heard of us. If you're from Maine you almost certainly have – in Vacationland, we're bigger than Moxie and whoopie pies. Besides yours truly, Jesse Maze, on guitar, there was Phil Cabana on drums, Cameron Nelson on bass, and Danny Crane on vocals. The four of us had a lot in common – during our freshman year at Apple Brook High School we spent much of our free time playing Dungeons & Dragons, making us the sort of social outcasts that were more likely to be ignored than picked on. Most importantly, and no doubt related to the number of weekend hours we spent playing D&D, we were all virgins.

None of us could play instruments, at least not well. Maybe that's not entirely true - Danny was the top alto in the freshman chorus. But it didn't take long for us to improve. A dedication to learn and to score with hot chicks burned like a California wildfire through our pubescent veins, and by the end of the summer we had a set list of four songs we could play reasonably well and two others that we sort of made up as we went along.

Our first gig was on Labor Day Weekend, just before the start of our sophomore year, when Kenny King asked us to play at his sixteenth birthday party. We jammed on our four tunes, took a break to scarf down some birthday cake, and then played them again. I felt up Tracy Landry later that night behind Kenny's shed, a first for me (though not for Tracy). The other guys also got some action, making our first gig a rousing success. It was clear that our destiny had been forged. On the way home from Kenny's that evening, the Dropouts promised to stick together for the rest of our career, all for one and one for all. We quickly decided on a democratic system of songwriting and decision making, much like the Beatles.

The Beatles were together for eight years. The Dropouts didn't last quite that long – five years – and our musical and cultural impact was considerably less than that of the Fab Four. But for four kids from Apple Brook, Maine, we didn't do too bad. By the time we broke up, we'd released two albums and three singles that made the Top 40 of the Billboard charts, including one which rose all the way to number 12 in 1986.

Yes, a band of four kids from Maine – we were still teenagers at the time – made it to the Billboard Top 20. Not the toppermost of the poppermost, but pretty damn close. The song was "Your Love Line", written by me and Danny in the basement of his parents' house while the other guys played ColecoVision upstairs. I had a cool riff that I'd been playing around with, Danny came up with some lyrics about a palm reader he'd gone to see one drunken night in Old Orchard Beach, and two hours later the song was written. It's funny. Lately I find myself forgetting why I walked into a room, yet I can vividly remember most details of writing songs from thirty years ago.

The Dropouts peaked with "Your Love Line", and the experience turned out to be the worst thing that happened to us. As it so often does, success bred greed and jealousy between longtime friends, festering like a disease that quickly infected and proved fatal to the band. We were being hailed as "Maine's Greatest Rock N Roll Band", and while not exactly a massive accomplishment in the annals of rock and roll, it was something to be proud of. The Dropouts were the biggest and the best to ever come from our area. Who knows how big we might have become.

After the band broke up, I became a sort of gypsy, travelling up and down the east coast as a guitarist for hire. I've been in too many bands to remember and played in gin- and sweat-soaked dives that even the rats stay clear of, but it beats working. My life and career were headed nowhere when, unexpectedly, "Your Love Line" returned from the dead. The song's revival came out of nowhere and didn't have quite the cultural impact as, say, the resurrection of Jesus, but it certainly changed my life for the better.

By now you've probably heard "Your Love Line". About three years ago, it was played on the CW on an episode of one of those popular teenage angst shows staring unrealistically good-looking actors. That was followed shortly afterward by the song's inclusion on the soundtrack of a Ryan Gosling movie, and from there it suddenly rose from the ashes of the rock and roll graveyard and back onto the charts, clawing its way all the way up to number 4. The Dropouts had a Top 10 hit, thirty years after it was first recorded and released. And next year, you'll hear "Your Love Line" in the newest Marvel movie-slash-CGI fest.

I don't know how or why it happened. Sometimes a long-ago hit song will chart again following the death of the artist. Prince is an example of this – two of his hits from the 1980s revisited the Top 10 following his passing in 2016. But no member of the Dropouts died. Our situation was similar to what happened in the 1980s, when older hits like "Stand By Me" and "Do You Love Me" re-entered the Top 10 after appearing on the soundtrack of a hit movie. Who knows why this happens. Probably, a young fan who liked the song as a kid grew up and got into the movie business. Or maybe the kid of some Hollywood executive stumbled upon the song on YouTube and liked it. Doesn't really matter. What does matter is that, out of nowhere, I'm suddenly loaded. Not Paul McCartney loaded, but wealthy enough to qualify as a well-to-do gentleman. The checks keep coming in, each one bigger than the last. I know this faucet won't run forever, but this time around I've been smart enough to see a financial advisor and make some investments.

Right now, I'm living in a Miami beachside condo with my girlfriend, Kendra. I'm already tired of Miami. The city was great when I first came here – everything happy and shiny and bright, from the ocean to the cars and buildings and perfect-looking people. But, like the old saying goes, you can't judge a book by its cover. Most of the people here are so fake and greedy and soulless that I sometimes wonder where they hide the horns and tails. The sunshine is wonderful if viewed from an air-conditioned area, but ten minutes out in the heat and humidity will wear you down until it feels like you're trudging through a jungle swamp. And after a good storm the ocean is washing through the streets – at the rate it's rising, the whole place will be underwater in the near future. I love my condo, but it won't be long before I move out of Florida.

Kendra, I fear, will not accompany me. She's twenty-four years old and a swimsuit model, like so many women her age in Miami. A seemingly endless supply of gorgeous young women with impossibly perfect bodies is one of the big selling points used by agents to target well-off middle-aged men (like myself) in search of high-priced real estate. Right now, Kendra's in the Bahamas for a couple of nights, doing a photo shoot. I like her, but our relationship has run its course. Kendra isn't to blame, not really. She's a bit empty inside, but who isn't at her age. And I was eagerly aware of what I was getting into with Kendra. When looking for a mature, intelligent woman of substance and culture, one would do best to avoid swimsuit models of half one's age. But I wasn't looking for intelligence, substance, or culture; I was looking for boobs.

The phone rings. I'm lying on my back in bed, slightly hungover and contemplating the direction my life is taking. After so many years on the road, going from band to band and gig to gig, to suddenly stop is like giving up drugs, cold turkey. At first you feel quite disoriented and possibly sick, but slowly, little by little, inch by inch, you feel better, like a whole new person. But the craving, unfortunately, never completely goes away. That's what I'm experiencing now – a craving for the road, for playing live in front of a loud, sweaty crowd. At this point, I'd play in a church choir just to get another taste of it.

I stretch out my arm and grab the glass of water I keep on my end table. I take a couple of long gulps. The water's warm but quenches my dry mouth. I set down the glass and pick up the ringing cell phone. While pressing the button to answer, I cough deeply, a thick smoker's cough earned from a lifetime of playing in damp, hazy nightclubs.

"Well, that's a classy greeting."

I recognize Megan's voice.

"Sorry, honey," I say, my head still groggy. "I meant to do that before I answered."

"Next weekend is Ellie's birthday."

"Ellie," I repeat carefully.

"My daughter," Megan snaps. "Your granddaughter."

"Hey, that's great," I say, hoping to cover my ignorance with hoarse cheeriness.

"Yes," she replies slowly, as though speaking to an imbecile, "it is great."

I don't think my happy voice worked. She sounds angry. But she usually sounds angry when talking to me.

"I was thinking you might want to come up for Ellie's party. She's turning fourteen. It's a big one."

I grab a remote from the nightstand and press the button to open the curtains. They part slowly, bathing the room in warm sunlight. Propping myself up on my pillows, I gaze at the Atlantic Ocean through massive French doors and watch distant yachts and cruise ships float through the Atlantic Ocean like tiny white figurines set upon a large, sparkling cake.

"Yeah, that's big," I say. "Wow, I have a fourteen-year-old granddaughter. I remember when you were fourteen."

"Do you? Because I certainly don't remember seeing you around very much."

One thing about Megan – she knows how to hurt someone. There's no fucking around, either; she finds a weak area and goes for it immediately. She'd be a hell of a swordsman. I can't fault her for what she says, though, because she speaks the truth.

"So, when's the party?" I ask.

"Saturday afternoon. We're having it at Mom's house."

A sailboat comes into view. It's heading east, away from the nearby harbor. They look so calm and peaceful moving across the water, but I went on a sailboat once. Puked my guts out. Never again.

"Sure, why not?" I say.

"Gee, that's fantastic," Megan says. "I'll tell Ellie that her grandfather was so excited to see her on her birthday, he said, 'Why not'. Every other gift will pale in comparison."

"Honey, I know you don't like me very much. Let's try to leave the past behind us and work on the present and future, okay?"

"Easy for the past to say."

I'll say this for her – she sticks to her convictions. Megan's dislike for me started when she was a teenager and has rarely wavered. Her disdain isn't without cause or reason, but I wish she'd move on. Megan, however, is not one to forget a slight, or what she considers to be a lifetime of slights.

"Can you get me a room somewhere? I'll try to fly in on Thursday. Is the Apple Brook B and B still open?"

"Yes," she says. "But Mom said you can stay with her. Ellie and I are living in the guest house now, so there's plenty of room at Mom's."

I consider the idea of spending three or four days with Rachel. It's been a long time since I've been to Apple Brook, and I imagine that spending a fall weekend in a big Maine lake house is still nothing to sneeze at. Rachel and I get along, we always have, but that may be because we've never addressed the past. Discussing Megan is as close as we get. Maybe it's time to change that.

"Yeah, okay. I'll stay with your mom. Why not."

"Hey, there's another 'why not' from Mr. Decisive," Megan says, but I think I detect more teasing sarcasm than festering anger in her words. I decide to get off the phone now, leave on a high note, like George Costanza.

"I'll see you in a few days, honey. I can't wait to see you and Ellie and your mom."

"I won't tell Ellie until you get here. No use getting her hopes up if you're going to pull your usual shit and not show up. That's something I remember well."

I start to tell Megan that won't ever happen again, those days are over, but she's already hung up. Maybe that wasn't playful sarcasm in her voice. But she did mention getting Ellie's hopes up, meaning my granddaughter's looking forward to seeing me. So that's something.

## 2

I was a shitty father. Still am, I guess. Can't deny it. In today's world they might refer to me as an absentee father. Doesn't matter what you call it; point is, I wasn't there. Plenty of men, especially in previous generations, put work before family. My dad did, out of necessity. If he didn't work sixty or seventy hours a week, we didn't eat or have clothes or a roof over our heads. Simple as that. What may have looked like putting work *before* family was really work *for* family.

For many years, I told myself I was doing the same thing. But there were some distinct and critical differences between me and my dad. First, I didn't live with my family. Technically, I had an ex-fiancée and a daughter who I'd left behind. My father's work was just that – work; hard, physical labor, installing swimming pools in the hot sun twelve hours a day, May through September. My father qualified for unemployment for the winter months but would never consider taking it. Instead he drove an oil truck, spending the long, cold Maine winter lugging a hose through deep snow and frigid winds to deliver oil, twelve hours a day. When I got older, he finally changed careers and started his own plumbing business. That was hard, too, and his back hurt him every day. He never complained, but looking back, it's clear that my old man sacrificed a lot of himself for his family. It's what a man was expected to do.

My job, on the other hand, involved playing loud, sleazy music in smoky bars and nightclubs until two in the morning, then getting drunk and screwing whoever was insecure enough to sleep with a guitarist she'd just met until the sun came up. Most of my gigs took place on weekends, leaving me with nothing to do but practice and loaf around the rest of the week. And make no mistake, playing music is not a job. It's not called *working* music, after all. What my father did was work, sacrifice. What I did was fun.

And yet, there was no time in my life for family. It wasn't long after the Dropouts broke up that I split from Rachel. Long story, but as you can probably guess, it was my fault. Megan was young, around two years old. I moved away from Apple Brook, down to Massachusetts, to start my solo career. I figured my manager would set up a meeting with the big record companies like Columbia and A&M and they could bid on me. Who wouldn't be interested in the guitarist from the Dropouts, writer of a Top 20 hit?

Pretty much everybody, I soon found out. There would be no solo album. I ended up bouncing from band to band, playing clubs all over New England. I'd like to say it got better, but it didn't. I eventually moved south, but nothing changed. I played in a series of mediocre cover bands and nobody knew me from the fat balding factory worker I'd replaced.

My excuse for not seeing my daughter was that I was on the road all the time, trying to earn a living. For whom, I'm not sure, because I almost never sent money to Rachel or Megan. Rachel's parents had money and I figured they'd be all set. But that doesn't explain why I couldn't write, or at least call once a week. At the time I attributed it to being young and ambitious. Looking back, it's clear that I was just selfish.

And yet, when I got older, I somehow didn't get any wiser. I didn't go out of my way to make it up to

Megan. Maybe I felt like I'd already blown it. That was my reasoning, anyway. But worst of all, I had a chance at a clean slate. I had a granddaughter. And what did I do? The same goddamn thing, which is nothing. I showed up when Ellie was born, stayed a few days, and promised to get back up there to see her soon. And two years later, I finally got around to it.

Over the years I've seen Ellie a handful of times, most recently when she was around nine or ten, right around the time when "Your Love Line" was making its comeback. Sad, when I think about it, that I don't measure time using milestones from my granddaughter's life – her first steps, her first day of school, things like that. Instead, I measure time by using the only proof of professional success I've ever had. In case the verdict about me was still out, the scales should now be tipped heavily in favor of selfishness.

There had just never been a compelling reason to go home to Apple Brook. It sounds absurd when said aloud, but I've truly felt this way for much of my adult life. I've been seeing a psychiatrist and she's helped me realize that it may not be my hometown, but instead my own humiliation that keeps me away. The hotshot kid with a Top 20 Billboard hit at 19 years old, leader of Maine's Greatest Rock n Roll Band, etc. – all that shit designed to lift you up will eventually slam you to the ground, harder and faster than a falling tree. And the bigger you are – particularly in your own head – the harder you fall. My shrink believes it isn't a lack of love for my daughter and granddaughter or anyone else that's kept me away, but a fear of appearing as a failure before them.

Very few people know that I'm seeing a shrink. Just Kendra and whoever she blabbed to. She promised to keep it quiet, and Kendra's not dishonest, but I know women well enough to know that she'll have to tell someone. And if that sounds like I understand women, let me clear that notion up right now by stating for the record that I know next to nothing about women. And next to nothing may be a grand overstatement. It's just that I've dated enough young women like Kendra over the years to recognize some consistencies in their actions.

The reasons for my seeing a psychiatrist are many and varied, as is often the case. It started simply enough with anxiety and trouble sleeping. For most of my life pills and booze had dulled my consciousness and kept my awareness at bay, a drunken foot pushing into a trash can so I could stuff it with more garbage. But now the can is overfilling, according to the psychiatrist. Has a lot to do with my younger years, unresolved relationships, all that happy horseshit. Happens often to people my age.

The psychiatrist is supposed to be one of the best in Miami. She charges like she is. I don't know. I've never been to a shrink before, so I have nothing to compare her to. It seems like she's helped me. I'm going back home in a couple of days, so I suppose we'll find out soon enough.

3

The perceived length of a three-hour flight varies according to whether one is seated in first class or coach. A lifetime of flying coach had me prepared for a long day of horrors which might include screaming children, old man farts, grouchy flight attendants and occupied restrooms. Instead, my first-class ticket entitled me to roomy seats, smiling faces, and free drinks. For those accustomed to such digs, it's just another day in paradise. To me, it's what I imagine the shuttle to heaven will be like.

When we land, I'm not in heaven, but instead in Portland, Maine. I walk through the terminal with a pretty good buzz, courtesy of three free Jack and Cokes. All I've brought with me is an old beat up carry-on bag and an acoustic guitar in a black case. The rental car counter is up ahead but I shouldn't drive yet. This may sound like common sense, but to someone with a long track record of alcohol abuse and making the wrong choices in general it's a real sign of maturity.

I wander around the small airport for a couple of minutes and then enter Shipyard Brewport. I sit at the bar, where a young man with a 1990s haircut and long sideburns takes my order. I skip the beer and instead order a water to go with my burger and fries. He pours me an ice water and I sip it while waiting for my food.

It's mid-afternoon and the place is about half full. The other bartender is female, a bit on the heavy side but young and cute enough to pull it off. She smiles at me and I smile back.

"Can I get you a drink?" she asks, walking over.

"No thanks," I say, shaking my head. "Already had a couple on my flight."

"I'm the same way, I can't fly without a few drinks." She stands on her toes and looks at the stool next to mine, where I've placed my bag and guitar. "Are you a musician?"

I nod and sip my water.

"You any good?"

I nod again.

"Are you anyone I know?"

"If I was, you'd probably know," I say, and she laughs. "My band, the Dropouts, had a pretty big hit in the eighties."

"Wow, the eighties," she says, like it's hard to imagine such a distant time.

"The song's become a hit again recently. It's been on a couple of CW shows and a movie with Ryan Gosling."

"I don't watch TV and Ryan Gosling's not my type. But I'll ask my dad if he's heard of you. I'm pretty sure he was alive in the eighties."

She moves along to wait on a well-dressed younger couple down the bar. My food arrives shortly afterward, and I move to a table to eat my burger and lick my wounds.

Less than an hour later I'm headed south on 95 in my rented SUV, toward Apple Brook. I don't need to use the GPS because I remember Rachel's address, 122 Far Shore Drive. Another one of those things I remember so clearly from long ago. I recall her phone number, too, from when we were in high school and it was her parents' house. She still has a landline, same number.

While driving I notice that people up here seem to drive faster than they used to, and more impatiently. Maybe it just appears that way because I'm on the downhill side of middle age. It's nothing like Miami, though. I dread driving there. Here, I don't feel at risk of being shot because I accidently pulled in front of someone. I find a country station – another hazard of middle age – and cruise along, lost in thought.

In less than half an hour I'm passing the *Welcome to Apple Brook: A Quaint, Friendly Community* sign. Long ago, at the height of my band's success, there was talk of changing the sign to *Welcome to Apple Brook: Home of the Dropouts.* Thankfully, some of the more rational leaders in the community – including the entire school committee – refused to get caught up in Dropoutmania and prevailed in the battle for common sense.

Far Shore Drive winds like a black ribbon through tall, thick trees and past the homes lining the western shore of Carpenter Lake. It's October, the normal onslaught of summer traffic is over, and from high above colorful leaves flutter downward like confetti, their previously fallen brothers and sisters radiantly coating the road like a welcome mat to autumn.

I drive slowly past two curving miles of lake houses. Some of them are still summer camps, boarded up and winterized for another year. But most have been converted in the years since my youth to lakeside McMansions by Massholes who've bought up most of Maine's waterfront property. You can take the boy out of Maine, but you can't always take Maine out of the boy. Doesn't matter where I am, when I see a Massachusetts license plate, my brain says Masshole.

Rachel's house is located on a large peninsula that juts out like a mossy green finger pointing to the east. Her parents left her the largest property on the lake, nineteen acres, with over a mile of shoreline, including a small inlet beside the house known as Hook 'em Cove because of its reputation as a prime fishing hole. Lazy Daze, Rachel's four-thousand square foot home, is located at the tip of the peninsula and surrounded by water on three sides. A few hundred yards away is the lakeside guest house where Megan and Ellie live. It's a beautiful log home, with lots of windows and a separate entrance from the road, but does not rate its own name.

Across the cove is a small fishing camp where Rachel's father, Mr. Brennan, and his buddies used to gather on Friday nights for poker games. It's also the place where Rachel and I took each other's virginity on a warm and rainy summer night after the longest six months of my life. I wrote a song about the experience and called it "Getting Wet in Hook 'em Cove", but never recorded it because Rachel found it embarrassing and asked me not to.

I turn down the long, curving drive to Lazy Daze and see Rachel sitting on a rocker on the front porch, reading a magazine. It's a cliché, I know, but from a short distance she looks just like the girl I fell in love with in high school. She could be a model for an LL Bean flyer – long auburn hair resting on the shoulders of her flannel shirt, faded jeans, bean boots, with a background of bright falling leaves and a peaceful lake.

She smiles and waves as I draw closer to the house. My heart skips and my stomach flips, an involuntary reaction no other woman has ever brought out in me. I step out of the car and am immediately hit by the cool lakeside breeze. The sweet scent of decomposing leaves wafts like a powerful perfume through the air. I take a deep breath and smile, soaking it all in.

Rachel sets down her magazine and steps off the porch to give me a warm, tight hug.

"You still look like a rock star, Maze," she says, reaching up to gently brush my hair and touch the small hoop in my left ear.

"And you're still beautiful," I say, and mean it. Up close, small lines have formed around her big brown eyes and the corners of her mouth and only serve to make her more stunning.

She blushes. "I see you haven't lost your charm."

Then something changes in her eyes, as though she's caught herself doing something wrong. Still smiling, she lowers her arms from my shoulders and takes a step back.

I reach into the SUV and grab my bag and guitar.

"It's been years since I've seen fall in Maine. I've missed it. I didn't realize how much until now."

"It's beautiful," Rachel says, tilting her head up to gaze at the trees. "Summer on the lake is wonderful, but fall is still my favorite season. It's so peaceful and quiet, like a passage from *Walden*. I love everything about it. It's the only time of year I enjoy the rainy days as much as the sunny ones."

"I remember that about you." For a long moment I watch her stare quietly into the trees. Then I turn my head toward the house. "Is Ellie around?"

"She's at soccer practice. I thought we'd go watch. She's on the freshman team."

"Really? I didn't know she played soccer."

As soon as the words are out of my mouth, I feel like an ass. Of course I don't know Ellie plays soccer. I haven't been around enough to know anything about her. I remember that Megan played soccer, but only because Rachel would occasionally send me newspaper clippings.

Rachel gives me a curious look but is thoughtful enough to say nothing. She turns to the house and I follow her inside. The door off the driveway – not the front door, which I don't ever remember seeing used – opens into a fashionably rustic kitchen. To the left is the entrance to the living room, and straight ahead is the stairway leading upstairs and a hallway leading to the two first floor bedrooms. Rachel tells me that she's in the master bedroom and has set up the other room for Ellie, who sleeps over a couple times a month. She's getting older now and those days are likely coming to an end, she says, though it's obvious she wishes they'd last forever.

Remembering the house well, I climb the stairs to the second floor and drop my bag and guitar in the first bedroom. There are four large bedrooms, all empty, along with two full bathrooms and a cozy, well-stocked library on the second floor. I could have my pick, but I choose the first bedroom because I'm too lazy to walk down the hall and it's the closest to a bathroom. The things that take priority about when you get older.

When I come back downstairs Rachel is standing at the kitchen island, pouring steaming hot water from a kettle into a stainless-steel travel mug.

"Which would you rather have, coffee or hot chocolate?" she asks, setting the kettle on the stove and putting the top on her mug. "The wind blows pretty hard across the soccer field, and the temperature drops quickly this time of year once the sun dips below the trees."

"Hot chocolate, please." I watch her pour powder from a packet into my mug and fill it with hot water from the kettle. "I should have married you."

She glances up at me while placing a lid on my mug.

"You getting sappy on me, Maze?"

"I don't know what the hell's going on. Probably shouldn't have said that."

"Well, I'm glad you didn't marry me," she says, with a slight smirk.

"Really? I have to say, that's not the answer I expected. Why are you glad?"

"Because now you realize what you missed out on." She hands me the mug and heads toward the front door. "Only took you thirty years or so to figure it out."

I watch her for a moment before following her outside. She's wrong. I figured it out long ago. I was just too stubborn to admit it.

4

1983

Rachel Brennan was a beautiful sophomore with big, soft eyes and shoulder-length auburn hair when we met on the lawn by a side exit during a school fire drill. She came from a privileged family and hung out with the popular kids, while I was a junior with little going for me except long hair, a growing collection of concert t-shirts, and a rudimentary-but-steadily-improving knowledge of the guitar. On that day I was wearing my usual school uniform – scuffed boots, tight faded Levi's, and a faded Levi's jean jacket, opened in the front to reveal the Motley Crue t-shirt I'd purchased during the previous week's concert at the Cumberland County Civic Center, in Portland.

It was a cold and gray December morning, the kind where the frozen grass crunches under your feet. I kept glancing at Rachel – she was so good-looking, it was impossible not to – and noticed she was shivering, even in her sweater. She had her arms wrapped around herself the way girls do, and for some reason she was standing a little way off by herself. In the middle of a conversation about the previous night's episode of TJ Hooker with Phil, my band's drummer, and a couple of other guys, I wandered off and approached Rachel. Having never actually approached such an attractive member of the female species before, I moved slowly and awkwardly, like a lion cub on its first hunt. When I finally reached her I just stood there staring at her, forgetting to talk.

"Can I help you?" she finally said, but not in an unfriendly way.

"Uh, no." Long pause, more staring. "You look cold."

"Yes, I am." She gazed past me, toward the school. Her breath came in small white clouds that I imagined smelled like lavender and tasted like strawberry. "I hope they let us back in soon. It's freezing out here."

I took off my jean jacket and handed it to her. "Here."

She stared at the jacket as though it was covered in snot. I rarely, if ever, washed my jacket and it may have actually had a bit of dried snot on the sleeves, down by the wrists, but it was certainly not *covered*. Finally, wearing an expression that left no doubt she was doing so against her better judgement, she put the jacket on. It was a little long for her, the sleeves hanging down past her fingertips.

"Thanks," she said. Then her face crinkled up, and she looked at me suspiciously. "Why's it smell like pot?"

"Oh . . . that's because I've been smoking pot."

"Today?"

"Well, not since school started."

Then she laughed, and it was like a choir of angels singing from heaven above. The most wonderful, glorious, life-altering sound I'd ever heard, like the merging of Motley Crue and Van Halen. She stared at me with a curious expression before sticking her hands in the jacket pockets.

"Let's see what we have in here, Mister Pot Smoker. I may have to call the principal over here and get you suspended."

"Hey, you're the one wearing it, not me. I've never seen that jacket before in my life."

She laughed again and pulled her left hand from the pocket. In the palm were several guitar picks.

"What are all these for?" She stared at me for a moment, until her soft eyes widened slightly in recognition. "Oh, you're in that band, right?"

"Yeah, the Dropouts."

"But you haven't dropped out, I assume."

"Oh, I have. I just show up for fire drills so I can stand in the cold and talk to pretty girls."

She giggled. I glanced over her shoulder at my friends. Phil, arms out wide as though hugging a big tree, was humping the air. Another friend, Nate, was making out with his hand. Still others were laughing and making obscene gestures while watching us. I had some very immature and disrespectful friends. Funny as hell, though. I couldn't wait until one of them talked to a girl, so I could do the same thing to him.

"You play guitar." Rachel put all of the picks back in the jacket pocket except one, which she held up between her thumb and index finger and peered at.

I nodded.

"Why guitar?"

"I couldn't fit drumsticks into my pockets."

She laughed again. "You're funny. So, is your band any good?"

I'd been asked that question so many times. One of these days, I thought, I'm going to answer, No, we suck. But now was not the time.

"Yeah, we're wicked good. You should come watch us practice sometime."

She nodded. "I'd like that. Can I bring a friend with me?"

I looked over at Phil. He wore an expression that might have been brought on by either ecstasy or burning diarrhea and was pretending to jerk off while staring at Rachel's ass.

"Yeah, I think that'd be okay."

The bell rang for us to go back inside. Rachel and I walked back together, slowly, hanging behind the other students. I don't know if it was done on purpose or not. It was on my part.

When we reached the doors, she started to take off my jacket.

"Keep it," I said. "You can come see my band practice after school today, if you want."

"Sure, where?"

I gave her directions to Cam's house. We practiced in his basement until five, when his mom got home from work.

"I'll give you your jacket back then. There's nothing in the pockets that'll get me in trouble, right?"

"Nah. Just make sure you keep the top left pocket buttoned," I said.

"You're so funny," she said with a big smile.

I watched her walk to the end of the hall. Reaching the corner, she turned around, smiled, and waved. I waved back, locked in the same spot. I hadn't moved. I was still in shock that I'd been so cool with her, like Burt Reynolds or something. I'd never spoken to anyone as good-looking as Rachel, aside from in daydreams. Lots of staring, but no talking. And I made her laugh! She looked so good in my jacket, if she'd asked I'd have let her keep it.

I wasn't kidding about the top left pocket, though. There were two fat joints and a pack of matches tucked away in there.

We were together almost two months before I was invited to her house. The Brennan Lakeside Compound, as I liked to call it. Rachel had been to my house a few times already, met my mom and dad. I'd brought her home a week after that fateful fire drill, desperate for someone in my family to see me with this knockout. Within a month she'd met both sets of grandparents and my Uncle Marc who I usually only saw at Christmas.

My mom welcomed her warmly, as she did everybody I was friends with. They talked cooking and hairstyles and school and cute actors and plans for college, almost like mother and daughter. At times I felt like a third wheel and would go watch TV in living room while they talked and laughed in the kitchen. And my father, to my immense surprise, was funny and charming in her presence. This was the man who, according to family lore, when asked, "Do you, Walter, take Charlene to be your lawfully wedded wife?", looked at the priest and answered, "I already paid for the room, so I guess I probably should."

After Rachel's first visit, during which my father spent thirty light-hearted minutes playing the same Atari games with Rachel that he could never be persuaded to play with me, the old man pulled me aside and said, "Wowza. Now *that's* a pretty young woman. And it's not just looks; she's the whole package. Smart, feisty . . . I like her. Looks like the old Maze charm is working for you. Chip off the old block!"

My mom rolled her eyes. "Settle down, Tiger."

"I was thinking it was the guitar," I said.

"Could be," my dad said thoughtfully. "Well, I'm glad to see it's finally paying off."

I wasn't mad at Rachel for waiting so long to introduce me to her parents. Everyone in Apple Brook knew her dad. He owned his own law firm and was a very well-known and powerful man in our area. He was on nearly every Board of Directors in town, from the library to the hospital, and was first selectman of Apple Brook's Board of Selectmen. He also owned Brennan's, the area's best and most upscale restaurant. Expectations for Rachel were high.

I pulled up to Lazy Daze on a cold Sunday afternoon in a 1974 Chevelle that I'd borrowed from a friend for the big occasion. The loud rattle of the glasspack exhaust resounded off the surrounding trees as I drove too fast up the winding drive. It was one of those winters when the air was frigid but we'd gotten almost no snow. I pulled up to the house and stomped on the gas for one more impressive roar of the Chevelle's powerful engine before shutting it off. I stepped out wearing a white-collared button-up shirt from Chess King under my jean jacket. My long hair was pulled back in a pony tail and tucked under my jacket collar to make it appear shorter, a suggestion from Rachel. I was very nervous and could have used a beer or a hit from the joint in my top left jacket pocket, but I chose to abstain because this was important to Rachel.

Rachel flew down the front steps and gave me a quick hug. She looked even more nervous than me.

"Ready?" she asked, as we approached the front door.

I nodded, and we went inside.

My first impression was that it looked like the interior of a hunting cabin. The walls of the kitchen, hallway, and living room were knotty pine, and the stuffed heads of several small animals were mounted on the hallway walls. Mrs. Brennan stood at the counter near the kitchen sink cutting up meat on a cutting board with a large knife. For a woman of her advanced years – I'd guess she was approaching 40 – Mrs. Brennan was attractive, the type of woman who made chopping up deer meat appear classy. When Rachel introduced me, Mrs. Brennan smiled warmly and said she'd love to shake my hand, but it would have to wait until she was finished preparing dinner.

"Why don't you introduce Jesse to your father?" Mrs. Brennan said.

Rachel held my hand until we entered the living room. The room was massive and featured a large stone fireplace over which a huge moose head with antlers at least eight feet wide gazed helplessly straight ahead. The room was well lit, with several large windows on the three outside walls. Mr. Brennan sat in an armchair, absently spooling line onto a fishing reel while watching a deer hunting show on TV. A pair of black reading glasses hovered near the end of his nose. He appeared oblivious to our presence even though we were well within his peripheral vision.

"Daddy, this is Jesse," Rachel said, in an abnormally high voice.

Mr. Brennan finally looked our way. He took off the reading glasses, set down the reel, and slowly stood up. He wore a sweatshirt with a fishing logo, along with tan khakis and slippers. I'd seen him around town many times and he'd always had a tie on. It was strange seeing him dressed so informally, like entering the Fortress of Solitude to find Superman lounging in sweatpants.

"Hello, Jesse. Nice to meet you."

He was a tall man, with wide shoulders and big hands, built like an athlete not long past his prime. When we shook his hand felt rough and calloused, like my father's. I hadn't expected that.

"Hey," I said.

He sat back down in his chair and gestured to a nearby couch. Rachel and I sat a proper distance from one another. Mr. Brennan put his reading glasses back on, slow and deliberate, and went back to working on his fishing reel. There was a long, uncomfortable period of silence.

"Rachel says you're a junior," Mr. Brennan finally said.

"Barely," I said, with a laugh.

"Junior year is a big one," he said, ignoring my attempt at comic relief. "Time to get serious about your future. What do you plan to do after graduation?"

*Throw a bitchin' all-night keg party*, was the first thought that came to mind. Luckily, Rachel spoke before I could.

"Daddy, leave him alone! He's not on trial here!"

He glanced over his glasses at her. "I don't believe I was being hard on Jesse. It's a question I'd ask of any young man his age, particularly one who wants to spend time with my daughter."

"I don't really have a plan," I said. "I'm in a band. I play guitar. I figure we'll probably make a record and go on tour, see how that goes. We're really good so I don't think it'll take us long to get famous."

"They really are good," Rachel said helpfully.

"I'm sure," said Mr. Brennan. He'd stopped working on the reel and was now fixing me with a very uncomfortable stare. "I'm assuming you play rock and roll?"

I nodded.

"That explains the long hair and the earring." He held up a hand to Rachel, cutting her off. "I'm not being disparaging. Just making an observation." He smiled at me. "And what is the name of your band?"

"Uh . . . The Dropouts."

Mr. Brennan's face turned a frighteningly dark shade of red. His eyes flicked back and forth between me and Rachel as though weighing how angry she'd be if he removed me forcefully from the house and how such an act might affect the family dynamics. Then he stood up, excused himself between clenched teeth, and left the room.

Rachel smiled tightly and gave my hand a quick squeeze. Not reassuring. I heard mumbling from the kitchen – a deep, angry rumble, followed by a higher, sharper hissing. This went on for several minutes, until there was a loud noise like a pan being slammed against the counter, followed by silence. A few moments later, Mr. Brennan returned to the living room. In his hand was a glass of caramel-colored liquor. He sat back down in his chair and took a quick gulp from the glass.

"So, Jesse," he said pleasantly, as though there had been no interruption. "Do you have a job now?"

"Sort of. My dad's a plumber and I help him out sometimes after school when I don't have band practice, and on weekends."

"A plumber, huh?" Mr. Brennan sat up a little, and for the first time, he sounded pleased. "That's a helluva good trade. If the, uh, rock and roll thing doesn't work out, it's something to fall back on."

*No fucking way*, I thought. But what I said was, "Yeah, maybe."

"There's always work available for a good plumber."

"That's true." I smiled. "Like my dad says, everybody's gotta shit."

Rachel put her hand to her mouth and turned away to muffle her giggles. Mr. Brennan stared straight ahead at the wall and took a deep swig from his glass. He started to get up, glanced toward the kitchen and, sighing deeply, sat back down.

"Uh, yes. Confucius couldn't have put it better himself." Mr. Brennan looked at the moose head, then me, then back at the moose head. Then he smiled and stared out one of the room's large windows for a long moment. "No plans for college, I'm guessing?"

"No. I'm not good at school," I said. "I hate it, to be honest."

"Hence, the band name," said Mr. Brennan.

"He's really smart though, Daddy," Rachel said.

"Yes, I can certainly see that, honey. So far, all signs point to 'really smart'."

There was another loud bang from the kitchen, the same pan being slammed once again on the countertop. Mr. Brennan glanced over his shoulder and frowned. Then he rubbed his eyes and, staring straight ahead, picked up his glass and, in one desperate gulp, downed the rest of his drink. With a satisfied grunt, he once again turned to me.

"I apologize if I'm being a bit hard on you, young man. But you must understand my point of view." Looking at Rachel, his eyes softened. "My daughter is intelligent, ambitious, outgoing, and beautiful; vice president of her class, a member of Key Club and Student Council, as well as the varsity soccer and softball teams. She also volunteers at the cancer center and the nursing home."

"Yeah, she's awesome," I said, smiling at Rachel. She smiled back.

"Yes! She is awesome," Mr. Brennan said. "Very good, Jesse. I couldn't have summed it up any better myself. And being so smart and outgoing and beautiful, my daughter obviously has her choice of boyfriends. I'm expecting football captains and class presidents and valedictorians. The crème de la crème, if you will. So, you can imagine how I feel when she brings home a long-haired kid with an earring who plays guitar in a rock band called the Dropouts, a kid who's entire lifetime plan can be summed up in one simple sentence – "Play guitar and get famous" – a kid who, by his own admission, hates school and places no value at all on education. Do you see the problem here, Jesse?"

Up until now I'd been well-behaved and polite because of my feelings for Rachel and the way I'd been raised. But now I'd been pushed too far. Mr. Brennan was a powerful man, both professionally and physically. He was five or six inches taller than I was and outweighed me by at least fifty pounds. But none of that mattered. He'd done nothing but insult me since the moment I'd walked in and I was ready to strangle the old fart, to see how he'd like to join his furry friend Marty Moose hanging over the fireplace.

Just as I started getting to my feet, fists clenched, a hundred and forty pounds of denim and attitude, there was a loud bang from the kitchen. I mean *loud*, like the refrigerator had tipped over. At the same time, Rachel started yelling at her father. I looked over, stuck in a sort of half-crouch between sitting and standing, and was surprised to see Rachel on her feet, chin out, tears streaming down her flushed cheeks.

"I can't believe you'd do this to me! How could you embarrass me like this?" she screamed at her father. "I hate you!"

She grabbed my hand and pulled me out of the room. I was so surprised, I forgot all about kicking her father's ass. As we passed through the kitchen her mother tried to stop us.

"I'm so sorry, Jesse. Please don't leave. Dinner will be ready in a few minutes. Why don't you kids go listen to some music in the den and cool off?"

"We're leaving," Rachel said, giving my arm another tug. "I no longer have an appetite. I think I'd puke if I had to look at *his* face across the table." She jerked a thumb toward the living room.

"Please don't leave! He didn't mean it. I'm sure he wants to apologize."

"Too late," said Rachel. "I don't know when I'll be home."

She pulled me out the door, then let go of my arm and stomped to the Chevelle. We got inside and for a minute neither of us said a word. It was cold but I didn't start the car. I watched through the foggy windows as Mr. Brennan walked from the living room to the kitchen. Mrs. Brennan lit into him, yelling furiously while waving a wooden spoon and a skillet. Mr. Brennan poured a drink, doing his best to ignore her.

"I like them," I finally said.

"I hate them. My dad, at least."

"I wanted to punch him," I said.

"You should have." She paused. "Well, maybe not. My dad used to be a boxer. He took second place in the New England Golden Gloves when he was a teenager."

"I don't give a shit," I said. Inside, Mrs. Brennan, still waving her spoon, followed her husband into the living room. "You still want to leave?"

Rachel nodded. I turned the key and the Chevelle came to life with a thick rumble. Mr. Brennan looked out the window but stayed seated in his chair.

"Where to?"

"I don't care." She reached down to turn up the heat and then slid over in the seat to sit next to me. I put my arm around her. "Let's just drive around for a while."

I turned the car around and headed slowly down the driveway, away from the house. As far as meeting the parents go, it couldn't have gone much worse. But it worked out in my favor, because Mr. Brennan couldn't have found a better way to push his daughter to me.

5

We walk onto the large field, where the smell of freshly-mown grass warms me like an aphrodisiac and puts a smile on my face.

"Field's a lot nicer than I remember."

Rachel nods. "Bigger, too. This is just the practice field now. There's a separate field for games on the other side of the fence."

She's dressed in a warm fall coat, with a cute wool hat and matching scarf, while I have only a leather jacket designed for fashion, not function. The sky is gray, and the temperature seems to be dropping by the minute.

"Remember when we used to come park down here and I'd defile you in the backseat?"

"Sometimes the front seat, too," she says, smiling.

We walk to the right of the field, where the girl's freshman team is practicing. The field borders a small wooded area where, in my day, kids would go to drink beer and smoke pot and feel each other up. Now they probably go in there and text each other non-offensive, gender-neutral greetings.

We stand by the sideline with a group of adults, parents and grandparents like us. A few teenagers hang around nearby, boys and girls, laughing and yelling and screaming. And texting. Along the far sideline I spy Megan, moving back and forth while yelling encouragement and tips to the team. I scan the players on the field and am embarrassed to realize I can't pick out my granddaughter.

"There's Ellie," Rachel says, as though reading my mind. She points. "Ponytail, to the right of the goal. Oh, she's got the ball!"

I watch as she speeds around one opponent, stops on a dime, and delivers the ball to an open teammate, who puts it in for an easy goal. Ellie is thin and gangly but moves with a smooth grace that I've never had, except in my fingers. Definitely a Brennan trait. Ellie casually slaps hands with the other girls, and for a brief moment I'm in a time warp, watching her grandmother back in high school.

"Whoa, she's pretty good," I say.

"Yup, team captain."

Ellie jogs past, glances at us, and does a double take. Breaking into a huge grin, she sprints over and hugs me tightly. I don't let go until she giggles and says she has to get back on the field.

The team continues scrimmaging. One of the players makes a quick cut and immediately drops to the ground, holding her ankle. A whistle blows and practice stops as Megan hurries onto the field and kneels over the girl while the other players gather around. Standing over them is a tall, thin black man with a kind face and a whistle around his neck. The coach, I assume. After a couple of minutes, the injured girl gets up, places an arm around Megan's shoulder, and limps to the bench on the far sideline.

"Is Megan the trainer?" I ask.

"Assistant coach. The tall guy is head coach. Milton Taylor. He was a great soccer player in his day. Played Major League Soccer for a couple of years, back in the nineties. He's a firefighter here in Apple Brook now."

"You seem to know a lot about him. You writing his biography?"

"We're friends. I dated him for a short time."

I look over at her. "And now?"

"We're still friends. But we aren't dating," she says, with a hint of a grin.

I finish the hot chocolate in my travel mug. It warms my mouth and stomach, but the rest of me is freezing. To try and keep my mind off how cold it is out here, I focus on what's happening on the field. Watching Ellie certainly distracts me from everything else. Her resemblance to Rachel is remarkable. She looks even more like her grandmother than Megan does. Moves like her, too, back in the day.

All at once an oddly confusing combination of awe, pride, and nostalgia washes over me. Typical grandparent feelings, I assume, but I'm not used to this grandparent stuff and it makes me feel old. Really old. Rocking chair, prune juice and denture old. I'm overwhelmed with a need to get away and collect my thoughts. To run from my emotions, as my shrink would say.

I set my empty mug down on the cool grass.

"I think I'll go for a walk around the field," I say to Rachel.

She tilts her head and looks at me kind of funny, but then she nods and turns her attention back to the field.

People are watching me. I'm generally not a paranoid person. I've been performing onstage since the age of fifteen, so I'm used to people looking at me. This is different. There's no guitar in my hand, no amplifiers, no spotlight. Yet heads are turning. Double-takes. Fingers pointing and mouths whispering. Discreet and not-so-discreet cellphone photos and videos.

I stroll over to the other side of the field, where the high school varsity team is practicing. The smells and sounds of fall in New England, including the grey skies and cool wind, are enticing. But it's difficult to enjoy myself when I feel like the unwitting butt of a joke that everyone else is in on. Even members of the boys' varsity team begin whispering and nudging each other after one of them sees me walking by. I check to make sure my zipper's up and wipe my nose in case there's a booger hanging out.

I walk the outskirts of the field, hoping to avoid people. I never appreciated the beauty of a stroll on a cool fall day when I was a kid growing up here. No child does. Each kid is the center of his or her own narrowly-focused universe, one that does not include a nostalgic recognition of the little things, including the natural beauty which surrounds us. That sort of appreciation comes only with age and a rising comprehension of one's own mortality. Once again, I feel old. Really old.

By the time I finish walking the field and return to Rachel's side, dusk is approaching, and the temperature is dropping. I'm no longer cold, though. I'm too paranoid to be cold. There is now a small pack of middle-aged women trailing a safe distance behind me, whispering and giggling like schoolgirls.

I explain to Rachel the stares, the pointing and whispers and picture taking from both adults and teenagers. Then I mention the women who've been following me for the past ten minutes.

"Don't be obvious," I say, "but they're standing over by the snack shack, looking at us. Why the hell is everyone looking at me?"

Rachel glances discreetly over her shoulder, then turns and waves, a big sweeping gesture through the air. "Hi Kerry! Hi Amy!" she calls to them. They smile and wave back, at least one doing so while staring into the cellphone she's pointing in our direction.

"Nice. Real discreet," I say.

"Oh, it's okay. I know them."

"Obviously. But I don't. So why are they following me?"

She shakes her head and looks at me with the sympathetic expression of a mother speaking to a kind, gentle, dim-witted child. "You really don't know?"

The women by the snack shack continue to stare and wave and smile. Glancing around, I notice at least two of the parents standing nearby on the sideline pointing phones at us, either taking pictures or video. Even a couple of Ellie's teammates on the field are sneaking glances our way and giggling. Megan glares at the girls from the far sideline, and then at me. I've seen that look from her before. It means that I, somehow, am to blame.

I shrug. "Nope."

"It's because you're famous, dummy. You're the guitarist from the Dropouts, remember? A bona fide rock star, from our little town."

"Yeah, but that was a long time ago. Most of these people weren't even born when we were together."

"Same as always. Cute, but thick." Rachel turns to face a man standing just a few feet away with his phone pointed at me and somehow manages to convey with just a look that it would be in his best interest to put the phone away immediately. After he turns and walks away, she continues, "In case you've forgotten, "Your Love Line" has made a massive comeback. The parents know it from the radio, the kids from TV and movies. The Dropouts, particularly you and Danny, are big stars around here. Your being here is obviously a really big deal. It's like if Elvis Presley had shown up at a baseball game in Memphis in 1970."

"Thank you very much, little lady," I say, using my best Elvis drawl.

"Stick with guitar," Rachel says.

I look around the field, doing my best to ignore the phones pointed at me.

"I hate to change the subject, mainly because the subject is me, but is there a bathroom around here?"

"They're locked. They only unlock the bathrooms during games," she says. "But there are a couple of porta-potties over there."

She points to two green, grungy-looking portable toilets standing near the woods in a corner of the field, about fifty yards away. I notice the grass around them is dead and faded.

"No, I don't use portable toilets, unless I'm really drunk. Looks like these people" – I gesture around me – "are about to get a real treat because if I don't take a leak soon, I'm going to wet myself."

"That's nice," Rachel says. "I'd suggest the woods."

"Yeah, that's a really good idea," I say. "It's been a long time since I took a piss in the woods. That's one thing I really miss about Maine. No woods to piss in down in Miami. Well, you could go into the Everglades, but you're likely to get your pecker bitten off by a snake or a gator."

She stares at me. "That's what you miss about Maine? Peeing in the woods?"

"Yes. Well, pissing. Men don't call it peeing."

"Of course not." She shakes her head. "Okay, well, have a good time."

I walk around the practice area as inconspicuously as possible, head down, collar up. Without looking back to see how many phones are trained on me, I enter the woods.

The shadows are heavy and it's much darker among the trees, but I'm not worried. I remember this area well from my teen years. There's a trail that starts from the road and leads to a clearing atop a small hill where kids used to smoke cigarettes and pot and drink alcohol stolen from their parents' refrigerators and liquor cabinets. It's been a long time, but I believe the clearing is about thirty yards ahead.

I look back and can still see the field, which means they will be able to see me if I decide to drain the lizard here. I don't even want to think about the TMZ headline for that one. I'd never even thought about being on TMZ until now, because I wasn't famous in Miami. Usually it's the young and athletic and beautiful (and often shallow and untalented) that are in vogue down in South Florida. An old fart like me who has a hit song from thirty years ago doesn't register very high on the Miami star meter. I was like the Ford Mustang of celebrities down there – I'd attract a modicum of attention, until a glossy Lamborghini or Bugatti showed up.

Continuing forward to the outskirts of the clearing, I hear the soft murmur of voices. Teenage voices. For some strange reason, it warms my heart to know that kids are still meeting in the woods to catch a buzz and feel each other up. It's nice to know that the good things in life carry over from one generation to the next.

I stop behind a tree, unzip my jeans, and commence to whizzing.

"Yo, Gramps," says a nearby voice, causing me to jerk backwards and piss on my shoes. I look to my left and see a gangly black kid with a trim afro watering a tree a few feet away. His stream is like a high-pressure firehose compared to my low-pressure sprinkler. Not to be outdone by a kid, I push, but my enlarged prostate refuses to cooperate and I stop before I herniate a disc.

"Where the hell did you come from?" I say.

"The clearing." The kid finishes and zips up. He looks over at my embarrassingly feeble stream. "Better hurry up, Gramps. It's gonna be dark soon."

"Thanks for the advice, kid. It might help if you don't stare."

I'm almost finished and my feeble stream weakens to a dribble. The kid notices.

"Hey, dude, you should probably get that checked."

"What're you, a fucking urologist?" I shake it and zip up. "So, what's going on at the clearing?"

The kid shrugs. He's tall and thin, I'd guess about fifteen years old. "Drinking a couple beers, dude. There's a couple joints being passed around, but I stick to beer."

"Your parents must be very proud."

He looks me up and down. "You look pretty lit, for an old guy. You want a beer, bro? Might help you with that problem. Beer always makes me want to piss."

The problem isn't in the wanting, it's in the doing. But I can't tell that to a wiseass fifteen-year-old kid. Besides, I could use a beer.

"You drink a lot, do you?"

"Well, straight up, this is only my second time," he says.

"And it always makes you want to piss? All two times?"

"Dude, do you want one or not?"

"Sure, why not," I say. "What's your name, kid?"

"Tyler. How about you?"

"Jesse."

"I like Gramps better."

There are three other teenagers in the clearing, two male and one female, all white. The girl has bright purple hair and there's a badly-drawn tattoo of what looks like Thor's hammer on each guy's scrawny left forearm. Maybe they got a two-for-one deal. They're sitting on a slanted rock about the size of a dinner table, passing a joint around. There are two beers under a nearby tree. Tyler picks one up and tosses it to me. Old Milwaukee. Warm. But beggars can't be choosers. I pop it open and take a swig. I'm wiping my mouth with the back of my hand when I realize I'm being stared at. Again.

"Hey Ty, like, who's the old guy?" asks the girl.

"Just call him Gramps. I met him taking a piss. He's cool."

"But, like, is he going to tell the cops about this place? Or our parents?"

"Most of your parents probably already know about this place," I say. "I used to come here when I was your age. And please don't call me Gramps."

I look around the clearing. In addition to empty beer cans, liquor bottles, and condom wrappers, there are several used needles scattered on the ground. Some things have changed here over the years, and certainly not for the better.

"Wow. That must have been back in the stone age," says Purple Hair.

"The stoned age," says one of the Thor Twins, and they all burst into a slow, stoned giggle.

I don't have to take shit from a bunch of glassy-eyed teenaged burnouts. On the other hand, I really want a beer. I decide to stay, but drink really fast.

"So, you got a grandkid on the soccer team, Gramps?" Tyler asks, with a smirk I don't care for.

I nod and take another swig of warm beer. I'm almost finished when Tyler tosses me the other beer.

"You can have the last one, dude. I'm meeting someone in a little while and I already had one. I don't want to show up with a buzz."

"That's what I like to see in young people today. Responsibility." I toss my empty can to the edge of the clearing, where it lands among dozens of other dead soldiers, and open the last one. "Is that your dad out there? The soccer coach?"

"No, why?" Tyler's laid-back expression darkens, and his voice is tight as he continues, "Oh, I get it. Because he's black and I'm black, right? We must be related? You throwin' shade, Gramps?"

The Thor Twins avert their eyes, as if they've done something wrong. Purple Hair stares at us and says, "Looks like Gramps is a racist."

I smile and sip my warm beer. "Racism can't exist without intent, honey."

"Huh?" she says vacantly.

"If I didn't intentionally say something racist, it's not racism." I take a long swig from the second beer.

"It was just a question. Unless things have changed a lot since I lived here, there are probably ten black people in all of Apple Brook, meaning there's a relatively good chance that the soccer coach is at least related to our friend Tyler."

"The correct term is African American," says the Purple Hair.

"You ever live in Africa?" I ask Tyler.

"Nope."

"You kids need to lighten up," I say, because somebody has to. "I didn't try to offend you. And if I did, that's your problem, not mine. Stop being a bunch of pansies. You kids don't know what offensive is. The Holocaust was offensive. Slavery was and is offensive. Assault weapons in schools are offensive. Referring to Justin Beiber as an artist is offensive. But asking a kid if a soccer coach is his father is not offensive."

"Settle down, Gramps. Don't need to go all extra. I'm not offended. And the coach isn't my father." Tyler smiles. "He's my uncle."

I run my hand through my thick hair. I'm one of the lucky few my age who hasn't lost any. I wear it long, around shoulder-length. It's light brown, with not a gray or white hair in sight, thanks to monthly visits with a very talented and expensive stylist. I take pride in my youthful appearance. I'm wearing a leather jacket and tight thin jeans, with Vans on my feet. I'm tired of this kid calling me Gramps. I decide to change the subject to the one I know best, one with no race, gender, or age restrictions.

"You play any instruments?" I ask Tyler.

"He plays skin flute, dude," says the shorter of the Thor Twins.

"No instruments, but I rap," Tyler says.

"So, no musical talent at all, then."

"Old white guy don't like rap," Tyler says. "Big surprise. How about you? What do you play?"

"Skin flute," says the other Thor Twin, and they giggle. Purple Hair continues to stare at us, slack-jawed.

"I play guitar," I say.

They don't seem to care. Weird. When I was their age, a guitar was about the greatest aphrodisiac out there, the reason thousands of skinny geeks like me took it up in the first place. It's how I met most of the friends I have in life. It's clearly the main reason women are drawn to me. I have no illusions of great looks or natural sex appeal or a winning personality. It's all guitar. If I'd never picked up a guitar, there's a very good chance that I would still be a virgin.

I glance around the clearing and notice how dark it's become. With two long swigs I finish my beer and toss the can among the other empties. I thank Tyler for the beer, nod to Purple Hair and the Thor Twins, and walk out of the clearing.

"Hope it helps with your pissing problem, Gramps," he calls after me.

I hate teenagers.

Practice is just breaking up when I get back to the practice field. It's not yet completely dark, but dusk is settling in nicely and it won't be long. Megan and Ellie are standing with Rachel, gazing around the field. When they see me approaching Rachel and Ellie wave happily, while Megan shakes her head.

"I was getting worried," Rachel says. "If you didn't show up in five more minutes I was going in after you."

"It wouldn't be the first time he didn't show up," Megan says.

Rachel gives her a sharp look.

"Hi, Grampy," Ellie says. "I'd give you another hug but I'm really sweaty."

I pull her into a tight embrace. "I won't let a little sweat bother me."

Stepping back, my hands still grasping her upper arms, I gaze closely at her young face and see Rachel's big brown eyes, auburn hair, and bright smile. I don't see anything of myself in her, but I must have passed something down.

"What do you ladies want for dinner?" I ask. "Anything you want, my treat. What's Apple Brook have for restaurants these days?"

"Actually, I'm making dinner tonight," Rachel says. "Homemade macaroni and cheese, Ellie's favorite."

"Hey, that was your mom's favorite, too," I say to Ellie. I look over at Megan, but she only stares at the ground.

"I have a friend coming over," Ellie says shyly.

I put one arm around her and swing the other around Rachel. "I must be the luckiest guy in the world. I'll be dining with four beautiful women tonight."

"Actually, you'll be dining with three beautiful women and one handsome young man," Rachel says happily. "We're going to meet Ellie's boyfriend tonight."

"Boyfriend? At thirteen?" I ask Megan.

Her eyes narrow, and I quickly realize I should have kept my mouth shut. But before Megan can say anything, Ellie says, "I'll be fourteen in a couple days. And he's my friend, not my boyfriend."

"But you like him, right?" Rachel asks.

Even in the growing darkness Ellie's face visibly turns red. Then she goes up on her toes and her ponytail bobs as she waves excitedly across the field. "Oh, there he is!"

I follow her gaze across the field and inwardly groan as I watch Tyler smoothly making his way toward us. Then I burp, loudly. Damn Old Milwaukee.

6

Dinner is a bit tense, but not like the heavy unease I used to feel every time I was around Mr. Brennan, when I could sense him fighting with all his willpower the paternal urge to tie me up and throw me in the lake with a cement block strapped to my leg. I don't want to throw Tyler in the lake or hurt him in any way. He seems like an okay kid. And he did give me a couple of beers. This is more of an awkward, hastily-formed pact between me and the kid, an unspoken agreement to both keep our mouths shut because each of us can take down the other.

Ellie and Tyler had come home with us from the soccer field, with Megan following in her car. When we were about halfway home, Rachel said, "It smells like beer in here." Not an accusation, but an observation. In the passenger side mirror, I saw Tyler chewing on a big wad of gum, staring out the back window. He looked worried. When Ellie said that she, too, smelled beer, his hand went over his mouth.

"That's me," I said. "When I went to take a leak there were some college students hanging out in the clearing. They offered me a beer and I took them up on it. That's what took me so long in there."

Keeping both hands on the wheel, Rachel glanced at me. "Why would college students be drinking in the woods in Apple Brook? The technical college is ten miles away."

"I didn't ask. I've found in life that if someone offers beer, you don't ask too many questions."

"Maybe they were high school students."

"Maybe, but they looked older," I lied. "I think a couple of them had beards."

"Kids look older today." Rachel shook her head. "That wasn't very smart, Jesse. If you were drinking beer with high school kids, you could get in real trouble."

I gazed into the passenger side mirror and locked eyes with Tyler. "I'm sure they'd keep their mouths shut. They'd just implicate themselves if they said anything."

His hand still over his mouth, Tyler gave a slight nod.

The homemade mac and cheese is delicious, and I'm quickly working on my second heaping plateful. Homemade food is a very rare indulgence for me. I'm admittedly useless in the kitchen, and Kendra is even more so – she's a twenty-four-year-old swimsuit model. When you look that good it often isn't necessary to develop certain life skills, like the ability to cook or carry on a meaningful, intelligent conversation. There are some great restaurants and takeout places in our area of Miami, but they all pale in comparison to a delicious homemade meal.

I could use a beer, but I've already had two and the last thing I want to do is get drunk the first night I'm visiting my daughter and granddaughter. I eat, sip my water, and listen politely as Rachel and Megan give Tyler a gentle inquisition. I have to give it to the kid; he handles the grilling beautifully. Much better than I did at that age, and in this very house. Giving answers to Rachel and Megan's soft questioning is not the same as being interrogated by Mr. Brennan – it's like the difference between a warm summer breeze and a Category 4 Hurricane – but the kid is smooth and probably would have impressed even the old man. By the time the plates are being loaded into the dishwasher – by Tyler, extra points for him – he's charmed them into thinking he's a great kid.

"We're going to the game room," Ellie says. She's changed into ripped jeans and a sweater and looks very cute.

"Sure," Megan says, glancing at her watch. "For about an hour, then I'll bring Tyler home."

I try to channel Mr. Brennan and give Tyler a threatening look, let him know there'd better be no hanky-panky going on in the back room, but intimidation just doesn't come naturally to me. Some fathers make a big show of cleaning their guns when a boy comes to pick up their daughter. Others deal with it a different way, welcoming the kid in and showing off their car or TV or guitar collection. I did neither – I was an absentee father. But, had I been around, I would have been the friendly, welcoming sort. Probably too friendly. Friendly enough to drink a beer in the woods with the kid.

"I'm going home to shower," Megan says, standing up. "I'll be back in about an hour."

I say goodbye and she nods to me. It's not much, but it's something. After the door closes behind Megan, I turn to Rachel. "Since when do you have a game room?"

"It's Daddy's old den," she says. "We converted it into a game room. Pool table, sixty-inch TV, foosball, ping-pong, video games. A teenager's dream."

"Sounds fun." I stand up from the table. "Maybe I'll go join them."

"Oh, no," Rachel says. She goes to the kitchen sink, begins to fill it with hot water, and tosses me a towel. "You can help me with the pots and pans."

After the dishes are washed and dried, I pour a glass of white wine for Rachel and grab a Bud Lite for myself.

"I don't know about that kid," I whisper across the kitchen table. From the game room I hear laughter and the sharp clack of billiard balls. "He's no good for Ellie."

"Listen to you, pretending to be a responsible adult. About thirty years too late."

That hurts, and I tell her so.

Rachel smiles sadly. "No offense, Jesse, but you don't know anything about either of those kids. Fortunately, Ellie seems to really love you. Kids seem to be very forgiving of grandparents, just like grandparents are quite forgiving of their grandchildren."

"I really don't think she has much to forgive me for." I realize I sound like a sulky teenager but plow on. "Lots of people don't see their grandchildren often. It's all about quality time."

"Sounds like a Facebook meme."

For a minute neither one of us speaks. It sounds like the pool game is already over. The only sound heard from the game room is the occasional giggle from Ellie.

"What are they doing in there?"

"Oh, lighten up," Rachel says. "They're young. Let them enjoy themselves."

"Remember how we used to enjoy ourselves at that age?" I say, raising my eyebrows.

"Shh," she says, looking toward the game room. Her cheeks blush red with embarrassment. I always loved that look on her. "We were older than they are."

"Not much. And kids today are older. I read that a twelve-year-old today knows as much as an eighteen-year-old in our day."

"I heard you mention to Ellie that you're still writing songs," she says. It's an obvious attempt to change the subject by bringing the focus back onto me. And it works.

"Yeah. Just wrote one that I think is pretty good."

"Will you play it for me?" she asks.

I gaze across the table and see the earnestness in her eyes. With a nod, I head upstairs to the guest bedroom and grab my guitar. When I return, Rachel's sitting on the couch in the living room with her refilled wine glass in one hand and my half-empty bottle of beer in the other. The lights in the room are dimmed.

"Mood matters," she says, grinning slyly. It's what I'd say when I used to play for her.

I sit on the couch beside her and strum the guitar a few times, fiddling with the knobs until the guitar is tuned properly. It's a good quality acoustic and it doesn't take me long. I smile at Rachel. She hands me my bottle of beer. I take a swig and set the bottle on the coffee table. Then I start playing.

I wrote the song two days ago on my balcony while looking over the ocean and thinking ahead to my trip to Maine. Kendra had returned from her photo shoot in the Bahamas the day before and told me that she'd taken up with a photographer she met there. There was a real spark, she said – "like, whammo!" – and she was moving out of my place and into his. To some people that might be the definition of moving quickly, but those people have never dated a model. I'm lucky (or unlucky) enough to have dated a few of them – playing guitar will do that for you – and have discovered that contemplation is not generally one of their strong suits.

There was nothing malicious about it on Kendra's part. I could see that she was sad about leaving, and she broke it to me as gently as she could. I was proud of her honesty in coming right to me with her feelings instead of sneaking around. She's young and beautiful, and what she wants sometimes changes with each sunrise. For my part, I've been through this sort of thing often enough that I dealt with it well. I wasn't in love with Kendra. Parts of Kendra, yes, but not Kendra herself. What hurt most was that she took up with a man who is successful, artistic, and presumable younger and better-looking than me. Maybe richer, too. If I plan to continue dating younger women, I should probably get used to it.

Sitting in the shade of my balcony, strumming my guitar while drinking a beer and watching the sun sparkle gold on the ocean, I found myself thinking about Kendra, and past relationships. My mind drifted back to my first relationship, the one I've never been able to let go of – Rachel. The song came quickly, as the best ones usually do. Time shifts during a burst of creativity, and two or three hours seem to pass in five minutes. I'm not Dylan when it comes to lyrics, but they're passable. I've never liked my voice. I sing in a low, John Mayer whisper. I can handle backup vocals, but I get embarrassed singing by myself. Guess that's why I'm a guitar player.

I'm not self-conscious around Rachel, though. Never have been. And so, I sing and strum and occasionally glance up at her smiling face.

*Well I remember the night I left, didn't want to be tied down*
*Time for me to move on, so put away that wedding gown*
*There's more for me out there, gonna be a big star*

*Looking back, I travelled a lot without going very far*

*We all fall in love, that's what the songs say*
*But songs don't tell us how fast it all fades away*
*I been there a few times, gone through the heartache and pain*
*And in the end, only one love still remains*

*Some things stay clear even when the past fades away*
*Thoughts of you so long ago still feel like today*
*I've made a lot of big mistakes in my life*
*But the only one I regret is not making you my wife*

*It's too late now, nothing to do but move on*
*And in the end I'll know why it turned out wrong*
*I won't cry or beg, cause that's not what I do*
*Instead I'll drink my beer and remember thoughts of you*

"I screwed up at the end, not sure if you heard that," I say, just after hitting the last note. When I look up, there are tears in Rachel's eyes. Her legs are pressed tightly together and she's pressing her steepled fingertips to her lips. Same thing she did years ago when I'd play a song she liked.

Before either of us can say anything, there's a loud burst of clapping from behind us. I turn to see Ellie and Tyler standing in the doorway. Ellie's clapping like, well, a girl, with her hands stiff and straight, slapping together with the quick and steady rhythm of a cymbal-banging monkey, while Tyler's nodding his head and clapping slowly.

"Dude, that was fire!" he says. "Straight up lit, bro! Gramps, you can play!"

"What the hell is he saying?" I quietly ask Rachel. "Is that code for 'I'm a moron'?"

She smiles, wipes her eyes with one hand and lightly slaps my thigh with the other.

"He's being nice. Just using teenage slang," she whispers.

"I wonder what Gramps is slang for."

"I think it means 'old fart'. Or something along those lines."

Ellie comes over and sits on the arm of the couch. I notice she's holding Tyler's hand.

"That was so good, Grampy." She turns to Tyler. "Of course he can play guitar. He's great. Don't you know who he is?"

"Yeah, I know who he is. Dude's your grandfather." He looks from me to Ellie. "Why, is he famous or something?"

Ellie looks at Tyler in a way that states, nonverbally, "Duh!"

"Yeah, he's famous! You've heard of that old song "Your Love Line", right? It was in the Ryan Gosling movie?"

"Oh, yeah. I've heard it." Tyler begins singing in a squeaky falsetto. "Baby, I'm not the kind to step over your love line . . ."

"Right! It's by The Dropouts. That's Grampy's old band! He played guitar and wrote the song!"

"Co-wrote," I correct her.

"Wow!" Tyler stares at me, wide-eyed. "You're famous. I can't believe I drank beer with a famous person."

"What?" Rachel and Ellie ask, at the same time. I grip the neck of the guitar tightly and consider bringing it down over the kid's head.

"Ah, I mean I'm watching him play and drink beer. I don't know what I'm saying. I've never met anyone famous before."

"I have that effect on people," I say.

"Maybe we could write a song together," Tyler says excitedly. "You play, and I'll rap. Dude, it would be so sick!"

"Yeah. Sick. But no."

My negative reply has no obvious effect on Tyler's mood. The excited smile remains on his face and I know that in his head there's some sort of acoustic rap mashup forming. The optimism of youth is not easily deterred, even when the idea is moronic.

"Will you play at my birthday party, Grampy?" Ellie asks.

"Of course, honey. Do you have any requests?"

"Well, "Your Love Line", of course. And how about that song you just played for Grammy?"

"Sure," I say. "What's funny is that, when I wrote it, I heard it being played by The Dropouts. I could actually hear it in my head. It sounded incredible." I pause to ponder the memory. "It's been a long time since that's happened."

"Dude, maybe you could get the band back together for the party," Tyler says.

From behind us, Megan says, "Ellie, it's time for us to bring Tyler home."

We all turn around. She's standing in the wide doorway, hair pulled back into a ponytail under a thick winter hat bearing a Patriots logo. She's also wearing mittens. Megan never did like the cold. I glance out a window, hoping that something in the darkness will show me the temperature. There's no thermometer but I notice condensation around the edges of the glass. Yup, it's cold.

Ellie and Tyler go into the kitchen to put on their coats, and Rachel follows them. I hear the kids talking excitedly, Ellie bragging about me and Tyler replying with a few 'lit's' and 'sweet's'. When I hear him say my playing is "pretty sick for an old dude", I can't help but smile.

"You want to come back over here after you drop him off?" I ask Megan. She's still standing in the doorway separating the kitchen and living room, arms crossed. "Maybe we could hang out and talk, have a drink together. It's been a long time since we've talked."

She shakes her head. "Not tonight. I'm tired."

"I'm only here for a couple of days, honey," I say. "I'm hoping we can get together."

She looks me in the eye and sings, *"We'll get together then, Dad, you know we'll have a good time then."* Then she disappears into the kitchen.

7

I don't know how long I sit on the couch after they leave, staring out the window, deep in thought. At some point, Rachel taps her knuckles gently against the side of my head.

"Hello? Anyone home?"

I smile, lean forward, and begin softly strumming the guitar. My shrink in Florida says I use the guitar as a form of protection, a six-stringed shield to keep the unwanted away from me. It's why I carry a guitar most everywhere I go. If a situation becomes uncomfortable, I can just hold my guitar in front of me like a barrier. It's said that Hendrix used to sleep with his guitar. I haven't gone that far, although I have passed out while playing, if that counts.

I don't even have to play my guitar in these awkward situations. Just having it there, hanging in front of me like – well, like a shield – relaxes me. It really does. I think the shrink was on to something with this, because I never once brought a guitar to her office and I always felt uncomfortable as hell.

"I was just thinking, maybe the little rapper had a good idea. About getting the band together to play Ellie's birthday party." I look at Rachel. "It's been so long, though. I don't even know if the guys are still around."

"When's the last time you saw any of them?" Rachel asks.

"Let's see." I lean back against the couch and run my hand through my hair. "Danny was at Megan's wedding, so that was what, fifteen years. Wow." I whistle softly. "Phil and Cam, I haven't seen since the band broke up. Over thirty years. Phil sent me an email congratulating me when Ellie was born. Sort of an olive branch, I think." Though I should have been the one to extend it, not Phil. "Not sure how he got my email address, but it was nice hearing from him."

"I gave it to him," Rachel says, surprising me. "I still see him once in a while."

"So they still live in Apple Brook?"

Rachel nods. "Danny and Cam do. Danny lives just down the street, on the lake. You passed his place on your way here. Cam lives in the Prince of Peace Church, on Pine Street."

"You said he lives in the church. You mean near the church, right?"

"No, I mean in the church."

I think about this for a minute. By saying Cam lives in the church, she probably means he's there often enough to live there, like a person who works a lot lives in the office, or an alcoholic lives in the bar. Then I consider Cam going to church, and it becomes even more unclear.

"Is he a monk now, or something?"

"Cam had some rough years after The Dropouts broke up. Went out to the west coast, got addicted to crack, lost everything. He was a real mess – living on the streets and in shelters. Even spent some time in jail. He eventually cleaned up, and a few years ago he moved back to Apple Brook. He became really involved in the church, did a lot of volunteering, and became music director. He plays with the band every Sunday, usually on drums. When the money from "Your Love Line" started rolling in, Cam decided to donate most of it to the church in exchange for an apartment in the back of the church."

"Must be a big church," I say.

"It's very big, since the money started coming in," Rachel says. "And getting bigger all the time."

"Did you say he's playing drums? What about bass? He's a bass player."

"I think he plays whatever they need him to play. He even sings sometimes."

"Wow. Those people must really love God if they're willing to listen to Cam sing."

Cameron Nelson, dedicated to the church. This was the guy who used to come home drunk on Friday nights and peek in the basement window to watch his father and stepmother have sex in the hot tub.

"How about Danny?"

"Danny sang in a few bands in Boston, then somehow got involved in the theater and moved to New York. He did very well and had parts in several Broadway musicals. He also took up playwriting, and one of his plays was nominated for a Tony. Danny's a very talented guy."

"Always was," I say. "Why'd he come back here? Let me guess: got married, had kids, wanted to raise them in a nice, quiet place like Apple Brook."

"You're way off," Rachel says. "He just got tired of the city lifestyle, the drugs and the crime and the never-ending parties. And yes, he did meet someone, a wonderfully kind person whom he recently married. I went to the wedding, in fact. But they won't be having kids."

"Too old?"

"Too gay," Rachel says.

It takes me a moment, but then I get the joke. I laugh for a few seconds, until I realize she's not laughing with me.

"Wait . . . hold on. Are you saying that Danny's wife is gay?"

"Yes, he is."

"He? He's a guy? And gay?" I look out the window into the darkness. "Holy shit. That would mean Danny's gay."

"Ding ding, give that man a prize!"

Rachel gets up and leaves the room, I assume to give me some time alone to process this unexpected news. In the background I hear the refrigerator door open and close, but it barely registers. I tightly grip my shield (I mean, guitar) and strum the chords of "Your Love Line", whispering the words while staring straight ahead at nothing. I couldn't be more staggered if Rachel had told me that Danny was dead. In fact, Danny's passing would be far more believable than this. Danny was the cock of the walk, the David Lee Roth of our band. He banged more chicks than the rest of us combined. Even if I wasn't in a committed relationship with Rachel back then, he'd have outdistanced me by a long way. Women loved him. I probably couldn't have admitted it then, but I can now. Danny Crane, gay. Man. It's like finding out The Fonz was gay.

Rachel returns and hands me a cold beer. "I thought you might need this."

I nod, tip my head back, and down half of it. "No kidding?"

She shakes her head and smiles kindly. "No kidding. I've talked to Danny about it. He says he was embarrassed and confused when he was younger.

People weren't allowed to be gay back then, especially singers in rock bands."

"But they were," I say. "Look at Freddie Mercury and Rob Halford." I play the riff from "Living After Midnight".

"They didn't come out, though. Not for a long time. When Danny moved to New York, he discovered that being gay or bisexual is nothing to be ashamed of, that there's nothing wrong with him. And now, in the twenty-first century, he can feel safe and secure living as a married gay man, even in a small New England town like Apple Brook." Rachel sips her wine next to me. "We've come a long way, baby."

I grab my beer and finish it. Danny, a married gay man. Those two words just didn't belong in the same sentence. Nothing against being gay. I have plenty of gay friends. I just didn't realize Danny was one of them.

"You said he lives down the road?"

Rachel nods. "The old McCarthy place. You remember it?"

"Yes. I noticed it earlier when I drove past. The house looks like it went on steroids and swelled to five times its original size."

"Danny's made some changes," she said with a smile.

I lean my guitar against the couch and try to ignore the popping and creaking of my joints as I stand.

"Let's go see him."

Rachel checks her watch. "We could. It's a little past eight o'clock so he should be up." She looks at me with concern. "Maybe I should call first, just to be sure we aren't interrupting something."

"Where's the excitement in that?" I say. "Come on, let's surprise him. It'll be fun."

She still looks worried, but she goes to the kitchen and takes her jacket from the coat rack. I do the same. "It'll be fun. Isn't that what you said the night you took my virginity?"

"And I was right, wasn't I?" I say, with a big grin.

Judging by the numerous spotlights illuminating the house and the front yard, Danny's place is about the same size as Rachel's, with far less land. It's lit up like a prison break. I follow her up the wide, curving cobblestone walkway. The front door is massive and looks like something found on an old European castle or abbey. In the center is a large round iron door knocker. Mostly decorative, I guess, as Rachel presses the doorbell. I'm reminded of the line in *Young Frankenstein*, when Gene Wilder says, "What knockers!" to Teri Garr, and I can't help but smile.

After half a minute or so the door opens. It's Danny, looking ready for bed, dressed in plaid flannel pajama pants and a t-shirt. He doesn't look much different than I remember. He's wearing glasses, which is new. Like me, he's kept most of his hair and wears it long, though there's a lot more gray in his. He squints into the brightness. "Rachel? Is that you?"

"Hi, Danny," Rachel says. "Sorry to bother you so late, but someone wanted to visit you and he couldn't wait until tomorrow."

His gaze turns to me. For a moment he squints at me without recognition. Then his eyes widen, and he flashes a smile as bright as the outside lights. I'm guessing teeth whitening.

"Jesse Maze! I don't believe it. Well, this is certainly a nice surprise." He steps back and waves us inside. "Come in, you guys, come in. It's freezing out there."

We step into a well-lit entryway. Danny gives Rachel a hug and motions for her to take off her jacket and hang it up on a nearby coat rack. Then he turns to me, still smiling. We silently stare at each other for a few moments before I pull him into a tight embrace.

When we separate, I notice tears in both Rachel's and Danny's eyes. For some inexplicable reason, a salty discharge seems to be welling up in mine as well. We all laugh, a little embarrassed. Danny and I both wipe our eyes with the back of our hands, while Rachel takes out a tissue.

"Jesse, you're looking great!" Danny says. He grabs both my shoulders and looks me up and down as if I'm a piece of art he's thinking of purchasing. "You don't look much different than the old days."

"You're looking good too," I say.

"You must be home for Ellie's birthday party?" he says.

"Yeah. How did you know?"

"I'm Megan's godfather, remember?"

I look at Rachel. She raises her eyebrows as if to say, "Seriously? You forgot that?"

"So, Danny," I say. "Rachel tells me you're a fag now."

The smile drops from Rachel's face like a sunset in fast motion, and I think perhaps I should have brought up the subject of homosexuality with a bit more tact. But after fixing me with a long, silent stare, Danny bursts out laughing.

"You shouldn't say fag. It's more acceptable if you say queer."

"Man, when I think of all the times you saw me naked while changing backstage," I say. "Makes me wonder what you were thinking."

"I was thinking, poor Rachel," Danny says, and Rachel begins laughing with him. A little too enthusiastically, in my opinion, although I soon join in.

We follow Danny into the living room. It's very big, with high ceilings and a large black woodstove throwing heat from one corner. There's a huge sectional couch in the middle of the room, facing a television that appears to be at least ninety inches. A small man with straw-colored hair, dressed similarly to Danny in flannel pajama pants, is tucked into the corner of the sectional, surrounded by comfortable-looking blankets and pillows. He stands when he hears us enter the room. I can see that he's at least ten years younger than us, or he has a great surgeon.

Danny introduces me to the man, his partner, Andrew. He's already met Rachel and they hug. We take a seat on the couch. Andrew goes to the kitchen and returns with two bottles of wine and four glasses, and over the next few hours we get a little drunk and talk and laugh about the unforeseen paths life has taken us down since the days of the Dropouts. There's little mention of our time in the band, and for that I'm grateful.

8

1985

Everything changed so fast. Just the year before, I was eighteen years old with a hot-looking girlfriend who I was really in love with and a band that was playing regularly at high school dances and even a few clubs in Portland. I was still living at home, but to the surprise of many I'd graduated high school and taken a part-time job at Strawberries, a record store in Portland.

Outside of music and Rachel, I had no plans or ambitions. The Dropouts recorded an album (funded by our parents and girlfriends and everyone else we could scrounge money from) on an independent label the same month we graduated high school. A couple of the songs got airplay on WBCN in Boston, leading to a gig at The Rat backing up a lousy punk band with angry, aggressive fans. It wasn't a good mix – the Dropouts weren't punk. We also didn't sound or look like the metal bands that were popping up everywhere at the time like a leather-and-lipstick-clad, guitar-driven venereal disease. We were more a mix of Aerosmith and the J Geils Band and normally would have gone over fine in Boston, had we not been playing in front of the city's last remaining punk fans. We played and sounded great but they didn't like us, showing their displeasure by spitting and hurling bottles at us.

As chance would have it, there was one person who was impressed by our performance that night. An A&R guy from Epic by the name of Ken Pike was visiting the city with his family and heard our song on WBCN, saw our name on the marquee later that day outside The Rat, and decided to come check us out that evening.

Artists and entertainers always like to say they made it because of talent, but in most cases, including ours, there's a corresponding amount of luck or fate or serendipity, whichever name you prefer. Phil once said it was shit-house luck, and to me that described it perfectly.

Despite the bottle throwing and spitting, Ken Pike liked what he saw and heard. He talked to our manager, Derek, one thing led to another, and soon we were signed to a record deal. They wanted product quickly, Danny and I had a backlog of songs we'd written, and our second album was recorded and released on Epic at the start of 1986. Suddenly everything went from zero to a hundred and nobody warned us to strap ourselves in.

In mid-January, Rachel told me she was pregnant. At the time, I was still living at home with my parents and driving a brown 1973 Pinto Wagon that burned two pints of oil a week. Most of the money I'd earned working part-time at Strawberries and playing high school dances with the Dropouts had gone toward helping pay for a van to haul our equipment to gigs. The van cost $2,000 and we'd split it four ways, $500 apiece. That left me with about $200 in the bank. Not much to raise a family on.

We talked briefly about an abortion. Mostly I talked and Rachel shook her head. I didn't really want Rachel to have an abortion, but I was scared. Rachel was scared, too. We weren't ready to be parents. But Rachel had been brought up Catholic and so had I; eternal damnation was not acceptable to either of us, although at times it seemed preferable to telling her father about the pregnancy. I ended up emptying my bank account and buying a small, cheap ring, and at the age of nineteen I proposed to my girlfriend, a senior in high school.

Mr. Brennan was not happy about my getting his daughter pregnant. I could tell by the way he pointed his gun at me. I didn't really think he'd shoot me, because a man like Mr. Brennan had too much to lose. Even so, it was by far the scariest moment of my young life. Like having an epiphany, I became vividly and uncomfortably aware that anyone staring down the cold dark barrel of a loaded gun for the first time is going to need a change of underwear very soon. For a few minutes there, the look in his eyes was that of a man who'd had enough of a pesky fly buzzing around his house and was going to get rid of it, once and for all.

My parents weren't happy, but they liked Rachel and offered to let us live at their house until we could afford a place of our own, provided we were married first. I guess they didn't want us living in sin. Rachel's father forbade his daughter to move in with us. She was to finish high school, have the baby, and go to college. The baby would stay with Mr. and Mrs. Brennan while she was away at school. There was a lot of arguing and crying and threatening between the two families over the next few months.

While all this was going on, almost unnoticed by me, our album, ingeniously titled *Dropping Out*, had begun creeping up the charts. First it crawled into the Top 200, by spring the Top 100, and by Labor Day it was comfortably nestled midway in the Top 40. It was only when we stopped gigging dives in Portland and Old Orchard Beach and started playing big clubs in Boston on a regular basis that I was able to put aside my personal unrest long enough to look around and realize, holy shit, something's happening.

"Your Love Line" cracked the Top 40 in August 1985, during the same week Megan brashly entered the world at Apple Brook Hospital. I never thought the excitement of holding my beautiful baby girl for the first time could be matched but hearing Casey Kasem on the radio that very weekend saying "And now, with their first Top 40 hit, here are the Dropouts" was a close runner-up. It was the greatest week of my life, never again to be equaled.

The night that Megan was born I slept in Rachel's room on a tiny hospital cot so I could be close to her and Megan. The next evening, I was in Hartford, Connecticut, playing a gig. The following weekend "Your Love Line" jumped fifteen places and the *Dropping Out* album entered the Top 40. A few days later we were in Boston doing a show with one of our heroes, Peter Wolf.

Our song and album were hits, the Dropouts were in demand, and I had a newborn baby girl. On top of that, I was still living at home with my parents (on my rare days off) and my girlfriend and daughter were living with her parents. I felt like a juggler who kept having more and more rings thrown to him from offstage. We were doing gigs, radio and TV shows, guest appearances, all while trying to write songs for the next album. Strike while the iron's hot, our manager kept repeating. Made sense, but he wasn't the one with a newborn baby at home. Or, even worse, at someone else's home.

One positive aspect of this crazy time was that Mr. Brennan's utter hatred of me quite unexpectedly lessened to a mild loathing. It might have been the sight of his beautiful granddaughter that caused it. Babies have a way of softening even the hardest of souls. Perhaps he felt that, as the father of such a beautiful angel, I couldn't be all bad. Maybe it was the way I'd stuck by Rachel's side throughout the pregnancy, even when he'd made it extremely difficult for me to do so. Most likely, though, it was the growing popular and financial success of the Dropouts that caused Mr. Brennan to lighten up a bit in his attitude toward me. The prospect of my earning a very good living, along with my diminishing presence from the everyday lives of his daughter and granddaughter due to work responsibilities, was enough to put a spring in his normally heavy step.

During the first two weeks of Megan's life I'd seen her three times. The rest of the time I was with the band, playing, practicing, writing, and partying. We were in New York when I got a call from Rachel to remind me that Megan was being baptized that weekend. We'd decided to name her cousin Sarah as the godmother and Danny as the godfather. Unfortunately, I'd forgotten to mention this tidbit of information to Danny.

"Hey, man," I said, as we drank beer and watched our equipment get loaded into the truck for a gig that evening. We knew we'd hit the big time when we stopped having to carry our own equipment. "I've got some good news and bad news."

"Bad news first," Danny said.

"I can't do the show Sunday night. Megan's being baptized and I totally spaced it. Rachel just called to remind me."

Danny watched a roadie struggle to lift a large amp into the truck. His expression showed he wasn't pleased with the bad news.

"And the good news?"

I flashed my most winning grin. "You're going to be Megan's godfather!"

His expression didn't change. Maybe this was his happy face and I'd never noticed.

"Dude, this is a lot of responsibility," he finally said. "I'm not ready to watch over a kid."

"It's not that hard, really," I said. And for me, it wasn't. I hadn't even had to change a diaper so far.

"What if I say no?"

"Well, I still can't play the show. I'm the father, I have to be at the baptism. I think Mr. Brennan is starting to like me. He hasn't growled at me in two weeks. And Rachel will never forgive you if you say no. Or me, for that matter."

He finished his beer and tossed the can aside.

"Fine. What's a godfather have to do?"

Danny wasn't Catholic. I'm not sure what he was. The topic of religion didn't come up very often in our band.

"Well, it's pretty easy. The worst part is when you have to take the scissors and snip him during the circumcision."

He jumped back about three feet.

"I'm just shittin' you, man." I laughed. "First of all, we don't do circumcisions at a baptism. Second, and most important, Megan is a girl."

"Oh, yeah." He laughed along with me.

"By being her godfather, you're basically saying that you'll help take care of Megan if anything ever happens to me or Rachel." I burp, loudly, and take a swig from my beer can. "And nothing's going to happen to us, don't worry."

He opened another beer. "What the hell, I'll do it. We could use a day off anyway. But you tell the other guys."

"No problem," I said. "And another bonus about going to the baptism – Megan's good-looking friends will all be there, and as the ceremony goes on, they'll start fantasizing about having cute little babies of their own. Then they'll start thinking about how babies are made, and they'll get all worked up." I said this knowingly, even though the last baptism I attended was my own. "It's better than foreplay. As the godfather, and a rock star to boot, all you have to do is smile their way and every one of them be ready to put out."

Danny nodded, looked away, and drank some beer.

9

Except for the trailers, Apple Brook High School looks pretty much the same as it did when I attended classes over thirty years ago. One side of the school, a field roughly fifty yards long where we used to have gym class on nice days – the same field where I first met Rachel during a fire drill, in fact – is lined with half a dozen mobile homes. Portable classrooms, Ellie tells me. The school is too small now, and apparently the solution was to build a trailer park. A new high school is in the works, she says, the biggest and most expensive in the state of Maine. It's going to include a vocational school and should be ready in three years, just in time for her senior year.

I drop Ellie off in front of the high school, where she gives me a big hug before getting out of the car. It's a great way to start the day. Driving away from the school I think about those ugly white trailers lined up in the old field. The students are taught to call them portable classrooms, as though talking about cute little classrooms that can be quickly set up on the lawn to hold algebra outside on warm spring days. At least the students will have something to complain about when they're old – *"back in my day we had to walk through snow and ice every day to get to history class."* But if those trailers had been there in my day, I never would have met Rachel during the fire drill, we wouldn't have had Megan, and Ellie would never have been born, like a genetic butterfly effect. It's a deep thought, something

I'm unaccustomed to so early in the morning, and I quickly turn up the radio to clear my mind.

Instead of going back to Rachel's, I swing over to Danny's house. He's ready, just as he said he'd be. The mouth-watering smell of pancakes and coffee drifts from the kitchen, and when Danny asks if I'd like breakfast I nod and follow him in, taking a seat near the French doors leading from the kitchen to a large deck overlooking the lake. The coffee is caramel-flavored, the pancakes blueberry, the maple syrup organic and local. While eating I watch the fog formed from cool air and warm water rise and float lazily over the lake. The sun is out and the fog will disappear soon, but for now I'm enjoying the view.

"You sure you want to do this?" Danny asks as we pull out of his driveway an hour later. "Cam isn't very fond of you, last I knew. For a long time, he blamed you for the breakup of the band, and the breakup of the band for the downward spiral his life took."

"So, in a nutshell, I'm to blame for all Cam's problems."

"Correct. He doesn't feel that way anymore, or at least he doesn't express those feelings. He's handed all his problems over to God. But I have a feeling that when God's not looking, Cam's still pissed off at you."

I turn off Far Shore Drive and drive toward town for the second time this morning. Normally I'm not even out of bed until around noon, so I'm feeling a bit out of sorts. The coffee helped a lot, but I'm still tired. It was a late night and I'd forgotten how early New Englanders tend to get up in the morning, as though racing the sunrise. Not all of them are up early, though. When I left Lazy Daze at quarter past seven this morning, Rachel was still nestled comfortably in her bed.

Danny and I are quiet for a couple minutes, listening to John Mellencamp sing about Sam Cooke playing on the radio. It's a comfortable silence between two old friends. When we arrive in downtown Apple Brook, I turn on to Main Street and say, "Rachel tells me Phil's doing well."

"Seems that way. We got together for lunch around this time last year. He's got a place on Wells Beach, big as a hotel. You probably heard that a few years after the band broke up, Phil invented a drum stool that was supposed to be the most comfortable around, really easy on your back. He sold a bunch of them, word got around, and next thing you know Tama offers him millions of dollars for it. All the Dropouts money we're making now is just spending money to him."

Danny points, and I turn down Pine Street and into the parking lot of the Prince of Peace Church. The building is vast and beautiful, white with a high steeple. Two mighty oak trees stand like sentries on either side of the front walkway. Behind the church is a small pond, with a white gazebo nearby. Along the edge of the pond are benches and picnic tables. In the background, stunning as the best work of a master painter, is a forest of vividly colorful trees.

I whistle softly. "Nice place. I don't remember this being here when we were kids."

"Back then, most people in town went to the Protestant and Catholic churches. The Prince of Peace was here, but the chapel was just that small part at the back. About the size of a trailer. The whole front part, more than ninety percent of the structure, was built over the past three years. There's a gym with a basketball court and weight room, a daycare area, conference rooms, commercial kitchen, the works. Parking lot, gazebo, benches, all new. I like to call it 'The House the Dropouts Built.'"

Again, I whistle. "This must have cost Cam everything he made. He'd better pray there really is a God. If not, he's made a very poor investment."

"Cam's a believer," Danny says, with a shrug. "Better than spending it on drugs."

I agree. We get out of the SUV and walk to a door on the side of what is now known as the back annex, aka Cam's house. Danny rings the bell. I stand a little back from him, gazing down at the pond.

After about a minute the door opens, and there's Cam. He doesn't look like the Cam I used to know – that Cam had pudgy cheeks and a blond mullet and a wispy teenage moustache curving over an ever-present grin and could often be found carrying a Dungeons and Dragons Player's Handbook. This Cam, the older, harder, life-bitten Cam, has thick, dark-rimmed glasses, with a heavily lined, slightly gaunt face half-hidden beneath a bushy gray beard. He's balding, and the longish gray hairs on the sides of his head stick out as though he's just pulled his finger from a light socket. The sleeves of his thick flannel shirt are rolled up to the elbows, revealing several faded green tattoos that don't appear to have been done by a professional. In his hand is a dustpan. When he recognizes Danny his dark eyes light up, and in them I see a brief but clear flash of my former bandmate and dungeon master.

"Dan the man," he says, with a slight smile. "How's it going, my friend?"

"Cam the man," Danny replies. "Lookin' good, brother. I brought an old friend with me. He wants to say hello."

I step forward, a bit uncertainly.

"Hey, Cam. It's nice to see you after all these years."

Cam squints into my face for a long moment, nods his head as though confirming a private thought, and throws a right hook that drops me like a wet sack.

The couch and the pillow under my head are soft and comfortable. The room is warm and relaxed and smells like a freshly pleasant combination of coffee and church. The bag of frozen peas pressed against my cheek is cold, and when I try to focus on Danny's face directly above me, I realize that my left eye is partially closed.

"What happened?" I ask.

"Cam punched you," Danny answers. "I'd say it was more a TKO than a knockout. You were floundering around but still conscious, and we had to help you inside."

"That's what I thought, but I hoped I might have dreamt it." Turning my head slightly, I'm relieved to feel little pain. "So, I suppose you're gay, right? I didn't dream that either?"

"Queer as a three-dollar bill," Danny says, still looking down on me. "Does it bother you?"

"That you're gay? No, I'm just surprised. But I'll get used to it."

He sits back on a chair near the couch. I take in my surroundings. It's a small, open apartment, very clean, very white. What stands out most is that there are no personal effects to be seen. My condo has my gold and platinum records hanging on the wall in the hallway, along with several photos of me playing onstage over the years. The only things on these walls are a cross hanging above the archway leading to the kitchen, a framed print of *Grace* by Enstrom on the wall next to the kitchen table, and a picture of Jesus on one wall of the living room. Thinking about it, this comparison probably shines a far more negative light on me than on Cam.

"Where's Cam?" I ask.

"Inside the church, praying for forgiveness," Danny says. "That's one tormented dude. He was almost in tears because he hit you, but I could tell he kind of wanted to do it again."

He smiles and chuckles lightly at the memory.

"Hmm." I pull the bag of peas away from my eye and sit up. "How's it look?"

Danny leans forward and tilts his head back slightly. "Well, the bad news is, you're still ugly." He peers closer. "It's a little swollen, so you might have a bit of a shiner."

It feels swollen, but the frozen peas are too cold to press against my face again. As I'm putting them back into his freezer, Cam walks through the door leading from his apartment to the church.

"Sorry about that, guys." He squeezes Danny's shoulder as he passes and sits on the couch. I sit beside him. He squints at my swollen eye through his thick spectacles. "I apologize, Jesse," he says formally. Despite his words and solemn expression, there's a glint of satisfaction in his eyes. "I don't know what came over me."

"Yeah, well, you have every right to be angry." I've thought for a long time about what I'd say to Cam if ever given the chance, and I'm discovering that it's far more difficult in person. Probably would have been easier if I hadn't been punched in the face first. "I was a stupid, selfish young man, and I threw away relationships with the people that meant most in my life

– my band, my girlfriend, my daughter. So, I'm here to apologize. I hope we can be friends again."

For a long time, he stares at the bare white wall across the room and says nothing. I glance at Danny, but he's scrolling through his phone and ignoring us. I don't know if it's the tension of the moment, but the throbbing in my cheek feels like it's getting worse. I consider getting up for the peas, but then Cam finally speaks.

"You really hurt me, Jesse." He looks at me and his eyes are filled with pain. Cam was always the most sensitive of the four of us, which is undoubtedly why he took the breakup so hard. "Danny hurt me too, but he wasn't as mean. And he apologized long ago. I haven't heard from you in over thirty years."

I nod and consider what to say. Many things come to mind: I didn't realize my selfishness bothered anyone; between playing in cover bands and getting drunk and screwing a long and forgettable succession of minor-league groupies, I just never had the time; my cell phone has bad reception. So many pathetic, inadequate excuses for never getting in touch with one of the best friends I ever had.

"You didn't even get the worst of the deal. Jesse went years without seeing his own daughter. Imagine how she feels," Danny says helpfully.

"Yes, Danny, thank you for that useful reminder." Turning to Cam, I say, "I regret how it all ended up. I truly do. The Dropouts should have stayed together and ruled the charts for twenty years. I should have married Rachel and lived happily ever after. I should have developed a good relationship with my wonderful daughter. But I fucked it all up." I cover my mouth. "Shit, sorry. I didn't mean to swear in church."

For the first time Cam smiles, and I catch a glimpse of the teenager I once knew.

"It's okay. We're not technically in church. And they're not as strict about stuff like that here as they are in the Catholic church."

I nod. "Anyway, I wish I could take it all back. I realize it's probably too little, too late, but is there anything I can do to make this right?"

Cam thinks for a moment, then shakes his head. "I don't think anything can ever make it right, to be honest. But you seem sincere, and I appreciate the apology."

"Maybe he could start going to church every week," Danny says, without looking up from his phone. I'm going to fucking kill him.

"That might be a good idea, Daniel," Cam says thoughtfully.

I look back and forth between the two of them. Go to church? It's not like I fucking killed someone. But, what the hell, if it'll mend fences.

"Uh, yeah, I suppose, if you really want me to. I could give church a try . . ."

Cam and Danny look at each other. First Cam smiles, then Danny, and then they burst into laughter.

"You don't have to go to church," Cam says, still laughing. "I wouldn't want the building to collapse around all the innocent parishioners just because of you."

It's great to share a laugh, even at my own expense. Sometimes those are the best ones. The tension seems to have vanished from the room and we spend the next hour talking about old times, tiptoeing around the breakup. Cam tells us about playing in a couple of bands after the breakup, but never finding the same thrill as when he played with his three best friends. He started to get heavily into drugs, and his girlfriend decided a move to California would be the best thing for them. With its sunshine and warmth and yoga and organic restaurants, they could start over with a healthy lifestyle and be anyone they wanted. Turns out it *was* the best thing, at least for her – less than a year after the move, Cam's girlfriend met a guitar player in a hair metal band and decided that was where her future lied. When grunge did to hair metal what a dart does to a balloon Cam should have been happy, but by that time he was too strung out to care.

He admits that the next decade or two is pretty fuzzy. Much of it was spent high, homeless, and hopeless. There were a few short stints in jail. Cam had real musical talent – he was a hell of a bass player and could also play drums and piano – but he didn't touch an instrument for over twenty years, until he got cleaned up. Wasted years, as he bitterly describes them.

"By the time I got sober I'd had enough of California and decided to move back to Maine," Cam says. "Out there, you just can't trust anyone. I'd thought many times about coming back here and getting a job at a music store, or even opening my own, but it wasn't my calling. Right before I went to rehab, when I was as low as I'd ever been, I discovered God. He's the reason I decided to get cleaned up, and I knew I wanted to serve Him somehow." Cam scratches his beard and glances up at the cross over the doorway. "And, besides God, the biggest reason I'm sitting here now is because of Phil."

"Phil?" I say.

I glance at Danny, but he must already know this story because he doesn't appear surprised. He's slowly poking at his phone, texting.

"He's one of the first people I called when I got sober and came back to Maine. I was never angry with Phil; he was in the same boat as me when the band broke up. Phil knows a lot of people around here, and when I told him what I wanted to do, he got me a job cleaning and doing maintenance at the church. I stayed at his house for a few months while I got back on my feet, and then "Your Love Line" started making money again." He shrugs. "And now I live here. Still cleaning the church, just got a lot more to clean and maintain now."

"Whatever happened to the girlfriend?" I ask.

Danny lowers his phone and looks over – now he's interested. Cam gets a faraway look in his eyes, smiles slightly, and says, "She ended up posing for Playboy. A Playmate of the Month in the mid-nineties. I don't know what happened to her after that."

"Well, she isn't going to top that." I glance around the apartment. "You don't happen to have a copy lying around anywhere, do you?"

Cam shakes his head and chuckles. Danny mentions that our next stop is Phil's house, down at the beach, and he invites Cam to join us. At first, Cam declines. There's too much work to do around the church, he says. But it's obvious that he wants to go with us, and it doesn't take much cajoling before Cam's in the back seat and we're on our way.

10

I'd forgotten about the stench of the marsh that surrounds the Mile Road connecting Route 1 with Wells Beach, but as we travel the short two-lane, I'm quickly reminded. The wet, grassy marsh is wide open and continues as far as the eye can see in both directions. It smells, in the words of many a child who has travelled this road, like a bad fart. The windows are up, but the odor finds its way inside. I love it. To me, the smell brings back pleasant memories of childhood. This, to me, is what the beach smells like. You don't get this smell at the beach in Miami.

Travelling the Mile Road also serves as a revealing test of maturity which, at fifty-plus years of age, we all fail miserably. We aren't more than a hundred yards down the Mile Road before Cam says, "Smells like Danny ripped one", and we all crack up like teenagers.

Phil's house is located on the ocean side of Atlantic Ave. The place is massive, twice the size of Danny's house. It's crammed onto a double lot and there is no room to park in the small driveway because a BMW and a Lexus SUV are already parked there. We use the public lot about a quarter of a mile away and walk back. There are several vehicles in the lot, which Danny says is surprising at this time of year. With the ocean breeze it feels much colder here than it does in Apple Brook. I jam my hands into the pockets of my leather jacket and hunch forward, trying to block the wind. Cam is dressed in just a flannel shirt with the sleeves rolled up, but the cold doesn't seem to bother him at all.

I ring the bell and woman in a wheelchair answers the door. She's attractive, about our age. Behind her is an enormous, high-ceilinged living room, and behind that I catch a glimpse of a kitchen full of stainless-steel appliances. Even from here I can see that the countertops are lower than normal and the appliances are custom-sized, similar in size to those found at a children's daycare center.

I smile and ask if Phil is home. She tilts her head and looks at me as though she knows something that I don't. Then she notices Danny and Cam. With a smile as soft and white as a daisy petal, reaches her arms up to them. First Danny bends down for a hug, then Cam. She holds Cam tight and presses her lips to his hairy cheek. I follow them into the house, confused, and forget to close the door behind me.

"And you, Jesse, obviously don't remember me," she says teasingly, after Cam straightens up.

I gaze at her face for a moment before it hits me. A girl Phil met one night at a show in Worcester. Tall, brunette, beautiful. Originally from Lynn, Massachusetts. A junior at Worcester Polytechnic Institute, which is easy to remember because engineering majors didn't tend to date members of the Dropouts. What I can't remember is her name.

"Lynne," she says helpfully. Then, looking behind me, "Cam, would you close the door? It's so cold out."

"I remember. Lynne from Lynn, City of Sin." I shake my head. "Wow, I knew you two were getting serious, but that was so long ago. I guess it worked out, huh?"

She smiles and steers the wheelchair to an intercom on the wall near the front door, set lower than it normally would be. I finally realize the reason everything seems so short is because the home is designed for a person in a wheelchair. She presses a button and says, "Phil, can you come upstairs for a minute, please?"

Releasing the button, she turns her wheelchair and says, "He's trying to avoid my friends."

I follow her gaze to a hallway leading toward the back of the house and become aware of female voices and laughter coming from that direction. Like curious squirrels peering out from a backyard hole, a blond head leans out from a doorway, followed quickly by another. Then, as quickly as they appeared, they're gone. There's a silent pause, and then a high-pitched, multi-voiced burst of female laughter.

Shortly afterward Phil enters from a different doorway, which I realize leads to a stairway. As soon as he steps foot in the hall, several women call out, "Hiii, Philll" in unnaturally high, teasing voices. He rolls his eyes and then sees us. At first he doesn't move, just stands there and blinks, as though not believing what he's seeing. Slowly, a grin spreads across his face and he crosses the room to us.

"Am I late for band practice?"

I'm first to be pulled into a tight hug. My first thought is that Phil smells really good, like a rich guy should smell. He definitely looks like a rich guy – short stylish gray hair, trendy jeans, a button-down shirt that fits so perfectly it must be custom-made, and Gucci slippers that probably cost more than Cam's entire wardrobe. After releasing me he hugs Danny, and then Cam. Cam's hug lasts longest, and like his wife, Phil gives Cam a peck on the cheek. Then he pulls us all together for a group hug.

"Looks like he's happy to see you guys," says Lynne, smiling brightly.

"Come in, guys," Phil says excitedly, looking us over like his favorite Christmas present. "Let's go downstairs. It's quieter down there."

He gives Lynne a meaningful look and nods toward the back of the house. She replies by sticking her tongue out at him.

We follow Phil through the doorway and down a wide staircase to the first floor. Just before passing through the doorway I notice a huge sunroom with floor-to-ceiling windows at the end of the hall with a beautiful view of the frothing Atlantic Ocean. Across the hall is an elevator. I hear my name whispered by several women who've come into the hall to see what's going on. They're also whispering Danny's name and the word 'Dropouts' with what sounds like a greater level of excitement.

The front half of the first floor is taken up by a heated two-car garage. The other half is split into a large game room and a soundproofed music studio, complete with a showroom's worth of instruments and PA's, along with a few laptops. After carefully looking over the guitars in the music room, I grab a Gibson Custom and take a seat on a stool.

For a while we talk – me on the stool, softly strumming, getting the feel of the guitar, the other guys seated comfortably on a long brown leather couch. Phil tells me (the others already know the story) about Lynne and the car accident that paralyzed her two years after their wedding. It was incredibly difficult, especially at first, but humor got them through it, he says. Humor and love. They couldn't have kids, thought about adopting, but in the end decided against it. Leaving her, taking the easy way out, never crossed his mind.

We laugh about the fun early days of the Dropouts, do a good job of tiptoeing around the bad times at the end, and get caught up on each other's lives. Because the other three have seen each other, if only occasionally, over the past thirty years, I do a lot of the sharing and listening.

While we talk, each ex-band member – in a manner so fluid and natural that it goes unnoticed – slowly drifts toward his chosen instrument. Phil takes a seat on one of the drum stools that made him a fortune, gently tapping his sticks on a tom; Cam wanders over to a bass guitar leaning against a wall, puts the strap over his shoulder, and starts gently plucking away at it the way he used to – no pick, head down, staring at his fingers; Danny stretches out on the now-empty couch like a lazy cat and watches us with a detached expression, the same thing he always did when the real musicians were working.

At some point, I plug in and play the into to "God of Thunder", by KISS. The other guys all smile. Cam plugs in, Phil starts banging away on the drums, and Danny summons the energy to rise from the couch, get behind the mike stand, and go through a few vocal exercises. I notice him looking into a mirror on the far wall as he does so. Young or old, straight or gay, rich or poor, it's comforting to see he's still got the ego of a lead singer.

Before long we're running through a set of cover songs we played when we were kids – "God of Thunder", "The Reaper", "Get Back", "Rip This Joint", "Sign of the Gypsy Queen", "Slow Ride". We sound rusty and Cam struggles at first, but there's still something there. I haven't enjoyed playing this much in a long time and the smile rarely leaves my face as we go through song after song.

I don't notice the women crowded in the studio doorway until we finish "Slow Ride". I'm not sure when they showed up, but there are at least five of them. Each wears a smile while staring into a cellphone pointed in our direction.

It's quiet for a moment. I'm all for having attractive women watching me play – I mean, that's the main reason I started playing guitar – but cell phones really turn me off. Even on stage in a club, I shut down every time a phone is pointed at me. For one thing, it's weird to see people staring into a phone while I'm playing 20 feet away. Makes me want to go rap my knuckles on their foreheads – "Hello, McFly! I'm up here!" A live performance is meant to be viewed live, not through a tiny screen.

What I really don't like is the idea that anything can be put out there for everyone to see within seconds. So, if I'm having a bad night and my playing's off, everyone sees it, not just the people in the club or theater. Same if I get in a fight with the lead singer onstage (which has happened more than once). Or maybe I sneeze and a booger is hanging out of my nose. It seems like people want to catch you at your worst now. I grew up in a generation where people said, "You had to be there." Now you don't, and I hate it.

When I realize the phones are still aimed at us, I don't start playing again. Instead, I turn away and look in Cam's direction. He's even more uncomfortable than I am and has turned and backed into a corner, like a child being punished for misbehavior. Danny is nonchalantly pretending to ignore the women, running his hands through his hair with his right side to them because he's always believed that's his better side. His glasses, I notice, have somehow disappeared.

"Are the Dropouts getting back together?" one of the women asks breathlessly. "I hope so, I really love your music. I grew up on it. Are you coming out with a new album, or touring?"

I look over at Phil. He's still seated behind his drums, looking very annoyed. In a strained tone, he asks the ladies to please put away their phones and go back upstairs. Reluctantly, they put away the phones but only take a step back from the doorway and continue to stare at us with star-struck smiles. Phil looks at the ceiling and yells for Lynne, but there's no reply from outside the soundproof music room.

"Should've closed the door," Phil grumbles, getting up from his stool. He goes to the intercom on the wall and says, "Lynne, a few of the horny cubs have strayed from the pack. Could you please send someone down here to round them up?"

If the women are bothered by being referred to as horny cubs, they do a fantastic job of hiding it. They continue to stare while whispering and laughing.

"I'm sending someone down now," says Lynne half a minute later, her voice slightly distorted by the intercom speaker. "Sorry about that. We heard music and they wanted to see the Dropouts play. Thought you might be practicing for a reunion."

Seconds later a couple other women appear and begin pulling their friends from the doorway. While the others eventually acquiesce to being led away, a pretty woman with bright red fingernails and skin the color of light cocoa steps forward and walks up to Danny.

"Hi, remember me?" she asks.

I can smell her perfume. I don't know if she's doing it on purpose or not, but her hips are moving gently back and forth. My knees grow weak. Danny appears unaffected.

"Sorry, no," Danny says, not impolitely.

"It's been a long time. We met after a show at The Rat."

Danny shakes his head and shrugs. "Sorry."

She smiles and steps forward until her breasts are pressed against him. "Maybe I could remind you."

Smiling like he'd really like to take her up on it, Danny leans over, gives her a soft kiss on the cheek, and says, "No, thank you. But I truly appreciate the offer." The woman touches her cheek and, rejected with her self-esteem intact, turns to join the other ladies.

"Once a rock star, always a rock star," I say, after they've gone upstairs.

"Lynne's friends from college are here for a week," Phil says, once again seated behind the drums. "Thirty-year reunion, I think. Twelve women from all over the country, spending a free week at Casa de Cabana. All food, drinks, and entertainment included. Oh, and who do you think paid for all of them to get here?" Phil pauses and shakes his head. "Sorry about that. Lynne's happy, so I'm happy. But I'll be happier when they go."

"I wish they hadn't taken videos," says Cam. "The last thing I want is to be seen playing with the Dropouts, like we're getting ready for a reunion. No offense," he adds, "but those days are behind me and I'd like to keep them there."

Phil nods, and it's unclear whether he really feels the same way or is just trying to empathize with Cam.

Danny and I look at each other and shrug. I was having a good time, and I'm sure being propositioned by an attractive fan didn't hurt Danny's ego.

"I could try to confiscate their phones, but you know how that will go," Phil says. "The videos are probably on YouTube by now, under the title, "The Dropouts Reunion.""

Cam groans a little, unplugs the bass, and sets it back against the wall. Phil puts his sticks down. I feel like one of those magical, spontaneous moments in life that can never be replicated has just come to an end. Danny looks like he's feeling the same way, but he goes and sits on the couch with Phil and Cam.

I set the guitar against the wall and grab an acoustic. "Tell me what you guys think," I say, and then play for them the song I played last night for Rachel.

When I finish, I look up at their expressionless faces and wonder if this was a mistake. Cam and Phil have every reason to bash it, just for spite. I wouldn't blame them either.

"You'd think your voice would have improved a little over the past three decades," says Danny. "But, no. Other than that, I really like it. I could sing the hell out of that song."

I agree. He could.

Phil says he likes it too, then gets to his feet and grabs a nearby laptop. He brings up a couple of songs he's recorded and plays them as we quietly listen. They're rough but recorded well and have the bones to be really good songs. I can tell he's a little uncomfortable sharing them, but he wants our approval. I understand how he's feeling and heap out the praise in heavy doses.

"Phil, your voice is worse than Jesse's, if that's possible," Danny says. "But the songs are good. I could sing the hell out of those, too."

I feel myself getting excited about music, like in the old days.

"Why don't we get together tomorrow and record a few demos?" I say. "You've got all the equipment, Phil. Maybe it leads to something, maybe it doesn't. Either way, it'll be fun."

Danny nods. Phil nods. Cam shakes his head.

"No way. Those days are over for me, in the distant past, where they should stay. I ain't going back."

"Come on, Cam," I say. "It's just four old friends getting together to jam. Nobody ever needs to know about it, unless we decide different."

Turning his head slowly in my direction, Cam glares at me through his thick glasses. I know what's coming – the verbal follow-up to the right hook he nailed me with earlier.

"Don't you mean, unless *you* decide different? Because at the end, you made all the decisions. You decided to break up the band. You decided to leave your fiancée and your daughter. And now, when I've made it clear that I don't want to do this, you're trying to force me into it, because *you've* decided it's what we should do. Fuck you, Jesse!"

Cam stands up, arms stiff at his sides, fists clenched, and begins pacing back and forth at the back of the room. "I'm not a violent man, but it felt so good to deck you this morning, I'm struggling not to do it again."

Phil leans back and claps his hands together. "*That's* why your eye's all swollen! I thought you might have had an allergic reaction to something, or you just

looked like that now. It has been a long time, you know."
He stares at me and nods. "This makes a lot more sense."

I'd like to tell Cam that I'm not trying to force
him to do anything, but he appears past the point of
reasoning with. He paces and mumbles prayers and
squeezes his fists so hard the knuckles are white. It's like
a dark cloud has enveloped the room, blanketing us in
heavy, uncomfortable silence. I hold my guitar, as my
shrink would say, like a shield. I strum the chords to
Dave Mason's "We Just Disagree" quietly, soft enough
that Cam can't hear. I'm afraid it might tip him over the
edge, and I'll end up with another painfully swollen eye.

Phil finally breaks the silence.

"I'm kind of with Cam on this," he says. "I
wouldn't mind getting together to jam on the new songs
and see where it goes. Maybe we even end up putting
some stuff down. But right now, my life is good. Aside
from the home invasion, that is." He glances at the
ceiling. "It's been great seeing you guys, and this has
been fun. Really fun. But if Cam's out, so am I."

We all were. The Dropouts weren't the Beatles
or Led Zeppelin, but we operated the same way, as a
democracy. Until the end, that is. As Cam was kind
enough to remind me.

"So . . . I guess we're done jamming?" Danny
asks, looking disappointed.

Phil looks back and forth, from me to Cam. "I'd
say so, yes."

I set the acoustic guitar back in its stand, being
careful to stay out of arm's reach from Cam. A minute
later Cam has calmed down enough to shake my hand
and mumble an unnecessary apology. We each hug Phil,
and I offer him an invitation to Ellie's birthday party the
following evening. He's noncommittal, though the idea

of getting away from the home invasion seems to appeal to him.

Little is said on the drive back to Apple Brook. Danny offers the front seat to Cam, but he silently declines. I'm a little relieved because Cam still seems angry and I'd hate to get punched while I'm driving. He does shake my hand when we drop him off at the church. I make him the same offer I made Phil, an invitation to Ellie's birthday party. He's also noncommittal, but it's obvious the idea doesn't appeal to him. He mentions saying a prayer for me and gets out of the SUV.

"You believe in God?" Danny asks me, as we watch Cam bend over to pick up some litter in the parking lot. He moves stiffly, like an old man. Packs a hell of a punch though.

"Sometimes. I don't know. Maybe not the God I learned about in the Catholic Church. I was an altar boy, you know, and just saying something like that still fills me with guilt." I gaze up through the windshield at the church's bell tower, where a few birds have gathered. Probably planning their upcoming trip south. "Sometimes I think of God and the church as a placebo. If you believe in him, whether he's real or not, you'll probably get something out of it.

"I believe in God," Danny says.

For a moment we silently watch Cam fumble for his keys.

"You know, God hates gays," I say.

"Not the God I believe in."

Cam finds the right key and disappears inside the church.

"Looks like I ruined Cam's day," I say.

"That's not how he looks at it. He thinks you ruined his whole life." He smiles at the look I give him.

"He felt the same way about me, too, though for some reason I've been forgiven."

I pull out of the parking lot, heading toward Carpenter Lake.

"Probably because you had the balls to apologize without waiting thirty years."

"That's what I was thinking, too." Danny nods. "But he'll be fine, once he turns it over a few times in his mind. I believe this was a positive experience for everyone involved."

"Sure you do," I say. "I get punched in the face, and you get propositioned by a gorgeous chick."

Danny smiles. "It was always interesting with the Dropouts, wasn't it?"

I nod my head slowly. There's no arguing that.

## 11

### 1986

Rachel's father was the first person to suggest dividing up the writing credits. This was shortly after we got our first checks for "Her Love Line". Mr. Brennan meant well, although I don't believe it was my best interests he had at heart. He was a lawyer and I was the disgraceful father of his granddaughter, his future son-in-law, and he wanted what was best for Rachel and Megan. At one point, after we'd had a taste of success, Mr. Brennan also suggested that we fire Derek and hire him to manage the Dropouts. That, I believe, was simple lawyerly greed. My immediate response was, No Fucking Way, although I phrased it a bit more politely than that.

More and more voices began whispering in my ear, telling me that as the songwriters, Danny and I were the ones with the real talent and deserved more than the others. The people I loved and trusted – my parents and Rachel – said something different: Cam and Phil contributed to the songs and deserved to be treated as equal songwriters, I should stick to the deal we originally made, and friendship was worth a lot more than a little money, especially in the long run.

This made no sense to me. First, it wasn't a little money; it was a lot. Especially if I continued to write hits like "Your Love Line", which I undoubtedly would. And what did I care about what happened in the long run? I was twenty years old, on my way to the top, and one of my primary goals was money. I'd have all the friends I needed when I was rich.

Danny was hearing the same things. Even more so, because he was the lead singer. He'd been contacted by a few managers, urging him to sign with them and go solo. For some reason, Danny had a much stronger moral compass than I did. He was in agreement with my parents. He said he'd rather fail with his friends than succeed without them. Money would come and go, but friends were forever. He sounded like a fucking Hallmark card.

I did something I should have done more of in high school – I got out my calculator and did some math. With Mr. Brennan's help, I calculated the amount Danny and I had received from our first songwriter's checks, split four ways, versus the amount we'd have made if it was split two ways. I estimated the amount we'd make from our second single, and how much money we could expect to lose over five years if the songwriting credits remained the way they were.

Two things I knew about Danny: he wasn't greedy, and he hated confrontation. He was impressed with my math work, but it didn't change his mind. Eventually the constant badgering by me and everyone else got to him, and he reluctantly agreed to change the songwriting credits on future songs. He refused to confront Phil and Cam about it, though; that dirty job was left to me.

I decided to talk it over with Rachel. The band was leaving in a couple of days for a three-month tour of the South and Midwest backing up The Firm, which featured Jimmy Page and Paul Rodgers. It was our first extended length of time on the road and the whole band was excited, especially me. I was going to meet Jimmy Page, my favorite guitarist ever.

"When did you become so greedy?" Rachel asked as we ice skated on the frozen lake outside her house on a frigid winter day. I was never much of a skater – I could lurch forward but had trouble with turning and stopping – but Rachel was athletic and coordinated and took to it as naturally as she did most every physical activity.

"It's not about greed, it's about getting what's owed to me," I said, repeating what I'd heard so much of lately. When she frowned at me, I added, "Your dad thinks I'm doing the right thing!"

My eyes watered from the cold wind whipping across the lake, but I could still see Rachel's frown deepen. Under the swish of our blades, the ice thumped and moaned an incredible melody in the quiet cold. I pulled off a glove and wiped the tears running down my cheeks, surprised they hadn't frozen.

"Since when do you pay attention to anything my father says?" She skated over smoothly, coming to a stop in front of me. She was rosy-cheeked and looked very cute in her matching pink hat, scarf, and gloves, and a puffy white ski jacket that I referred to as 'The Marshmallow'. "Why not just keep things the way they are?"

Her body was steady as she gazed at me, perfectly balanced. Meanwhile, I was rocking back and forth like a passenger on rough seas, waving my arms and trying not to fall on my ass.

"I'm doing this for you," I said. "You and Megan."

"You really think we need the money? Look at this place." Rachel gestures toward the shoreline, at her parents' house, in a grand, sweeping gesture. "We don't have to worry about money. Keep things the way they are. You'll make enough money, and most importantly, you'll have your friends!"

"I want to buy a house for me and you and Megan. I'm tired of living with your parents."

"What's the rush? You're on the road all the time anyway. In a couple of days you're leaving, and we won't see you for three months. It's easier for us to stay here, where my mom can help out with Megan."

She stood up on the front of her skates and kissed me. Easy for her, not for me. I began windmilling my arms, trying unsuccessfully to maintain my balance. Rachel grabbed my jacket to slow my fall, but I still landed on my ass. It hurt – that ice is hard. With her help, I got back up. I looked toward shore and hoped her father hadn't seen anything. I felt emasculated enough around him.

"I'm putting a down payment on a house with my next check," I said, trying to sooth my injured ego. "You have three months to pick one out."

"You don't need to change the songwriting credits." Rachel took my hand and we started skating together, though it was more like a graceful mom leading a stumbling child. "Don't let your ego get the better of you. You're better than that." My expression must have clouded, because she flashed me her best smile. "Money and ego break up bands, Jess. The Dropouts have a great future, unless somebody gets greedy. Think it over during your tour."

"You're right. I'll think about it."

"Don't say a word about it while you're on the road, either. To anyone. Everybody's focus should be on one thing, the music. This tour is a big deal for you guys."

"No shit, really?"

I leaned over to kiss her, stumbled, and fell on my ass again.

A lot happened over the next three months. The Firm tour was the most fun we'd had in our lives. We held our own with Paul Rodgers and Jimmy Page, both on stage and off. Derek, our manager, was lining up another tour in a couple of months. He was throwing around names like Aerosmith and REO Speedwagon for headliners and suggesting that with another hit or two we'd soon be headlining. Danny and I had written several songs on the road and were excited to get back in the studio. Cam had tried cocaine for the first time and by the end of the tour was hooked. And, for the first time ever, I cheated on Rachel.

It happened in Detroit, on the third night of the tour. We'd just come off stage when I saw her in a group of girls standing outside the dressing room, waiting to meet us. It hadn't taken us long to discover that the quality of female fan on a national tour was far better than what we'd experienced on our typical New England bar gig. And this girl was the prettiest I'd ever seen. I refer to her as 'this girl' because I'm not sure I ever caught her name. If I did, it didn't matter – I'd forgotten it by the next morning.

I drank some whiskey after the show, chatted her up for a few minutes, and next thing I knew she was giving me a blow job. It sounds silly to describe it that way – "I don't know how it happened, honey; one minute we were talking, and then she had my dick in her mouth" – but with whiskey, time and place become a little altered. Admittedly, I was very inexperienced sexually – up to that point, Rachel was my one and only – but it's safe to say this girl had done this sort of thing before. If not, well, she was a natural, a Mickey Mantle of blowjobs. It was over in about a minute. If she was displeased, she didn't show it. In fact, she thanked me. I replied in kind, then rejoined my bandmates for more partying.

The next morning, I was racked with guilt but reassured myself that, because there was no penetration, Rachel was still my one and only. This and booze eased my mind for a couple of days, until I met another unnamed young lady after a show somewhere in the Midwest. This time, there was penetration. Most of my guilt was overridden by the fact that I really, really enjoyed it. The rest I kept at bay with copious amounts of alcohol. I became like Cam was with cocaine, taking every opportunity to do it over again. I called Rachel every other day, but otherwise I almost never thought about her. I was having too much fun.

By the time we returned to Maine it was springtime, the time of rebirth. The snow was gone, the grass was turning green, and the leaves were budding. But my relationship with Rachel, as I saw it, was as cold and gray and barren as a January morning. It felt empty, and the reason was no fault of hers. She loved me just as much as always and had spent the three months apart planning for our life together. She had previewed many houses in the Apple Brook area, eventually deciding on a log cabin-style home on twenty acres of beautiful rolling hills and forest.

The change was with me. Living the life of a touring rock musician had opened my eyes to an endless world of drunken debauchery, and I took to it like a fat kid to sugar. No responsibilities, no consequences. We were treated like gods (minor gods, perhaps, but gods nonetheless) by the fans, promoters, and nearly everyone else, and I began to believe the hype. Everything was easy and free. Up all night, sleep all day, one town rolls into the next. Living the rock and roll lifestyle for three months and coming home to the responsibility of a fiancée and daughter was hard enough, like emotional whiplash. But coming home to a family, and living with Rachel's parents, was like having my swelling head twisted completely around.

After a couple of days at home I left for Boston, using the excuse that I had to be there because we were recording our next album. That wasn't a complete lie – we were recording our album in Boston, but we weren't scheduled to start for another week. I spent the week alone, partying, living the life of a single rock star on a level far above where I was actually at. My ever-increasing ego had carried me up another few notches.

Before long Rachel discovered what I'd been up to on the road. She'd been understandably confused and hurt by my coldness and distance since returning. I'd barely said hello to her or the baby in the two days I was home and had shown no interest in looking at the house she had hoped would become our family home.

After I left for Boston she started asking around, trying to find out what was wrong with me. When she confronted me with it over the phone, I admitted to my infidelities. She cried and I felt bad, though alcohol and an inflated sense of entitlement will do wonders for washing away blame. She wouldn't tell me how she found out, other than to say it was someone in the band.

The Dropouts reconvened the following week in a Boston studio. I was in pretty rough shape, but the other guys weren't doing much better. Cam, especially, looked like shit, like he'd slept in a gutter, and his mood matched his appearance. Danny, like me, had been drinking too much. And Phil was smoking pot by the bagful to help with his back pain. I'm not sure if it helped his back, but his personal hygiene was definitely suffering.

Danny and I had written about twenty songs together, plus we both had a few of our own. Before the band got down to playing and narrowing down the list of songs to be included on our next album, I had something to say.

"Listen, guys, before we start, I want you to know that there are going to be some changes to the songwriting credits going forward. Instead of every song being credited to The Dropouts, the songs will now be credited to whoever wrote it."

"Meaning you and Danny," Cam said.

I sipped my beer and looked over at Danny, who'd suddenly become very interested in something on the bottom of his shoe.

"Yeah, well, whoever writes the song. You and Phil are free to write songs, too."

"And who decides if my song, or Phil's song, gets on the album?" Cam asked. He was seething, and I knew we were getting into dangerous territory.

"We'll put the ten best songs on. If yours is one of them, great."

"Well, it fucking won't be, because I've never written a fucking song in my life. And Phil's no fucking songwriter, either."

From Phil, slouched down and sunk deeply into his side of the studio couch, came a slow stoner's laugh.

"This is just about money, right?" said Cam, his voice growing louder. "So you and Danny can make more than us? We agreed a long time ago that all songs will be credited to the entire band, but now you've decided, on your own, to change things. What happened to band democracy? All for one, and one for all? Now you're going to wield your power over us, keep us non-songwriters at the back of the bus. What do I look like, Rosa Parks?"

Phil giggled again. Danny checked his other shoe. I smiled. Big mistake. Cam's face reddened like a tomato in August. I tried to be diplomatic.

"Look, Cam, comparing this to segregation is a bit of an exaggeration. The Beatles split up their songwriting credits. So did Zeppelin. The Stones. Aerosmith. Almost every band does it."

"I may not write the songs, but I come up with the bass line. Phil plays the drums. We write the parts for our instruments. You don't."

"Danny and I give you guys the freedom to play your parts. We let you express yourselves that way. It's not exactly songwriting."

"Oh, you *let us*?" Cam was up on his feet now. "I suppose you *let us* play in your band. And it's nice of you to *let us* go on tour with you." He grabbed a bottle of scotch from a nearby table and took a long swig. "Maybe we should change the band name to 'Jesse Maze and the Dropouts.' Will you *let us* do that?"

Cam had made it clear how he felt and was pacing back and forth, shooting angry looks at me every time he spun around. It was obvious why Danny wanted me to deliver the news to the others. None of Cam's anger was being directed toward Danny. Just me. A classic case of shooting the messenger.

"Anybody else have anything to say about this?" I said. "If not, maybe we can take a break, grab a drink, and then start working on the songs."

Danny and Phil were quiet, but Cam had more to say.

"I should have known you'd do something like this, Jesse," he said, pointing furiously at me. "You have the greatest girlfriend in the world, but you cheat on her because you believe you're entitled to whatever you want. And now you think you're entitled to lead our band, too."

Danny looked up at the mention of Rachel. Even Phil's perma-grin momentarily disappeared. I stood up and threw my beer bottle against the wall. The studio engineers looked up at us through the window but said nothing. They were probably used to this sort of thing.

"I can get another bass player to play your part, Cam," I yelled. "You wouldn't be too fucking hard to replace, I'll tell you that!"

Danny finally spoke. "That's enough, Jesse. We're not splitting up. Cam's not going anywhere."

"If he's not happy with the way things are, he can leave," I said.

"If Cam leaves, I leave," Danny said.

"Yeah, me too," said Phil. "We decided that a long time ago. Like Zeppelin, man. If one member goes, we all go."

"We also decided to share songwriting credits a long time ago," Cam said, staring angrily at me. "I thought it was an agreement between four friends, four equal band members. But now I see you just *let us* believe that."

I did what any self-centered prick digging himself a hole would do – I attempted to pull someone else in with me.

"It's not just me. Danny's been thinking the same thing."

Danny looked back down at his shoe. He was probably thinking about throwing it at my head.

"Maybe he was," said Cam. "We all think about things we shouldn't. Hell, I think about banging Phil's girlfriend almost every day. She's great-looking, way too good for him."

I glanced at Phil, who smiled and raised his hand for a high-five.

"The difference," Cam continued, "is that I don't act on my thoughts, because I value our friendships more than anything. Even though Danny had the same thoughts as you about the songwriting, he didn't say anything about it. But you did."

I'd had enough.

"Listen. All of the songs we've put out so far will remain the same. But any songs from this day forward will be credited to the individual songwriters. Take it or leave it."

"Fuck you, I leave it," Cam said. "And I think I speak for Phil, too."

Phil nodded, his glassy, bloodshot gaze fixed on a picture on the wall behind me.

"You don't want to do this," I warned. "I can find another band like that." I snapped my fingers. Then, mimicking Cam, I said, "And I think I speak for Danny, too."

"You don't speak for me," Danny said quietly. "Only I speak for me."

I looked at each of them. Only Cam met my gaze, but I knew the others, even Danny, stood with him. Backing down wasn't an option. This band was nothing without me. I'd get what I was worth, or I'd leave.

For a full minute we faced off in silence. Then I decided to walk. Without another word, I grabbed my guitar and notebook full of songs and left the studio. It was over. I'd dropped out of the Dropouts.

## 12

I wake up at around ten o'clock on Saturday morning, my head a little foggy. It's how I've started most mornings of my adult life. The life of a rock and roller, I've always told myself. Only now I'm not a rock and roller; I'm just a hungover old guy with a drinking problem.

My full bladder forces me out of bed. After taking a leak, I look at myself in the mirror. What I see is a bleary-eyed guy with a coarse roadmap of lines etched across his forehead. Not as deep as some others my age but lined enough to say this isn't the face of a young man. I haven't shaved in three days and most of my stubble is white, as are a few hairs along the edges of my temple. Time to see the hairdresser for another coloring.

I brush my teeth and take my cholesterol pills. Yup, cholesterol pills. The doctor told me I should be able to lower my numbers by exercising regularly and changing my eating habits, including cutting back on the alcohol. Fuck that. I chose the pills. I consider shaving but decide against it. Nobody in Maine seems to shave, why should I? I turn on the shower faucet and, groaning like an old man, bend down to grab a towel from a low shelf. Setting the towel on a hook outside the shower, I test the water until it's nice and hot and then step inside.

The hot water soothes me, loosens me up, and my mind drifts to the previous evening's dinner. It was just the family – me, Rachel, Megan, and Ellie. I'd offered to take them anywhere and we'd ended up eating at George's Diner in Apple Brook. Ellie's choice, because she said they had the best cheeseburgers and chocolate shakes in the world. And she may have been right. They served a good bottle of Bud too.

Ellie talked a lot about Tyler and what a good singer and rapper he was. I mentioned that if he was a good singer he wouldn't be rapping, but my granddaughter's eyes narrowed and Rachel kicked me under the table and so I said no more.

Danny texted me during dinner to tell me a couple of videos of the Dropouts playing earlier that day at Phil's house had already made it on to YouTube. I immediately went to YouTube and checked them out. We sounded like shit, but that could have been because we were recorded on a cellphone. The videos were clear though.

Soon we were all watching the videos – Rachel with me on my phone, Megan and Ellie looking at Ellie's phone across the booth. I quickly grew bored and went back to my burger, but Ellie watched it a few times. Then she went on a few other sites.

"Grampy," she said. "You're trending."

"Huh," I said. "Can you pass the ketchup?"

"You should read the comments on here," Ellie said. She giggled. "A few women wrote that you're still really hot. A lot of women are saying Danny's hot. A guy here says the bass player looks old and can't play for shit."

"Cam's had a rough life," I said, my mouth half-full. Rachel frowned, and I swallowed before continuing. "And he can play, trust me. It's just been awhile. Once we got warmed up, he sounded great."

"Are you guys getting back together?" Ellie asked.

"No. That was just some old friends getting together for an afternoon."

"Seems like you had fun today," Rachel said. "Except for when you got punched, of course. But you can barely see it now."

"Which one punched you?" Ellie asked. "The old guy who plays like shit?"

"Yes, Cam. He's my age, he's just had a hard life. That's what drugs will do to you." I took a sip of my beer and pointed the bottle in my granddaughter's direction. "Remember that. And as I said before, he can still play. It's just been a long time, that's all."

"Why did he punch you?" Ellie asked.

"Your grandfather sometimes has that effect on people," Rachel said, patting me on the arm.

After dinner Rachel and I went back to her house, while Megan dropped Ellie off at a high school dance and went to a friend's house. A beer for me, a glass of wine for Rachel, and soon we were sitting on the couch under a big soft blanket with the lights out, a roaring fire in the fireplace, and *Legends of the Fall* on the television. Rachel's head rested against my shoulder. It was comfortable, like how I imagined a couple who've been together for many years would spend their Friday nights.

And then, of course, I ruined it. I kissed her on the forehead. She squeezed my arm, which I translated to mean, "I'd like you to kiss me on the lips." And so I did, a small kiss. All good. Then I went in for a longer kiss, which went well for about three seconds, when she pulled away.

"What are we doing, Jesse?"

"Has it been that long, you don't remember what kissing is?"

Rachel patted me playfully on the chest. The firelight danced in her eyes. "I have a healthy dating life, thank you. I mean, where do you see this going?"

"Down the hall, I hope," I said, nodding toward her bedroom.

That's one of the problems with being in bands and having relatively easy access to ready and willing females – you never practice your lines. I was about as smooth as a horny teenager trying to get his girlfriend into the backseat.

"Really?" She leaned away from me. "You think I'm going to sleep with you after two days together? You're charming, Jesse, but not that charming."

"Well, it's not like we're strangers. We've done it before."

"Not since we were teenagers! This is the longest we've been alone together in over thirty years. The last time we spent any time together was at Megan's wedding, and that was because we were seated at the same table."

"I wanted to sleep with you then, too, but you were married to Hairy Assface."

"His name was Harry Aspinall," Rachel said, trying not to smile.

"A guy with a name like that shouldn't have a beard."

She finally breaks into a grin.

"Yes, well, he made a lot of poor decisions. And I made one when I married him. But," she says, again turning serious, "I feel as though sleeping with you would be another poor decision."

"Why?"

Rachel spoke slowly and carefully, as though I'd suffered a concussion. "Jesse, these past couple of days have been wonderful. I'll admit, at times it's felt like the old days, like I'm the only girl in your life and you're the big rock star. You're my first love – maybe my only love. But it's not going anywhere. In a couple of days you're going back to Florida, and what'll we have? I'm not going to be just another roll in the hay, Jesse. I've never been that girl."

"You'll never be that. I've been happier with you these past couple of days than I can ever remember. Being around you, Megan, and Ellie, I feel . . . content. It's a feeling I've never really experienced before."

"I'm glad, Jesse." She took a deep breath, as though preparing to jump off a cliff. "I'll admit, I feel the same way. It's made me wonder what a life with you would've been like. What it could be like, in the future. But I can't allow myself to think that way. I'm just trying to protect myself. You understand, right?"

The firelight gleamed brighter in her eyes, and I noticed tears. It had been so long since I'd dealt with real emotion that I felt my own tears welling up. My throat felt tight. My first instinct was to curse myself for being weak. I thought about running. But instead, I took her hand and said, "What if I stay?"

After staring at me for a long moment, she leaned back and started laughing. Not exactly the response I was looking for.

"Stay here, with me? Why? To get laid?"

Ouch. That hurt. I mean, I understand why she said it. It sounds about right. Half the things I'd done in my life were to get laid. But, still.

"No, not to get laid," I said. "Because I want to spend more time with you and Megan and Ellie. You're my family."

She stared at me. I stared at her. We'd reached a stalemate. I understood her reasoning. I wasn't exactly

Ozzie Nelson. More like Ozzy Osbourne, although by all accounts there's a lot of love between Ozzy and his family. So, basically, I was the worst. And my claim to want nothing more than to be more involved with my family may have been more credible had there not been a raging boner straining like a trapped anaconda against my jeans.

Pushing the blanket aside, Rachel got up from the couch and looked down at me. There was no anger in her expression, but it didn't look like I was about to get invited to her bedroom either.

"I'm going to bed," she said. "I want you to consider what you said about wanting to move back here. If you want to move back for the right reasons, to sort of mend fences and try to be the man we'd always hoped for, I think that's a wonderful idea. But if you are just doing it to get me in the sack, well, I'd rather you save both of us some time and hurt."

"That's not why I'm doing it. I want –"

She held up her hand to stop me. "Don't say anything tonight. Just think about it. If you decide you mean it, we can talk." She sighed and gazed into the fire. The room was growing darker as the flames began to die out. "And if you decide it was just your dick talking"– still looking into the fire, she smiled – "we can forget it ever happened. I'll never bring it up, I promise." She giggled. "Bring it up. That was a good one."

"Great. You're a real comedienne."

"Good night, Jesse. Don't stay up all night." Leaving the room, she laughed louder. "Stay up. I'm full of them tonight."

I listened to her walk down the hall, heard her bedroom door close. For a long time, I stared into the fading fire. Eventually I got up and threw another log on. I walked softly into the kitchen, where I found eight cold and lonely Shipyard beers in the refrigerator. By the time I went to bed, I'd drank them all.

I get out of the shower, towel off, and dress. After swallowing a couple of Excedrins, I head downstairs. There's a note from Rachel on the kitchen table, saying she had to run some errands and would be home in a little while. There's also a reminder of my lunch plans with Megan. Like I need reminding.

Opening the refrigerator, I'm faced with a choice of scrambling some eggs or microwaving the last piece of leftover pizza for breakfast. Pizza it is, along with roughly a pot of coffee and a gallon of water. I sit at the kitchen island and check my phone. There's an email from Derek, who I remain in occasional contact with because he's still technically the manager of the Dropouts. He's seen the videos of the band playing at Phil's house on YouTube and suggests getting together to discuss a tour. There are other emails from music industry types, all saying the same basic thing. I reply to none of them.

There's a text from Danny asking if I want to practice our Happy Birthday duet before we play it at Ellie's party. I text back that I think we can manage Happy Birthday without practice, but he may want to go over the words a few times to make sure he can remember them all in his old age.

Kendra sent a few texts. Long, rambling, and most likely composed while she was high, the overall gist is that she's moved everything out of my beachside condo but now she's having second thoughts because she found out the photographer she left me for is still screwing the last model he went out with. I delete the text, feeling a tinge of embarrassment because she's younger than my daughter and less mature than my granddaughter.

Rachel comes home a few minutes later, carrying bags filled with decorations for Ellie's party. Only when she asks how I'm feeling do I realize that she's cleaned up all the empty beer bottles from the coffee table. Really, I don't feel bad considering how much I had to drink. Decades of late nights and abusing my body with both legal and illegal chemicals has enabled me to shake off all but the worst of hangovers. Coffee helps, too.

We talk for a few minutes, mainly about Ellie's party. Neither of us mention our conversation from last night. I meant what I said – I'd like to stay here in Apple Brook and be the husband, father, and grandfather I never was. Like the saying goes, better late than never. Although both Rachel and Megan may disagree with that adage, at least in this case.

At noon I leave the house. It's a beautiful day, not too cold, the sky clear and the sun high in the sky. I slowly steer the SUV along the unpaved road leading from Rachel's house to Megan's. About a quarter mile long, it runs along the lake and is covered with a soft, colorful mat of fallen leaves and pine needles. Both houses have their own paved driveways from the road, and I can only guess that this road remains unpaved as an implicit symbol of independence between parent and daughter passed from one generation to the next.

The trail wasn't here when I lived at Lazy Daze, back when Megan was a baby. It was only after I abandoned my fiancée and baby for the lure of rock and roll stardom that the house was built for Rachel. She'd had her heart set on raising our family in the log cabin, but when I left, she was stuck living at her parents' house. Rachel needed some independence, but her parents weren't ready for her to move too far away, so they offered to build her a house on their land. It was the type of compromise only the rich can come up with.

Megan comes to the door in her jacket, ready to go. She locks the door behind her and gets into the SUV. When I ask how she is, she says fine. When I ask where Ellie is, she says at a friend's house. When I ask where she wants to eat, she says she doesn't care. We're not off to a rousing start but she hasn't cussed at me yet and I put a little check mark in the win column.

"We could grab some sandwiches and park by the bridge on the other side of the lake," I say. "That's always been a really nice spot. Or we could go back to George's Diner. I wouldn't say no to another cheeseburger."

Megan shrugs. "George's is fine."

The diner is less than half-full, not what I expected at this time on a gorgeous Saturday afternoon. Megan tells me there's a high school football game being played that afternoon, the only Saturday afternoon game of the season. Half the town will be there, she explains, but she doesn't have to. I remember. In a small town, some things never change.

We order – salad for Megan, another cheeseburger and chocolate shake for the old guy with high cholesterol – and for a long time neither of us says anything. I stare out the window next to our booth, thinking of what to say, while Megan stares at her phone. I'm surprised when she abruptly sets her phone down and speaks first.

"If you've got something to say you probably should do so now, since it'll probably be two to five years before you happen to swing by again."

"Well, I'll start with that," I say. "I'm thinking of moving back here so I can spend more time with your mom and you and Ellie. I know I can't make up for my mistakes of the past but I'm hoping we can have a better future."

That's not bad, I think. I'd like to pull out my little lyric notebook that I carry everywhere for those rare occasions when I have a good idea, but now is not the time.

"I'll believe it when I see it," she says.

The waitress arrives with our food. I put ketchup on my cheeseburger and take a bite. Just a bit pink inside and delicious. Two big greasy cheeseburgers in less than twenty-four hours, not to mention the tall, frothy chocolate shakes, aren't doing me any good. But I've ingested worse.

"I don't blame you for feeling that way." I watch her poke carefully at her healthy salad while I swallow a chunk of beef and cheese. "All I can say is it's different this time. I want to be there for Ellie because I wasn't there for you. I know that won't make up for not being there when you needed me, and I'm sorry. I really am."

She nibbles at her salad and doesn't say anything for a long time. I drink my shake too quickly and wince as brain freeze bursts behind my eyes and across my forehead. Some lessons never get learned, no matter how old a person gets.

"Do you know how difficult it is for me to believe you?" she finally says.

"About as difficult as it is for your mother to do so," I answer. "But Ellie seems to like me, and your mom appears ready to give me the benefit of the doubt. Pretty sure, anyway."

"Ellie has me and mom. She doesn't need you, so she has no reason to dislike you."

"You two have done a fantastic job with her. She's a wonderful young lady. I'm just hoping you'll let me be a part of her life. And yours."

I finish my burger and nibble absently at my fries, dunking them in ketchup. Megan continues to pick at her salad and says nothing.

"Is your dipshit ex involved with Ellie at all?" I ask.

For the first time, Megan smiles. It's warmer and brighter than the sunlight outside the window, and my heart lifts.

"He's a worse father than you," she says. My lifted heart plummets like an elevator with a snapped cable. But then I see the teasing look in her eyes, so much like her mother's. "Sid was a terrible husband, too, so I shouldn't be surprised. He lives in Massachusetts, less than an hour and a half away, yet he's only seen her a handful of times since we divorced. He's remarried, got a new family now. He usually calls Ellie on her birthday, but not always. At least you used to call me pretty regularly, and you always sent gifts for my birthday and Christmas."

"Stop," I say. "You're making me blush."

Megan laughs. It's the first time I've made her laugh in what seems like forever. Years. At the sound of it my throat begins to tighten and my eyes well up with tears. I blink several times, mumble something and hurry to the men's room. Staring into the small cracked mirror above the sink, I wipe my eyes and ask myself aloud what the hell is happening. I realize we live in an era where it's acceptable for men to cry and gender is never assumed and football players wear pink. But this isn't my era, and I'm not the crying type. At least, I *wasn't* the crying type. Now, apparently, I am.

A minute later someone knocks on the bathroom door. I check my face like a flustered school girl and return to the table. Megan is finishing her salad and only glances up when I return. Maybe she doesn't realize why I left.

"Just wanted to check if my eye is still swollen. You know, from yesterday," I say. Just call me Mr. Inconspicuous.

"I hadn't even noticed," she says. "It's almost gone. Your eyes are a little red, though."

"Probably allergies."

Inconspicuous, and smooth.

"I think it would be nice if you were able to spend some time with Ellie," she says. As my expression brightens, she adds, "But I'll believe it when I see it."

"I'd like to spend time with you as well. If you're interested." I put my elbows on the table and lean forward. "I know I was a shitty father. A shitty person. Only a real jerk would leave someone as wonderful as your mom and a baby as perfect as you. But I can't go back and change things."

"Would you? If you could?"

"Go back and change things?"

"Uh-huh."

"In a second," I say, and for some reason I'm surprised to find I mean it.

The waitress, a chubby, pleasant-faced woman of about twenty, arrives with our bill. I pull some cash out of my wallet and set it down on the table. The waitress, who hasn't left, scoops it up but still doesn't walk away. Instead, she nervously clears her throat.

"Are you one of those guys? In that old band, the Dropkicks."

"The Dropouts," Megan answers, smiling at me. "Yes, he's one of them."

"Will you sign this?" she asks, pushing the bill toward me and handing me a pen.

I'm tempted to sign Danny's name until she happily tells me that she's met Danny a few times in the diner and already has his autograph. She's hoping the other two come in sometime so she can complete her collection, but she doesn't think she'd even recognize them. I ask for her name, then write To Ava, from your favorite Dropout not named Danny, Jesse Maze. I hand it to her, and she thanks me with a big smile.

On the walk back to the car, I put my arm around Megan. Surprisingly, she lets me.

"I'm looking forward to Ellie's party tonight."

"She can't wait for you to sing to her," Megan says. "She wants all her friends to see her Grampy, the rock star. She's so proud of you."

"I remember your fourteenth birthday party," I say. "I sang Happy Birthday to you, too."

"And I was glad you did," Megan says. "It was a wonderful time in our relationship. But you ruined everything at my sweet sixteen party."

"Oh . . . yeah."

I hadn't forgotten about that one – not by a long shot – but I'd done my best to push it to the back of my mind. Judging by the rough way Megan pushes my arm away and moves away from me, that day is still painfully fresh in her mind. The memory is even worse for me, like someone jabbing at an old wound that didn't heal correctly.

I hold the passenger door open as she climbs into the SUV. We talk a little on the way home, mostly about the food we just ate and the party taking place in a few hours. It's not much, but at least we're talking. And, best of all, a small ray of light had flickered through a chink in Megan's armor. She'd smiled, and even laughed. It was brief, just a glimmer of warm sunshine on a rainy day, but enough to give me hope.

## 13

## 2001

Heads turned when I walked up the driveway to the Brennan's house for Megan's sweet sixteen party. I'd like to say it was the awestruck look a rock star always gets when he arrives at a party, but this was a different generation, one that had never heard of the Dropouts and preferred Britney Spears and 'N Sync to rock and roll.

No, the reason heads turned was because a group of teenagers was passing a couple of joints around in a hidden nook at the side of the huge house. They saw an old guy approach – I was 35, ancient to teenagers – and tried to hide the weed. But after years of heavy-duty partying I could sniff out pot like a K-9. Instead of heading up the front steps, I walked around the corner of the house to where the kids were getting high. A couple of them looked ready to run but most gazed at me with attitude, something that comes standard with most kids that age. Of course, they might've just been staring because they were too high to look away.

"How's the party?" I asked.

It was a perfect summer afternoon, blue skies and warm sun, around eighty degrees. From the lake side of the house I could hear the thumping beats of some music I instinctively hated, along with shouts and laughter, splashing water, and the smoky aroma of meat cooking on a grill.

"Good," said a teenage girl in tight shorts. "We're just out here getting some fresh air."

"Huh." I nodded toward the beachfront. "Air not fresh enough by the lake?"

The girl appeared confused and looked at a tall kid with curly hair, who looked at another kid, who looked at his girlfriend, and so on. It was like a game of stoner's dominos.

"Don't worry, I'm not here to bust you," I say. You'd think they'd have been able to tell – I was wearing baggy shorts, sandals and a Jimmy Buffett t-shirt. "I just want a hit of whatever you're passing around."

They all looked at each other again. Then the girl who'd first spoken up shrugged. She was obviously the leader. The tall curly-haired kid pulled a joint from his pocket, lit up, and handed it to me.

"Be careful, old-timer," he said. "This shit's really strong. Probably a lot different than the stuff you used to smoke at Woodstock."

I was thirty-five years old and this kid had me pegged as a senior citizen. I know everyone over thirty looks old to a teenager, but come on. I took a big hit, held it, and took another. By the time I handed the joint back, half of it was gone.

"Whoa," said the leader girl. "Better go find a chair to sit in."

I gave them my coolest smile, nodded, and walked on past, toward the lake. That would show them who's old. I'd been in rock bands for twenty years. A little pot wasn't going to faze me.

There were at least a dozen kids in the water or on the dock, laughing and splashing and screaming. The beachfront at Lazy Daze was about fifty yards of smooth sand, shaped in a curve as it went around the end of the peninsula. A half-acre of lush green grass and tall pines stretched from the house and beachfront, with several groups of teenagers and adults spread out in different areas. Near the house was a long table loaded with wrapped presents. I placed the envelope containing my gift to Megan – two Pearl Jam concert tickets – in a bare area near the edge. Working the large, smoky grill in the shade of the house was a thin man with a neat beard, wearing an apron that said, "Kiss the Cook." Mr. Brennan had always insisted that only he man the grill, stating that someone else could take over only after he'd died. As far as I knew, the old man was still alive.

For a moment I stared at the cook, trying to remember if I'd ever met him. And then, suddenly, it was as though I'd fallen through the rabbit hole and landed smack dab in the middle of a Jimi Hendrix song. I watched Rachel move gracefully across the grass to the grill and kiss the cook, just as the apron demanded. Everything felt weird, wrong. The curly-haired kid was right, that was some strong shit. I found an empty Adirondack chair on the edge of the lawn, near the beach, and sat down heavily. I was pleasantly surprised to find a beer in my hand. I took a long swig, felt the bubbles tickle my tongue, and watched a bird move slowly across the soft blue sky.

I'm not sure how long I sat there before Rachel found me. Might have been thirty seconds. Might have been an hour. She was standing in front of me, talking as if through a thin sound-muffling veil. I focused, and the veil dropped.

" – wish you would have let me know you were here. Megan will be so happy to see you!"

I nodded and went to take a sip of my beer, but the can was empty. Rachel bent over and gave me a quick peck on the cheek. She looked and smelled great, her tan legs still sexy and perfect in her tight white shorts. She waved her arms toward the lake, then pointed to me. I watched a pretty teenage girl emerge from the water with a smile on her face, and it was only when she got close that I realized it was Megan. I stood up to pull her into a tight hug and was immediately soaked. The cool wetness soaking through my clothing was not entirely unpleasant.

"Holy shit!" I hear myself say, as if from a distance. "You're all grown up!"

"No kidding, Dad." She pulled away and grabbed a towel. "Sweet sixteen, remember?"

Three things struck me as odd. First, I don't ever remember her pulling away from me during a hug. She'd always clung to me until I gently backed away. Second, she called me Dad, not Daddy. That was also a first. And third, for a moment I was so far off in another universe that I'd completely forgotten I was at her birthday party.

"I remember," I said. "I brought my guitar so I can sing Happy Birthday to you."

Megan smiled, then wrapped herself in a towel and went off to talk with a group of friends. Rachel took me by the arm and lead me to the grill. I wondered if I looked hungry. I certainly felt hungry. Megan stood beside the cook, took his hand, and said, "Harry, this is Jesse, Megan's father. Jesse, this is Harry. My fiancé."

I stared at the bearded cook, thoroughly confused. I'm certain Rachel said fiancé, but this was the first I'd heard of it. Surely, somebody would have told me about this. Maybe she said Beyoncé, like the singer. Why she'd say the cook was her Beyoncé I didn't know, but I was really high. Maybe he sang karaoke. Looking around for a beer, I was surprised to find another one in my hand. I wasn't sure how it kept happening, but I liked it.

"Hi, Jesse." The cook set down his spatula and stuck out his hand like a guy who shakes hands all day long. "I'm Harry. Harry Aspinall."

All I heard was Harry Ass, and the giggling started. Rachel glared at me, and I forced myself to stop. But a goofy grin was still plastered on my face, i'm sure of it.

"Hey, man," I said. I shook his hand, even though I normally didn't shake. Some guys believe that having an aggressive bone-crushing handshake is proof of their sexual prowess. As a guitarist, I couldn't afford to have my right hand squashed by an insecure one-pump chump.

"So, Rachel tells me you're a guitarist."

I took a long swig from my beer and nodded.

"I'm an accountant, myself," Harry Ass said. One arm was draped protectively around Rachel. "I have offices in Boston, Andover, and Portsmouth. Busy as hell. Got a few Red Sox and Celtics players as clients."

"Huh," I said. I really didn't know what else to say to Harry Ass except, who gives a crap? But I thought that might be rude, so instead I tipped my head back and finished my beer.

"I understand you were once successful," he said.

Rachel was comfortable in most situations, but I could see from her expression that this wasn't one of them. She pointed to the grill and reminded Harry Ass to flip the burgers because they were starting to burn. While he flipped the burgers, she looked at me with a mix of embarrassment and pity. There really wasn't anything more to say. My beer was empty, and for some reason another hadn't magically appeared in my hand. I turned away from Rachel and went in search of alcohol.

Two huge barrels full of ice were located not far from the grill. Dozens of soda cans and plastic water bottles in one barrel, beer cans in the other. I grabbed two wet cans of Budweiser, sticking one in the front pocket of my shorts and opening the other one. I pounded down half the can and stared at the teenagers splashing away in the water. I watched Megan run down the dock and cannonball a group of laughing boys. I was already really buzzed. In my experience, mixing pot with alcohol gets you twice as drunk on approximately half the alcohol.

I looked back at the grill. Harry Ass was carrying a tray full of burgers and hot dogs to a nearby picnic table. I felt like I could eat every burger and dog on the tray, but I wasn't going near them while that guy was around. Rachel was seated in a chair near the grill, in the shade. She wore sunglasses but it felt like she was watching me. Might have just been paranoia. Mr. Brennan walked down the porch stairs. I turned away and hoped he hadn't seen me. I felt him approach and ignored him, like an ostrich with its head in the sand.

"Jesse," he said.

With a burp and a sigh I turned to face him. We'd all aged, but Mr. Brennan had seemingly done so at a more accelerated rate. I'd seen him a couple of years ago at Megan's fourteenth birthday party and he'd aged a decade since then. His face was heavily lined and saggy, with a complexion that matched his thin gray hair. His large frame was slightly stooped, as though his strong body could no longer carry the many burdens he placed upon it. Even so, the old man still radiated a strength that could be felt just by standing next to him, and it was clear that, despite his physical frailties, he was still the most powerful man in almost every room he entered.

"Hi, Mr. Brennan. How are you doing?"

"Been better, been worse."

"I was sorry to hear about Mrs. Brennan," I said, trying not to slur. "She was a wonderful person. I always liked her."

"She was wonderful," he said, and for a minute he stared silently at the tree line across the lake. "She always liked you, too. I could never for the life of me figure out why."

Not much you can say to that. I opened my mouth, but instead of speaking I poured beer into it until the can was empty. I tossed the empty toward a trash can, missed by three feet, and pulled the full can from my pocket.

"Still drinking, I see," Mr. Brennan said.

I glanced over my shoulder at Rachel. The sunglasses were off, and she was definitely watching me now.

"Haven't found a reason yet not to."

He shook his head in disgust. "Don't you ever want to make something of yourself? I saw you talking to Harry. Now there's a young man who's going places. It's nice to see Rachel with someone who will be able to take care of her the way she deserves."

"Maybe that's why I left, because I thought it was best for her."

Mr. Brennan snorted like a bull. "Nope. You left because you thought you were the next Elvis Presley and would find something better. How'd that work out for you?"

I drank from my beer and said nothing.

"This could have all been yours," he said, gazing proudly at his property and the people on it like a king overlooking his kingdom from a castle tower. "When I die the house and property is going to Rachel. My partners will have to buy her out of my share of the law firm, so she'll make a huge chunk of change there. You're aware that she's working as a paralegal at the firm?"

No, I wasn't, but I nodded anyway.

"That's how she met Harry. Paths cross in the professional world, Jesse. You could have done very well for yourself. Hell, you could have taken over your father's plumbing business and made a good living. Built it into something." He looked down at me like a displeased headmaster. "But you threw it all away."

I didn't have to take this anymore. I may still smoke pot with high school kids, but I wasn't a teenager anymore. I finished my beer, thanked Mr. Brennan for the insightful criticism, and walked away. The shortest distance between two points is a straight line, and though I may have weaved slightly I went directly to the beer barrel. Sticking one beer can in each pocket of my shorts and carrying six more in my arms, I made my way back to my chair at the end of the grass. For a long time

I sat, drinking alone, watching boats race past and kids goof around in the water until I passed out.

It was dark when I awoke. My tongue was dry and sticky and felt like it was Velcroed to the roof of my mouth. My head felt thick and heavy. With effort, I sat up. The world spun around for a few seconds and then began to slow down as the ride came to an end. For most people, it might be the worst hangover they'd ever had, the one that brings on toilet-hugging pledges to God and vows of abstinence. For me it felt like just another day at the office.

I squinted in the darkness and attempted to get my bearings. There was a roof overhead and screens to the side, meaning I was on a porch. I remembered arriving at Megan's birthday party, but everything after that was just black, empty space. I put my hand down beside me and felt thin plastic. I felt around and, in the brilliant moonlight shining through the screens, realized there was a large trash bag under me. I tried to stand, tripped clumsily on the slick plastic, and landed on my butt with a loud thud.

To my right, on the wall without a screen – the wall attached to the house – there was movement. I squinted, and in the shadows saw the outline of someone seated in a chair.

"You're awake," said Rachel. She spoke quietly, but her voice carried in the dark.

"Barely," I said. "Where am I?"

"My father's porch."

I nodded. Ouch. Big mistake. More spinning.

"What time is it?"

There was a dim light as Rachel turned her wrist to look at her watch. "Ten forty-five."

I got up on one knee, very slowly, and looked through the screens. Distant lights twinkled like stars from across the lake, but there was nothing in the yard nearby. No campfire, no people. Just darkness.

"The party's over already?"

"Been over since eight o'clock, when some of Megan's friends discovered her father had passed out drunk and pissed himself in his chair."

I sat back down. The night felt darker and heavier. I reached down and felt my crotch. My shorts were soaked. I couldn't have pissed that much. I patted myself down and realized my shirt and my hair were also very wet. That explained the shivering and goosebumps. I thought it was just alcohol poisoning.

"Shit. Did Megan see?"

"Just long enough to break down crying and tell everyone to go home. She saw a group of kids laughing and throwing potato chips at someone passed out in a chair. They didn't know you were her father. How could they? Megan's only seen you a handful of times in her life, and her friends have never met you. Well, now they have. When Megan saw you passed out drunk, she was very embarrassed. When she saw the dark stain on your shorts and the puddle on the ground underneath, she was mortified."

I groaned and rubbed my cold arms. Normally Rachel was quite understanding about my absentee approach at parenting, but not tonight. Her quiet voice felt colder than my wet skin. I'd never heard her use this tone before. Clearly, I'd really fucked up this time.

"How did I get up here?"

"Harry and a couple of the other guys carried you to the end of the dock and threw you into the water, but you didn't wake up. Didn't even flinch. They dragged you back up onto the dock and wanted to leave you there, but I was afraid you'd roll over in the middle of the lake and drown. The thought delighted my father, but I convinced him to let us bring you onto the porch. Less paperwork if you aren't floating face-down in the middle of the lake come morning."

For a long time, the only sounds were the steady, high-pitched buzz of a million cicadas and the occasional croak of a bullfrog. A mosquito whined near my ear and I blindly swatted at it.

"Where is everyone?" I finally asked. "Where's Megan?"

Rachel's chair creaked as she shifted her weight. "Megan went to her room right before you were thrown in the lake and hasn't come out since. Harry is in there with her, I think, trying to cheer her up or just be there for her. Being a father figure to her, which you'd know nothing about. My father is in the den, most likely loading and unloading his rifle. I'm sitting out here to make sure you don't die on the porch."

"Thanks."

"Now that it's clear you're not dead, I'm going inside to console my daughter." She stood up, little more than a shadow with white shorts. "You can stay the night out here, but you should leave early. My father is up at six a.m., and I honestly believe that if he sees you out here, he'll shoot you." She paused at the door. "He knows enough lawyers and judges to get away with it."

I nodded as the door closed behind her. I lay back on the trash bag and stared through the screens at the star-filled sky. I could have used a pillow. And a blanket. Dry clothes. A couple Excedrin. But I wasn't about to go inside and ask. They'd let me live this long and I didn't want to push it.

For a long time I shivered and stared at the sky, feeling worse than I'd ever remembered feeling. You've really done it this time, Maze, I said to myself. I'd heard bad parenting stories, but if there was an anthology of shitty parenting, I'm pretty sure my story would be in it. Nights like this are what drive people to swear off drinking forever. I thought about it for a little while. Then I wondered if there was any more beer in the barrel.

Eventually I fell asleep. I slept fitfully and dreamt of rock stardom and diapering babies and teenage sex and shotgun blasts. When I awoke the sky was still dark but the stars were fading away with the first traces of light on the horizon. Sitting up, I felt like shit, and it wasn't just the hangover. I'd blacked out a few times in my life, not many. Each time, upon waking up, I've been hit with a heavy wave of unease, like Dr. Jeckyll wondering what drunken Mr. Hyde was up to the night before. Sometimes the answer brings laughter and enormous relief. Other times it brings embarrassment and regret.

This time, along with embarrassment and regret, it carried shame. Terrible shame. I sat on the floor of the porch, rubbing my heavy eyes with my knuckles, thinking of my parents and how embarrassed they would be if they were still alive. I'd have to find some way to make it up to Megan. But first I had to get my ass up and out of there before I got shot.

My clothes were still wet and heavy, and when I moved they felt cold on my skin. I slowly got up, quietly closing the porch door behind me. I carried my trash bag down the stairs and shoved it into a trash can near the still-open grill. Birds started singing, one at a time, until they formed a bright morning chorus announcing dawn's approach. For a moment I admired the serene lake and the soothing first reflections of light along the shore. Then, suddenly, my stomach lurched, and I threw up for a couple of minutes on a pine tree. Wiping sweat from my forehead and feeling much better, I circled to the other side of the tree and took a leak.

Suddenly hungry, I found an open bag of chips on a table and grabbed a handful. Stale and a little wet, but they hit the spot. I found a couple cans of beer floating in the barrel and carried them unsteadily around the house, to my car. Just the thought of drinking a beer almost made me throw up again, but I knew from years of experience that it was the only way to cure a hangover this bad. I stood by my car for a few minutes, watching the first ginger edge of the morning sun rise above the trees across the lake. This really was the most beautiful spot on the lake. I looked up at the house and wondered which guest room Rachel was sleeping in with Harry Ass the accountant. I thought about Megan and wondered if she'd slept at all. I didn't remember much about yesterday, but I could recall Mr. Brennan telling me that I blew it. And that was before I pissed myself. No way I could argue with that.

Then a bedroom light went on. I got into the car, opened a beer, and drove away before Mr. Brennan could get to his gun.

14

I bring Megan to Lazy Daze so she and Rachel can decorate and prepare for that evening's party. I don't understand how it can take hours to prepare for a birthday party. When I was a kid, decorating for a party meant sticking a few candles on the cake. Maybe a few balloons and party hats, if people were feeling particularly festive.

I follow Megan inside and offer to help out. Rachel realizes it's a half-hearted offer and tells me I can help by looking through a slideshow of photos on her laptop. The slideshow is going to be projected onto a screen in the living room during the party. While Megan and Rachel laugh and plan and listen to awful pop music in the living room, I sit at the kitchen table and watch the slideshow. It's fifteen minutes long and spans Ellie's life. There's the first photo ever taken of her on the day she was born, her first day of kindergarten, all of her school pictures, school concerts, plays, soccer and softball photos, parties with her friends. Everything I've missed, essentially. It feels like an indictment of poor parenting and grandparenting. I'm in a couple of the photos, but too few. Far too few.

By the end of the slideshow my damn eyes are welling up again. I hurry to the bathroom, place my hands on the edge of the countertop, and lean toward the mirror. What the hell is wrong with you, I whisper to my red-eyed reflection. The way today is going, I'm going to have to seriously consider investing in some Visine. I breathe deeply and dab at my eyes until I look somewhat normal, all the while watching myself in the mirror. My psychiatrist in Miami would have a grand old time with this. She's two thousand miles away but I can see the satisfied expression on her face. I scowl at my reflection before leaving the bathroom.

A beer would be good right now, but I resist, for two reasons. One, I'm pretty sure I finished off all the beer last night. And two, I won't drink before or during Ellie's party. I pour myself a glass of cranberry juice instead and close the laptop before I embarrass myself and burst into full-fledged tears.

"What do you think of the slideshow?" Rachel asks, coming into the kitchen for a glass of water.

"I think it's fantastic, absolutely beautiful. Must have taken you a lot of time."

"Not that long, surprisingly. I just hope the pictures don't embarrass her in front of her friends. You know how teenagers can be."

"I'm sure everything will be fine," I say, having had very little with teenagers since my own teenage years.

I follow her into the living room, where Megan is filling up balloons with a helium tank. There must be fifty balloons already, some tied to various pieces of furniture while the rest press against the ceiling as though trying to force their way upstairs. There's a bagful of unfilled balloons and I wonder if she's planning to fill them all.

At one end of the room is a small clear area, which Rachel says is for the DJ. She asks me to slide some furniture against the walls so the kids will have room to dance. Up high on the wall facing the entrance to the kitchen is a huge banner that says *Happy 14th Birthday Ellie!* Hanging on the wall above the fireplace where the stuffed moose head once looked down upon all who entered this great room is a soccer jersey.

After we move furniture Rachel starts dusting, even though the room looks spotless. Megan continues to fill balloons. There's a knock on the door. I answer it and two serious-looking women push past me with a huge cake, bigger and more elaborate than most wedding cakes, three tiers high and covered with red and white frosting, the colors of the Apple Brook Warriors. On the top is a female soccer player.

Rachel and Megan look the cake over while I stand by the door and soon declare it perfect. With many thanks they hug the cakemakers, and Rachel hands them a check for more money than many of my guitars have cost. I hold the door open, flashing my most winning smile, and they walk past me without a glance on their way out. Lesbians, for sure.

"Do you treat all of Ellie's birthdays so extravagantly?" I ask. I love my granddaughter and I'm all for spoiling her, but this seems a bit much for a fourteenth birthday, even for her.

"Not really," says Rachel. "We weren't able to do much for her thirteenth because she had mono, so we're making up for it this year." She smiles brightly. "It's fun, isn't it?"

I smile and nod, though the fun of so much time and effort being spent on a birthday party is lost on me. For my fourteenth birthday I got my favorite food, pizza, and a chocolate Betty Crocker birthday cake with fourteen candles that I blew out in front of my parents, my grandmother, and Danny. Trick candles, so it took three tries to finish them off, much to my mother's delight. My one birthday gift was a Dungeons and Dragons Monster Manual which Danny, Phil, Cam, and

I excitedly utilized that evening during a long D&D session in my basement. To me, it was a lot more fun than what is being planned for Ellie.

After helping move the cake to the exact right spot on the kitchen table, I sense that my usefulness in the party setup is quickly coming to an end. In this sad and confusing era where gender is not to be assumed and any perceived racist or sexist comment, whether factual or fictitious, is grounds for immediate job dismissal and social media lynching, I brave the consequences and state that decorating for a teenage girl's birthday party is woman's work. Pushing it even further, I declare that there isn't a straight man in the world who could find this enjoyable. I'm greeted with indifferent shrugs and nods toward the front door.

Happy to see that politically correct overkill hasn't infected my family, I hurry out to the SUV before Rachel and Megan change their minds.

I spend much of the afternoon driving around Apple Brook. Though I've visited the town several times since I left over thirty years ago, they've mainly been quick visits, in and out faster than a horny teenager losing his virginity. I've never had the time (or desire) to revisit the old town.

The thing about old towns is, they don't change much. People grow old and die, new generations take over, families move in and out, buildings are built up and torn down, businesses open and close. But, for the most part, the feel of the town stays the same. Rich and powerful families stay rich and powerful, only with new, similar faces. Like an ever-growing herd of T-Rexes, Walmart stores have stomped their way through small towns across America, flattening most small businesses and destroying much of what made America great along the way. But a few of the strong remain, allowing Apple Brook to hold onto the small-town charm and character that I remember.

Driving unhurriedly down Main Street, I see these old businesses standing as tall and proud as when I was a youth. There's Welch's Hardware, with its creaky warped floorboards and perpetual grease-and-sawdust, blue-collar smell that washes over me as I drive by like an aromatic wave from the past. Two doors down, next to a karate school that was a record store in my day, is Gene's Bakery. No fancy wedding cakes from Gene's, just the best donuts and pastries known to man. Every Saturday morning when I was a kid, my father would come home with two maple squares, one for him and the other for me. According to my mom's letters, my old man continued to get himself a maple square every Saturday morning until he passed away. What I wouldn't give to have just one of those mornings back again. I open my window as I drive slowly past and hope the sweet warm aroma of flour and sugar fills the air, but Gene's closes at noon every day. Disappointing, yes, but I'm happy to see that some things haven't changed.

Tune Town, the music store where my dad bought my first guitar, is gone, replaced by a Chinese take-out. McDonald's is still serving up their delicious artery cloggers near the center of town, and though the old brown brick building has been replaced by an even uglier white one, the line at the drive-thru is as long as it ever was. The Dairy Queen next door has added a drive-up window in the past few decades but otherwise looks the same. I'm willing to bet that some of the high school girls working there have mothers (or, god forbid, grandmothers) who worked the counter in my day and, aside from the big hair of the past and tattoos and piercings of the present, today's girls resemble those of the past.

I drive past my parents' old house on Charles Street, the house I grew up in. It's not my parents' house anymore. They died in a car accident twenty-five years ago, when I was twenty-eight. Doesn't seem possible that it could be so long ago. The money from their savings and my dad's retirement account was left to Megan. Everything else, including the house, was left to me. I came up for the funeral, stayed in the house for two days, then split. Barely even took time to see Megan, who was nine years old and devastated by the loss of her grandparents. Father of the Year strikes yet again.

There was never a thought about keeping the house. I wanted nothing to do with it or Apple Brook. I wanted to leave the past so far behind that it disappeared from the rearview mirror. Not because of anger or bad memories, but because I believed I was too good for this place. At the time I was playing in a country music cover band and living in a one-bedroom apartment in Houston with a coke addict stripper whose stage name was Saffron. Anyone with any objectivity, or half a brain, could see that I wasn't too good for any place. But I still expected to be back on top sometime soon.

I park on the side of the road, across the street from my parents' house. At the intersection up ahead, the one with the 7-11 on the corner, a couple of homeless people with cardboard signs and sad expressions work opposite sides of the street. I'd never seen a homeless person in Apple Brook in the entire time I lived here, but I've seen at least a half dozen in the last two days. Rachel told me most of them are part of an organized group from Portland who come in steady rotations to work many of the smaller towns in the area. Even homelessness is going corporate.

The old house has gone to shit. The black shutters that my father took down and painted every two years are now a faded, weather-beaten gray. The white paint is peeling badly and should have been repainted three or four years ago. My father's green, well-maintained front lawn is now mostly dirt, with numerous holes dug by two menacing rottweilers patrolling the yard behind a rusty chain-link fence. My mother's numerous flower gardens, which I sometimes helped tend, and which filled her with such pride and satisfaction, are just a colorful memory from the distant past.

The rest of the neighborhood, once an ideal place for a kid to explore and play games and feel safe, has gone the way of my parents' house. The rocking chairs that Mr. and Mrs. Soucy used to occupy every night of the summer while drinking cocktails on their front porch has been replaced by a ripped front bench seat from an old automobile. Rap music pounds and shakes like a musical migraine from passing cars. Used hypodermic needles are scattered on the sides of the road and sidewalk. Decline and decay are everywhere: cars resting on blocks in driveways, blankets and sheets hung in windows instead of curtains, crooked blinds, peeling paint, aggressive rottweilers and pitbulls instilling fear and foreboding where friendly labs and beagles once greeted strangers with a friendly bark and a wagging tail. In the span of little more than a generation it's gone from Mayberry to Breaking Bad.

Before arriving, I'd thought about knocking on the door of my parents' house and asking the current owners for a quick look around. The idea of seeing my old room and the basement where my friends and I evolved from Dungeons and Dragons geeks to wild rock and rollers was exciting. But after spending a few minutes gazing around the old neighborhood, I've changed my mind. I'd never get past the rottweilers, and who knows what I'd find inside even if I did.

I drive away and take a cruise past the childhood homes of my friends. Though their parents have all either moved away or passed on, the houses and neighborhoods look similar to how I remember them. Better than my childhood home, that's for sure. This saddens me even further. Despite what Thomas Wolfe said, you can go home again. You just might not like what you find.

There's a white brick Cumberland Farms near the center of town, across the street from McDonald's. I pull up to one of its ten gas pumps. Stan's Gas and Lube, with two grimy full-service pumps, stood here when I was a kid. Back then there were five gas stations in town and only two were self-service. The full-service pumps were usually run by either a crotchety old man with booze on his breath and a dirty rag hanging from his back pocket or a stoned-looking teenager with a cigarette in his mouth and a dirty rag hanging from his back pocket. Cam worked at Stan's for a week during our senior year, long enough for the smell of gas to cling to him like dirt clings to Pigpen. He complained that the fumes gave him a major headache, too. After a week he'd had enough and quit Stan's Gas and Lube. It probably didn't help that we asked Cam at lunch every day if Stan had given him a lube job. Of course, we had no idea who Stan was, or if there even was a Stan. But everyone cracked up at the lube jokes. Well, everyone except Cam.

Back then gas was under a dollar a gallon, and I'd put two dollars' worth at a time in the old Pinto. In the summer I'd go to the self-service because it made me feel cool to pump my own gas, like a man, but on cold winter days I'd go to the full-service and have it pumped. You want to see a pissed-off face, watch someone drag themselves out of a cozy chair in a warm gas station to trudge out into the icy Maine winter and pump two dollars' worth of gas into some punk's car. I haven't thought about that for a long time and it brings a smile to my face. Today, I put fifty dollars into the SUV.

A police car pulls up to the pump behind me. The wind is picking up and the temperature is dropping quickly, and as I screw the SUV's gas cap on I turn up my jacket collar. A short, thin man in a loose-fitting uniform steps importantly from the police car. The cop's head is bald, his expression serious, and he scans the area like the Terminator behind his mirrored sunglasses.

He locks in on me for a long moment. The smart thing to do is look away and get into my vehicle. But I have a long-standing hatred of authority which, admittedly, has not served me well over the years. A small part of my brain is signaling me to get into the SUV and drive away, but a much larger and stupider part locks my feet in place. This larger part of my brain has made most of the decisions in my adult life and should be fired.

Now the cop is sauntering toward me like he's king of the gun slingers. That small self-preserving part of my brain is now blasting a code red, yet I stand where I am, locked in a stare down with the officer until he's standing right in front of me. I'm not tall, just under

5'10", but I'm at eye level with the top of his shiny freckled head.

"Is there a problem, Officer?" I ask. I keep my eyes trained on the top of his head, just to be annoying.

"I thought that was you, Maze."

I glance down from the top of the cop's head. Slow and deliberate, he removes his sunglasses. His eyes are small and dark and too close together. I visualize him younger, with a nest of kinky black hair and a Wham! T-shirt, and it comes back to me.

"Dum Dum Dunham!"

"That's Officer Dunham," he says, beady eyes narrowing. "You'd be wise to keep that in mind."

"Hmm." I try to think of something nice to say and draw a blank. "Um, it sucks to be bald, but at least you don't have that ugly fucking nest of pubic hair on your head anymore." I smile. "So that's something."

I've never been a bully. Fighting always scared me. I've had one fight in my life, not counting the times I've made people angry enough to punch me. There are a lot of those. But I mean one in which I actively participated. It happened in second grade. Timmy Traves pushed me down on the playground, so I got up and swung at him. I missed. Then he took a swing at me. He didn't miss. He knocked me down, my lip bled, I peed my pants, fight over. As I got older my fighting technique developed into something more sophisticated – when a fight broke out, I moved to the back of the crowd, crouched down, and yelled really loud. I've always had a fear of being punched, and because I tend to piss people off so easily, I consider it to be a rational fear. Just yesterday I was punched by a middle-aged devout Christian, one of my best and oldest friends from childhood. It takes real talent to make something like that happen.

In my later teen years, I discovered that playing guitar made everyone want to be my friend. Freaks, geeks, jocks, burnouts, goths – everybody seemed to accept me. When they found out I was in a band, the tough guys would nod to me and sometimes try to befriend me. When we were together, me, Danny, Phil, and Cam, it was like we were a gang. Nobody could touch us. We walked the school halls untouched, quite a change from the Dungeons and Dragons days, when we more closely resembled a trembling group of level one monks in a cave full of hungry orcs.

I liked being liked, even if it was because of people's impression of me instead of who I really was. In high school, everything is shallow and based on impression. I was laid back and got along with everyone.

Except for Alex 'Dum Dum' Dunham, that is. Dum Dum had a crush on Rachel in high school. Not a big deal, because everyone had a crush on Rachel. She was perfect. In the opinion of many, her only flaw was her selection in boyfriends. Even I, the flaw, had to wonder about it from time to time. But I wasn't really the jealous type, and most guys were cool about it. On occasion someone would ask her out and she'd politely turn them down in a way that no feelings were hurt. In high school there were always plenty of girls to go around.

But Dum Dum didn't see it that way. He was a smart but arrogant kid who liked to openly laugh at people with poorer grades than his. He kept asking Rachel out, badgering her to the point where she felt the need to be rude. But even that didn't stop Dum Dum. He'd wait for her in the hallway after class, go to her soccer practices, call her at home. He'd tell her I was a loser, that I was going nowhere and someday I'd get bored and leave her and she'd regret going out with me. In some ways maybe Dum Dum wasn't so dumb, but we didn't know that at the time.

I didn't see him as a threat and tried to ignore the stalking until I heard him spreading rumors about me being with another girl. Rachel didn't deserve it, and neither did the other girl. Physical threats and confrontation weren't my style, so I retaliated by writing a song about Alex Dunham and titling it "Dum Dum Dunham". The nickname stuck, and it was cruel but I didn't feel badly about it. I don't remember all of the lyrics, but the chorus went:

> *Alex Dunham, you can call him Dum Dum*
> *spit in his locker, do it just for fun fun*
> *when girls see him coming, they start to run run*
> *Dum Dum Dunham, he's just a Dum Dum*

Not my best lyrics – if I'd submitted it as a poem my English teacher probably would have given me a D+ – but easy for teenagers to remember and laugh at. I recorded the song onto a cassette and passed it around to a few friends, who taped the song onto more cassettes and passed them around, until the entire school was singing it in the hallways and cafeteria whenever Alex Dunham appeared. I hadn't wanted to humiliate the guy in front of the entire school, but the song had spread quickly and was out of my control. Feeling guilty, Rachel and I approached him one day in the cafeteria, where he was eating lunch at a table by himself.

"Hey, man," I said. The racket of two hundred teenagers talking and laughing and eating buzzed all around us. "Sorry about that song going all around school. I just wanted you to leave my girlfriend alone, but it shouldn't have become this big a deal."

Rachel nodded solemnly in agreement. Dunham set down his bacon burger, stood up, and stuck out his hand. I wasn't so averse to shaking hands back then, and I reached for it. Then the little bastard pulled his hand back and hit me on the cheek with a mean left hook. All talking and chewing came to a sudden stop and the lunchroom went very still. From the floor I looked up, rubbed my jaw, and watched Dum Dum give Rachel the finger before walking out of the cafeteria.

I was a little embarrassed about getting knocked on my ass, but I wasn't a fighter – I was a guitar player. I spun it like a politician and was soon being told how brave I was for taking a fall for my lady. Things didn't turn out so well for Dum Dum. Everyone liked Rachel and when word got out about him giving her the finger and pushing her (the high school grapevine is lightning-fast and notoriously fallacious) he couldn't turn down a hallway without being shoved into a locker.

Over thirty years later, he clearly hasn't forgotten about it. For a long moment he stares at me, and I hope he doesn't zap me with his taser. Then he says, "How about another left hook, asshole."

I deserve that. I know I do. So there's absolutely no excuse for me responding with, "Want me to write you another song, Dum Dum?"

His left hand moves to his hip and now I'm certain I'm about to be tased. But I'm saved by the nervous approach of a woman and a teenage girl.

"Excuse me. This may sound silly, but I was wondering if . . . oh my goodness, yes, it really is you!"

Me and Dum Dum both turn toward the women, clearly a mother and daughter. The mother is about forty, heavyset but well-dressed, with blond hair and a very pretty face. The daughter, dressed in ripped jeans and a retro Oasis t-shirt, has darker hair and the same pretty face as her mother. Her body is thin with curves in all the right places, and she walks like she knows it. I look from mother to daughter, taking in what time and genetics are going to do to those curves.

"Can I help you, ma'am?" Dum Dum asks, puffing out his chest.

"Oh, no, I'm sorry. Not you. Him!" She points to me and somehow pushes Dum Dum aside without touching him. She gazes at me with that same glazed look on her face that so many people get in the presence of celebrity, no matter how minor. "You're Jesse from the Dropouts!"

I nod and smile. "I am."

The woman turns to her daughter and, practically bouncing on her toes, says, "It's him! You know the song, from that show you like, and that movie we watched on DVD that night. It's him!"

The daughter is pointing a cell phone in my direction. When I look her way, she smiles and waves at the screen. I have serious doubts about her generation.

"I can't believe this!" the mother says breathlessly. "We're visiting family in Apple Brook and we just stopped in for gas, and there you are, pumping gas like you're one of us!"

I've always tried to be nice to anyone who recognizes me. It's not always easy because people will approach you when you're eating, or out with family, or pumping gas. On the celebrity scale I'm rather low. If it were football, I'd be a second- or third-string quarterback. Maybe that's why people feel comfortable approaching me. For many of these fans, meeting me is the highlight of their day, or week, or year. It's a story they'll tell for years to come. Taking a few seconds out of my day to make someone so happy is not a problem. It usually makes me happy too.

"Even guitarists need fuel," I say. A really lame line, but the woman bursts out laughing like I'm Jerry Seinfeld.

"I'm Gina," she says. "This is my daughter Lily. Can I get a picture with you?"

Without waiting for an answer, she takes her phone from her pocket and slides up beside me, nudging Officer Dum Dum out of the way. She holds it at arm's length and snaps a photo of us standing beside my SUV while the daughter takes a video of her mom taking the photo. The idiocy that technology inspires is lost on them and most of society.

While giving Gina and her daughter a quick hug I look around at my surroundings. The combination of a police officer and squealing females with cameras has garnered some attention in the Cumberland Farms parking lot. I glance at Dum Dum and see his bald head now resembles an angry tomato. The look on his face is murderous. Now would be a good time to get out of here.

I wish the mother and daughter a good day. Then I slap Dum Dum on the shoulder and say, "Nice to see you, Officer Dunham. I feel safer knowing you're patrolling the gas stations and donut shops of the area."

I'm just grabbing for the door handle when I'm slammed face-first into the SUV. Things are a bit foggy after that, but I'm aware of warm blood running down my face, a woman screaming, and Officer Dum Dum saying, "Jesse Maze, you're under arrest for assaulting an officer," before dragging me to his police car.

15

It's been a few years since I've been inside a jail cell. It still sucks. The Apple Brook jail is small and old, located in the basement of the police station. The jail is standard – cold, cement walls painted a dull gray and steel bars. No windows. I've got my own cell and I don't see or hear any other prisoners. It's better than a drunk tank, where you're constantly in danger of being puked on or pissed on or punched. But it still sucks.

I don't know what time it is because the police took my phone during processing. I know I've been here for a while. I'm guessing that Ellie's birthday party has already started. I think about having to tell Megan that I missed Ellie's birthday party because I was in jail. She'll never forgive me, never speak to me again. Doesn't matter that I didn't do anything. I've screwed up too many times before.

My nose isn't broken but it's swollen and hurts like hell. There's a throbbing bump where my forehead met the SUV's back door and it hurts every time a hair brushes against it. My wrists are raw from the handcuffs being too tight. My knees are scraped from being dragged across the parking lot. I'm in a lot of pain and my family will never forgive me. The thought of getting out and murdering Dum Dum Dunham is the only thing keeping my hopes up.

At least my hands aren't damaged. I'm sitting in a corner of the cell, gazing at my hand and wiggling my fingers, when a door slams shut. Approaching footsteps echo off the cement. A tall police officer glances at me and unlocks the cell door. He pulls the door open and holds onto it without looking at me.

"Am I free to go?" I ask.

The cop doesn't answer, which I interpret as a yes. I slowly get up and walk out of the cell. My movements are stiff, my steps short and tentative. Two hours of sitting on a cement floor is tough on the body of a guy my age. How do you know when you're getting old? When sitting is a painful activity.

The cell door clangs shut behind me and I follow the cop to the door leading out of the jail. This isn't a high-tech facility like you see on the documentaries, with cameras everywhere and several security points for each entrance. It's just an old wooden door with a lock on the handle. The cop sticks a key in the lock and opens the door. As we pass a few offices I have a sudden thought – what if I'm not being released, but instead being transported to the county jail to stay overnight?

The cop unlocks a second door. I walk through it and into the lobby. The overhead fluorescent lights are bright. Gina and her daughter are seated in plastic chairs on the other side of the room, near the front door. When she sees me, Gina smiles and hurries over. Her daughter doesn't glance up from her phone. Through the glass front doors, I see darkness. The door clicks shut and when I turn around the cop is gone. He never said a word to me.

I ignore Gina and go to the front desk, located behind what I assume is bulletproof glass. I press a buzzer beside it. After a very long minute an overweight officer appears, takes a seat, gets comfortable.

"Yeah?"

"I was just released from a cell," I say. It hurts to talk. "Am I free to go?"

"You Maze?"

"Yes."

The fat cop gets up and walks away. This is the strangest experience I've ever had in a jail.

He returns a minute later and slides my phone, wallet, and keys to me through a slot. I take them but still have no idea what to do.

"So, is that a yes?" I ask. "Am I free to go?"

"We don't usually let people into the lobby and hand them their personal belongings if they're staying."

"Why am I being released? Not that I'm not pleased. By why?"

The desk cop leans forward and nods. "Ask her."

I turn around. Gina's standing right behind me as though we're in line for movie tickets. Smiling brightly, she holds up her cellphone.

"I recorded everything that cop did to you," she says breathlessly. "It's all here. He slammed you into that big vehicle for no reason. Twice! Then he put you in handcuffs and dragged you to his car. He didn't even let you get up!"

"I don't remember most of it, but that would explain why I'm so sore," I say, gently touching my forehead.

"I didn't have a chance to record it the first time he slammed you into the car – it happened so fast – but I got the rest. And Lily got it all from beginning to end because she was recording me talking with you. We followed the police car here and it took me forever to talk to someone. I showed an officer my video and threatened to put it on Facebook and Twitter and Instagram and YouTube if you weren't released immediately."

"And that's when I was released?"

"Not exactly," Gina says. "The officer watched the video and then deleted it from my phone. Prick. PRICK!" she yells, looking at the now-empty desk. I smile for the first time in hours. "But I'd already sent the video to Lily, and she had her own video on her phone as well. We sent it to the Apple Brook police department, found an email address for the police chief, and sent it to him. Then I sent it to my brother. That's who we're here visiting. He's a town councilor." She pauses for a quick breath. "Half an hour later there was a short meeting, and here you are! All charges dropped."

I give her a hug and thank her. The daughter looks over from her seat and without expression points her phone at us again. I'd ask her not to but that would be like asking a lioness not to hunt.

I look down at my phone. It's after seven, meaning I'm already an hour late for the party. There are calls and texts from Rachel and Danny, several from managers and agents who I don't know and don't care to know, and a few from Derek, the band's manager.

"I have to get going," I say, and I'm halfway out the door before I realize I don't have my vehicle. Certain that it's been towed, I walk back to the front desk and ring the buzzer. It's a full five minutes before the same desk cop appears. I tell the cop that, had this been an emergency, I could have been dead many times. He doesn't appear overly concerned. I find out that my vehicle was indeed towed and that I can pick it up at the lot behind the jail at any time, but it will take about a half hour to process. The fee is $100 but because it's after 7 p.m. there's an additional $50 charge.

There's no time to argue about the cost of getting beaten up and thrown in jail around here. There's also no time to wait for the SUV to be processed. Ellie's party started over an hour ago. The only choice is to grab an Uber and hope it doesn't take too long.

"We can give you a ride," Gina says, and I notice she's still standing close to me. "Where are you going?"

I give her directions, and fifteen minutes later we turn into Rachel's driveway. There are cars parked in the yard and lined up halfway down the driveway. The *thump, thump, thump* of loud music can be felt from the end of the drive, as can the yells and laughter of dozens of partygoers. I consider inviting Gina and Lily inside. I'd rather not, but after all they've done for me this afternoon, I feel I owe it to them.

Looks like a fun party," Gina says, watching lights flash and people dance through the big windows. "We've got a party of our own to get to, don't we, honey?"

Without taking her eyes from her phone, Lily nods.

"My sister-in-law's birthday is today," Gina says. "My brother took her to the movies tonight and we're having a surprise party for her when they get back, around nine or ten."

"That's great," I say, slightly relieved. "Listen, thank you for everything you've done today. Really. If not for you I'd still be sitting in that jail cell."

"Our pleasure. I can't believe we got to spend the afternoon with Jesse Maze!"

She reaches over for another hug. Her daughter watches, then surprises me by leaning forward for one of her own. I open the passenger door, stick a leg out, and then turn back to them.

"What are you planning to do with that video of me getting arrested?" I ask. "You told the police you wouldn't put it on the internet, right?"

"Nope," says Lily, and mother and daughter laugh. "We told them if they didn't release you, we'd put it on the internet. We didn't say we wouldn't if they *did* release you!"

"Wait. So you put my arrest video out there?"

"Yup. Facebook, Twitter, Instagram, YouTube. It's blowing up already. Police brutality videos do well. Add a celebrity, especially a fragile old guy like you, and it'll be huge!"

The walk up the driveway to the house is a quarter mile of frigid lake winds. The temperature has dropped at least twenty degrees since midday. But I barely feel the cold. I'm too busy feeling embarrassed about the world watching me get smashed head-first into the side of my car by Dum Dum Dunham.

The birthday party is in full swing. The squeals and laughter of teenagers having fun fills the air, with a background of thumping hip-hop music. Boys and girls talk and laugh in the kitchen and dance in the living room. Parents gather in small groups along the walls, quietly wondering where the time has gone. Presents are stacked on the kitchen table, next to the tall birthday cake.

At one corner of the table, arm-wrestling a fifteen-year-old boy, is Synthetic Sid, Ellie's dad. It's been over a decade since I've last seen him, but Sid looks basically the same. The short curly hair has just a touch of white in it and the goatee has flourished into a full beard, but the cocky grin and the tight shirt designed to show off his muscular upper body is still present. His blue eyes have a slightly sharper tint, and I wonder if he's wearing colored contacts.

He toys with the kid for a while, lets him push his thick arm halfway to the table before smiling and slamming the kid's hand to the table in a sharp banging arc. There's a collective murmur of appreciation from the small group of acne- and testosterone-riddled onlookers. The defeated boy winces and holds his smashed hand tight to his body as he walks away in embarrassment. Sid drinks from a water bottle and calls out for another challenger. Then he notices me.

"Jesse!" he yells, even though I'm less than ten feet away. "How the hell are you?" He does a double take. "You look like shit! Did you walk into a wall, or something?"

"No, a car."

I try to step past him, but he's on his feet and has my hand in a vice grip before I can pull away. Insecure wannabe tough guys like Sid are the reason I don't like to shake hands.

"I'm surprised to see you here, Sid." I finally extract my hand from his grip.

"I could say the same thing to you."

Good comeback, for Sid. He's normally an imbecile.

"Where's your whistle?" I ask.

Sid's a high school gym teacher and takes great pride in intimidating teenagers while wearing tight shorts and shirts. I'm just assuming this, of course. I've only met Sid a couple of times and that was enough. But I do know he loves his whistle. Sid's a weird guy.

"Back home," he says seriously. "I don't wear it on weekends unless I'm refereeing a game."

"Or getting married," I say. "Speaking of, I hear you have another family now."

"Yes, I remarried."

That's all he says on the subject. It isn't like Sid to avoid bragging about something, anything, given the opportunity. Most of what comes out of his mouth is fake, but that's never stopped Sid from delivering his lies with the earnestness of a Jimmy Stewart character.

"How's that going?" I ask.

"Honestly, we're having a tough time right now. But you know how it is. Couples fight sometimes."

"Uh-huh."

I see Danny across the room. We make eye contact and he begins making his way toward me across the crowded house.

"That explains why you're here," I say, after turning back to Sid.

"I'm here because it's my daughter's birthday!" he says indignantly.

"You're here to line up a backup plan. You want to move back in with Megan if your current marriage goes south."

"You were always an asshole, Jesse." The muscles in his forearms dance like piano wire as he clenches his fists. "You're lucky it's Ellie's birthday."

"Am I wrong?"

"Get away from me, before I kick your ass."

I nod and step around him. The way things are going, he'll have to take a number.

The house is very crowded. Danny follows me upstairs, where I toss my jacket onto the bed in my guestroom. There's nobody up here, unless a couple of kids snuck away to quietly fool around in one of the guest bedrooms. If they have, I don't want to know about it.

"Where have you been?" Danny asks. We're in the hallway and he's blocking my way back to the stairs. "Are you drunk?"

"No, I'm not drunk!" I'm offended, though with my track record it's not an unreasonable question.

"Then why are you so late? Rachel's angry. Megan's very angry." He leans in and peers closely at my face. "Are those new bruises? And blood? That's not from Cam, is it?"

"No, I haven't seen Cam. I was arrested." Before he can ask, I say, "I'll explain later. Right now, I need to find Rachel."

"Tread carefully, my friend. There's a tidal wave of angry estrogen headed your way."

We start down the stairs. At the bottom stands Rachel. She stares up at me, and her expression is a mixture of anger and hurt that momentarily freezes me. Taking a deep breath, I solemnly follow Danny down the stairs like a death row inmate walking the last mile.

# 16

## 2004

*Megan Maze & Sidney Wagner*
*Request the honor of your presence*
*on their wedding day*
*Saturday, the eleventh of June*
*Two thousand and four*
*at two o'clock in the afternoon*
*the First Congregational Church of Apple Brook*
*Drinks Dancing Shenanigans to follow*

I read the invitation a few times to be sure I was seeing it correctly. This was in part due to the four beers and two milligrams of Valium I'd ingested as an afternoon snack, but also because I had no idea my daughter was engaged or even had a boyfriend.

In the nearly four years since Megan's disastrous sweet sixteen party I'd heard nothing from anyone in Apple Brook. Sad, very sad, but not surprising. And certainly not Megan's fault. It's nobody's fault but mine. Embarrassment and a fear of rejection kept me from contacting Rachel or Megan. I found that burying my shame in a diverse assortment of intoxicants was helpful.

I'd been living in Virginia for about a year, playing with a Journey tribute band. I was living in a small one-bedroom apartment with a gorgeous Virginia Tech grad student who was intelligent but not very smart. How else to describe a young woman who has everything any man could want yet chooses to live with a drug-addled guitarist in a cover band? I was grateful to have her, but it was just another example of why I will never understand women.

We barely ever saw each other because the band was on the road a lot and she was busy with school and work. Distance helped keep the relationship alive, especially without the troublesome encumbrance of fidelity. It was upon my return from three weeks on the road playing several bar gigs near colleges in South Carolina and Georgia that I opened Megan's wedding invitation. It had arrived with the mail a couple of weeks earlier.

I checked the calendar. The wedding was less than a month away. The band – named Open Arms, which made us sound like a group of soft-rock fairies – was booked every weekend for the next six months. But this was my daughter's wedding and my way to get back into her life. The invitation was a huge step in the right direction, and the fact that Megan had made the first move wasn't lost on me. Then again, receiving a generic wedding invitation in the mail without so much as a note or phone call told me that Rachel was still angry with me. It was time to break out the old Maze charm and put an end to this estrangement.

Half a pot of coffee later, I dialed Rachel's number. My palms were sweaty as I paced back and forth in the small living room. I thought about what I'd say when she answered. So many questions to ask, so many apologies to make. I decided to go with a joke. Loosen things up. When a male voice answered, I was caught off guard. After a confused pause, I asked if I had the right number for Rachel Brennan.

"Sort of," the man said. "You have the correct number for Rachel Aspinall, formerly known as Rachel Brennan."

"Huh?"

"Who is this?"

"Jesse. Who's this?"

"This is Harry Aspinall," he said, with more than a hint of irritation. "Rachel's husband."

"Wait." Now I was very confused. I wished I'd waited to call when I was sober. "Harry Ass? Rachel married Harry Ass?"

He called me a shithead and hung up.

I poured another cup of coffee and tried to process what I'd just heard. Then I called back. This time, Rachel answered. The sound of her voice caused my heart to skip a beat and left me momentarily speechless, but then I forged ahead.

"You married Harry Ass?" I said, all thoughts of starting off with a joke forgotten. "What are you, nuts? That makes you Mrs. Harry Ass!"

There was a long sigh.

"Hello, Jesse. How have you been?"

"A hell of a lot better than you, Mrs. Ass! When did this tragedy befall you?"

"I married Harry last year," she said.

"And when were you going to tell me about this?"

"Well, Jesse, I didn't feel it was something that required your approval. I planned to tell you about it the next time we spoke. Which I'm now doing."

I chugged coffee until my mug was empty. It's a strange feeling, having a beer and pill buzz and then chasing it with strong coffee. Not the best combination if one wants to take part in a calm, rational conversation.

"Were you tricked into this? Is he holding you hostage? Should I call the cops?"

"I married Harry of my own accord," Rachel said patiently.

"You have to say that if you're being held prisoner. He'll kill you if you say otherwise."

"Why are you calling, Jesse?" Again, she sighed. "I'm guessing this is about Megan's wedding."

This was a diversionary tactic, and like throwing a ball to a hyperactive puppy it worked perfectly on me. I grabbed the wedding invitation from the kitchen counter and asked her why our daughter was getting married at nineteen years old.

"She's in love," Rachel said. "And she's almost twenty."

"She's way too young. We were in love at nineteen, but we were smart enough not to get married."

"I had a baby out of wedlock at eighteen. You left your baby and fiancée at twenty." For the first time, she sounded angry. "Using us as an example is probably not the best tactic."

"Hmm. So, who's this guy? It is a guy, right? I've seen women with the name Sidney. Usually it's spelled with a Y, but who knows these days. Is our daughter a lesbian? Not that there's anything wrong with that."

Rachel explained that, no, our daughter was not a lesbian. Sidney Wagner was indeed a man, a high school gym teacher a few years older than Megan. They met in an education seminar at the University of Southern Maine, where Megan was a physical education major.

"Great. He's a grown man who wears shorts and a whistle to work."

"Sounds like something my father would have said about you," Rachel said.

"I had a guitar. A guitar is a lot cooler than shorts and a whistle."

"True. A guitar is very cool."

I think about what's happened since I'd last been to Apple Brook. Rachel married Harry Ass. Megan graduated high school and was halfway through college. I had no idea she was interested in physical education. If I'd been offered a million dollars to say what my daughter was likely to major in, I couldn't have done it. She was an adult now, and it struck me how little I knew about her. My family and I were strangers, and it was entirely my fault.

"Why didn't you tell me about this before, instead of just sending me an invitation? I am the girl's father, Rach. I deserve to know."

"After that stunt you pulled at her birthday party a few years ago, you're lucky you got an invitation at all," she said. "To be honest, she wanted nothing to do with you. First you embarrass her – no, not embarrass – you *mortify* her – and then she doesn't hear from you for four years. Not even a phone call to apologize." She pauses. "I had to talk her into inviting you."

"I thought staying away was the best thing I could do," I said quietly.

"No, Jesse, I don't believe that. You're not Captain Cook, leaving home to discover new continents. You're just hiding. You felt humiliated, and rightfully so, because you behaved like an ass, and your pride wouldn't allow you to apologize. That's all. Running and hiding is what you do."

Sounded about right. For a minute I mulled over what she'd said. It's not pleasant having your flaws so accurately described. Necessary, maybe, but not pleasant. There was no sound from the other end of the line. Rachel knew she'd given me a lot to think about.

We ended up talking for another ten minutes. I decided to arrive in Apple Brook a couple days before the wedding so I could meet Sidney and try to patch things up with Megan. Rachel didn't seem to think a couple of days would be enough, but I'd always had great faith in my diplomacy skills.

Well, she was right – a couple of days was not enough. A couple of years might not have been enough. When I arrived in Maine, Megan refused to see me. She's stubborn like her grandfather and, like him, appeared to have developed a genuine loathing for me. Speaking of Mr. Brennan, Rachel informed me that the old man had developed dementia and Parkinson's and was now living in a nursing home. There was no love lost between us, but I respected Mr. Brennan for a number of reasons and was sad to hear about his physical and mental decline.

With her father in the nursing home, Rachel and Harry Ass now resided in the big house, Lazy Daze.

After she graduated from school, Megan and Sidney would be moving to Apple Brook to live in the smaller house. I first met Sidney at the big house on Thursday afternoon, two days before the wedding, less than an hour after I arrived in town. Harry Ass was at work and Megan sat quietly nearby, leafing through wedding magazines while Rachel introduced me to Sidney on the porch overlooking the lake. The same porch where I'd slept on a trash bag after passing out and pissing myself at my daughter's birthday party four years earlier. Sidney seemed okay. The tight shorts and whistle were a bit disconcerting, but some people love their job. He might have found my long hair and skull ring disturbing. If so, he was polite enough not to mention it.

We talked for half an hour or so, and then I made an excuse about having to meet a musician friend in Kennebunkport for a beer that afternoon. Sidney invited me to his bachelor party that evening, just seven or eight guys going out to dinner and then catching a Sea Dog game in Portland. The Sea Dogs were the Double-A affiliate of the Red Sox and were a relatively new addition to the state. It was a gracious offer and I welcomed the opportunity to spend more time with my soon-to-be son-in-law. I hadn't yet decided if I liked him or not, and an evening eating and drinking with his friends and family was sure to show me what type of person he was.

On my way out I gave Rachel a quick hug. Megan didn't look up from her magazine when I said goodbye. I bent over and kissed her forehead. She didn't acknowledge it, but she didn't push me away either. Sidney walked me out. When I got into my rental car, he gestured for me to unroll the window. Leaning inside, he said in a low voice, "We're not going to the ball game tonight. We're going to Mark's Showplace."

"What's Mark's Showplace?" I asked, though I had a pretty good idea of the answer.

"Oh, man." Sidney chuckled. "Mark's is the best strip club north of Boston. I know most of the girls that work there and they've promised free lap dances to my party because I'm getting married." He leaned in closer. "Probably more than lap dances, too. I've already fucked half of the girls that work there. Bring a condom."

He slapped the roof of the car and walked off, and I was left with a very distinct and revolting taste of the type of man my daughter was marrying.

It had been decades since I'd stepped inside a church. I'd attended a few weddings over the years but most of them took place in a lovely outdoor setting like the beach or were very small affairs presided over in the office of a justice of the peace or notary public. The most recent wedding ceremony I'd attended was performed in a cramped living room by a justice of the peace with the business name Marriage by Mitch. The bride wore black, the groom wore shorts and an Iron Maiden t-shirt, and we all drank whiskey during the ceremony.

The day of Megan's wedding was warm and sunny, a perfect Maine summer day. The church did not collapse upon my arrival, a good sign for all gathered. Megan was absolutely beautiful in her white gown and watching her walk down the aisle brought up imaginary images of what Rachel might have looked like on our wedding day. I sat alone and spent much of the ceremony gazing at Rachel and her husband because I couldn't stand to watch my daughter pledge her love and devotion in the eyes of God to that sleazeball gym teacher. I'd never be able look at him without picturing the smug look on his face at Mark's Showplace as he high-fived his friends and disappeared for an hour into a back room with two strippers. His own father cheered him on. He tried to slap my hand, but I got up and walked away. I'd never claim to be chief of the morality police, but this man was marrying my daughter in two days. Filled with disgust, I left the strip club and drove back to my hotel.

Telling Rachel or Megan about Sidney's infidelity wasn't an option. Megan was young and in love and would never believe it, particularly given the source. Rachel had usually trusted me and given me the benefit of the doubt despite all that I'd done to her. But her marriage to Harry Aspinall had raised a kind of implicit barrier between us and I now found myself being treated with a polite but cold indifference, which is probably what I'd always deserved. My daughter was marrying a bad man and because of my past behavior there was nothing I could do or say about it. Karma really can be a bitch.

The minister got to the part about "Do you, Sidney, take Megan to be your . . .", and I turned my gaze to the altar. Standing beside Megan were five bridesmaids dressed in white, all young and attractive, friends of hers since childhood. It was a painful realization that none of them were familiar to me. Staring into Megan's eyes as though she was the only one for him, Sidney was dressed in a white tux and wearing a ridiculous-looking gold whistle on a thin gold chain that would be perfect to strangle him with. His five groomsmen were also dressed in white tuxes and had all cheered Sidney two nights earlier when he took the two strippers into the back room with the intent of cheating on his fiancée.

The happy couple said their "I do's", the groom kissed the bride with his stripper-tainted lips, and everyone cheered and wept and headed to the lake for the reception.

A big party at Lazy Daze just didn't seem the same without Mr. Brennan, like the crowned head being absent from his kingdom's biggest celebration. Mr. Brennan's absence from the wedding of his beloved only granddaughter made me realize just how poor his condition must be.

There was some benefit to his not being there, mainly a freedom I'd never felt when the old man was watching my every move like a disapproving chaperone. Flying solo and not able to bring myself to kiss the bride for marrying an asshole, or to shake the asshole's hand, I'd left the church and arrived at the reception early. The wedding band, The Band of Gold, was finishing setting up, and after a couple of beers with the guys I'd convinced them to let me play rhythm guitar with them. Finding an extra guitar wasn't difficult. I had one in the backseat of my car.

The Band of Gold was quite talented, tighter than most wedding bands. There were several tables set up on the large and perfectly manicured lakeside lawn, and viewed from a camera's lens the setting was elegant enough to earn a spread in a bridal magazine. But while the backdrop was stylish and sophisticated, the party vibe was more casual. There was no assigned seating and the caterers had prepared a summer barbecue-themed meal with a selection of hot dogs, burgers, steak, and chicken, along with potato and macaroni salads. There was plenty to drink, including champagne and beer and soda and anything else a person could want at a party on a beautiful late afternoon by the lake.

After sitting in for a few songs with the band, I decided to get some food. I filled my plate with burgers and dogs and potato salad. I grabbed a beer but drank it slowly as I ate. No way was I going to get drunk today. I didn't remember much of the last party I attended here, but I sure as hell was going to remember my daughter's wedding reception.

Not recognizing many people, I sat at a table with strangers. They introduced themselves as the family of one of the bridesmaids and said they had known Megan since she was in first grade. She'd spend many nights at their house over the years and watching her get married was almost like watching their own daughter's nuptials. I introduced myself as Megan's father. They appeared confused and were too polite to say that they'd never heard of me. I focused on my food and didn't look up until a someone softly grabbed my shoulder.

"Good to see you can still play guitar."

It had been years but I immediately recognized the voice. I looked up at Danny and smiled, then got to my feet and pulled him in for a tight hug. Hit by a powerful wave of emotion, I realized how much I'd missed my old friends. There were no empty tables, so I grabbed my beer and the rest of my second burger and walked with Danny down to the water's edge, where we said again how great it was to see each other. There was no mention of the past, no recap of the last twenty years, no questions about how the other was doing. Danny was like a brother and we fell into conversation like it'd been days and not decades since we'd seen each other.

"Rachel looks good," Danny said.

I turned and found her sitting at the long head table with the happy couple and the groom's parents and a few of the bridesmaids and groomsmen.

"She looks beautiful," I said, taking a bite of my burger. "Always has."

"You fucked up letting go of that, buddy."

"Thanks, I wasn't aware." Rachel noticed us watching her and gave a small wave. Beside her, Harry Ass looked over and scowled. "What do you think of her husband?"

"I don't think I like him," Danny said. "Seems a bit arrogant. When Rachel introduced me to him as a singer, he asked what my real job was."

"Fucking geeky accountant. Ask him how many times pulling out his ledger has gotten him laid. Probably never slept with an attractive woman in his life."

Danny grinned. "I hate to point this out, Maze, but I'm pretty sure he's sleeping with Rachel."

"Maybe, but there's no proof of that. My proof is right there." I nodded toward Megan. I'd never seen a more beautiful bride. As I watched, she leaned in toward Sidney and laughed at something he'd said.

"Sorry, but we might need a DNA test to confirm it. Because that stunning young lady over there is far too attractive to be related to you."

"My mom was pretty. It's genetic."

"Your mom was *very* pretty," Danny agreed. "I just always assumed you were adopted."

For a while, neither of us spoke. I watched the activity on the lake. The water was still cold due to the cool June evenings, but even so there were people tubing and knee boarding from the backs of boats. I heard Danny laugh softly as a kid took a tumble from his tube. Our silence wasn't uncomfortable. On the contrary, the relaxing calm of it said more about our friendship than words could have.

The music stopped, and the *ping, ping, ping* of a spoon tapped repeatedly against a glass silenced the guests. At the head table the best man, a short, sweaty man whose back tattoo of Hugh Hefner had been on full display when he removed his shirt two nights previous at Mark's Showplace, stood up and said, "I should have done this before dinner but Sid had just realized he'd gotten married and I had to revive him with smelling salts."

After the laughter subsided, the best man delivered a short but eloquent speech about those lucky few who find that one true love to share their life with. He raised his glass to the newlyweds and winked at his own beaming wife as the guests clapped. The speech was well done and would have come across as genuine and honest to anyone who hadn't seen the best man slip a stripper three hundred-dollar bills before following her into a back room.

"You have an opportunity to meet the groom?" I asked Danny.

"Sure did. Like mother, like daughter. I've come to the sad conclusion that the Brennan women, beautiful and intelligent as they are, have appalling taste in husbands. Hell, Rachel would be better off with you, though that's not really saying much." He smiled at me, and then gazed for a moment at the head table. "You think Sid will take that whistle off during the honeymoon? Maybe he'll blow it every time he's ready to climb back on."

"Jesus, Danny."

He burst out laughing, and I couldn't help but smile. The band started up again. We watched Sidney lead Megan to the square area of grass that was cut as short as a golf course green and serving as a dance floor. The dance green. I took one last sip from my now-warm beer. I wanted another one but wouldn't do it.

"Hey, you want to see about doing a song with the band?" I asked. "It would be like half a Dropouts reunion."

"Sounds fun. But there's something you need to do first." I glanced at him questioningly, and he nodded toward the dance green. "The father-daughter dance."

*Shit*, I thought.

She purposely ignored me when I approached her as she walked back to her table. But when the band announced it was time for the father/daughter dance, Megan had no choice but to accompany me to the dance green. I thought I saw Megan glance toward Harry Ass, but that might have just been my insecurity kicking in.

The song was "My Little Girl", by Tim McGraw. I wasn't sure who chose the song. It wasn't me – I was lucky to have been invited to the wedding, never mind be consulted on anything. It certainly wasn't chosen by Megan. As we slowly dance, her arms were almost fully extended in an effort to stay as far away from me as possible, like a head cheerleader being forced to dance with the junior high school's biggest nerd. Her selection would likely be something along the lines of Harry Chapin's *Cats in the Cradle*.

It had to be Rachel who selected the song. I looked to the head table. Not surprisingly, Sid had his arm around a bridesmaid who appeared very intoxicated. The best man, he of the heartfelt speech about the joy of spending life with your soulmate, had just moments before removed his arm from around the drunken bridesmaid and was now being reamed out by his very displeased wife, who was thrusting her index finger like a dagger toward his flabby chest. Harry Ass sat with his phone to one ear and a finger in the other to block out those bothersome wedding noises.

Rachel was the only one at the table watching us, and the glow of love and happiness on her face was enough to make me smile. That tender expression left no doubt about who'd selected the Tim McGraw song.

"Honey, you look so beautiful," I said, trying to break the ice. "The most beautiful bride I've ever seen."

"You should have seen Mom on the day she married Harry. She was stunning, the happiest I've ever seen her."

Intended to wound, and mission accomplished.

"Your mother is the most beautiful woman I've ever had the privilege to lay eyes on. There's honestly never been a time when the sight of her didn't make my heart race." I smiled down at my daughter. "And that's exactly how you look today."

Megan looked up at me, a hint of a smile playing at the corners of her mouth. "Thank you. You don't look to shabby yourself."

"Are you happy? Is today what you wanted it to be?"

"This is exactly what I'd hoped my wedding day would be." Her face slowly curled into a big smile. "I'm the happiest girl in the world."

The head table was at her back and she tried to turn and look at it. I held her fast for a long moment, hoping she wouldn't see her new husband give the drunken bridesmaid a quick squeeze on the ass. If Megan noticed what I was doing, she didn't mention it.

For a little while neither of us spoke. I was aware of many eyes upon us, but a lifetime of being on stage made them easy to ignore. I listened to the lyrics describing a father's love for his daughter and was overwhelmed with emotion – love, pride, shame. I should have done things differently. So much lost time. Feeling myself beginning to choke up, I tried to force the feelings away. It wasn't easy to do without a bottle of whiskey or pills.

"I just wish Grampy could have been here," she said softly, and for a moment her smile faltered.

"All of your grandparents would have been so proud of you," I whispered. "Grandma and Grandpa Maze spoke of nothing but you every time I called them, and I'm certain Grandpa is giving God an earful for taking him before he had a chance to attend your wedding. Your Grammy Brennan would be crying nonstop and Grampy would have taken control of everything to make sure your day was perfect, whether you wanted him to or not. He'd probably have a helicopter flying overhead with snipers to make sure nobody got out of line."

Megan giggled softly. Then she pulled me closer. I wanted to say something, tell her how much I loved her, but talking never did me much good so I kept my mouth shut. That's how we finished out the dance, slowly turning, silently holding each other.

"I'm glad you came today," she said, pulling away from me. "It really means a lot to me. I'm sorry I've been a jerk to you. Just a lot of stress, I guess."

"I deserved it," I said. "And I'm glad you're happy. I wouldn't have missed this for the world."

I leaned over and kissed her on the cheek. She smiled at me, the same cherubic grin I remembered from when she was a little girl. When she walked away, back to the table with her sleazy new husband, my heart felt as though it might burst. Luckily, Danny grabbed my arm before I could do something stupid like cry.

"Hey, the singer wants us to play a couple of Dropouts songs with the band! Why didn't you tell those guys you were in the Dropouts when you played with them earlier?"

I shrugged. "I'd have been embarrassed if they'd never heard of us."

"Well, the good news is, they have heard of us." Danny grinned. "The bad news is, the reason they've heard of us is because their moms and dads were big fans."

I looked at him for a moment, and we both started laughing. Nothing like a strong shot of humility to lighten the mood. A few minutes later, when we took the stage to play "Your Love Line" with the Band of Gold, I was still smiling.

17

Rachel's angry. Really angry. She doesn't really say anything, just nails me with a scorching glare that could wilt flowers. I'd rather be yelled at. I try to explain that I'm late because I was arrested and thrown in jail, which does nothing to better her mood. It's only when Tyler rushes up, waving his phone in the air like an overgrown puppy shaking a stuffed toy, that she releases me from her Vader-like mental grip.

"Gramps dude!" he says, sliding to stop in front of us. "You're in a video online that has like a hundred thousand views!"

"Yeah, I know. It's from yesterday, when me and the other guys from the Dropouts got together and jammed on a few songs."

"No, dude. That one has, like, millions of views. This one is from today. It was just posted a couple of hours ago."

He holds out the phone. Rachel leans in next to me while Danny looks over my shoulder. The titillating title reads **Cop Beats Aging Rocker Jesse Maze Senseless**, which I imagine sounds unbearably thrilling to anyone not named Jesse Maze.

The video is about a minute long and begins with my hugging Gina in the Cumberland Farms parking lot. An angry-looking Dum Dum Dunham stands beside us, and three or four women are holding up phones while standing near gas pumps in the background. The hug is quick. I then smile and wave at the camera before giving Dum Dum a friendly pat on the shoulder and saying a few words to him. When I turn around to get into my SUV, Dum Dum places one hand on the back of my neck and grabs the back of my jacket in the other. He stretches out one leg to trip me, and as I fall forward, he slams me face-first like a battering ram into the side of the SUV. Then he pulls me back and does it again. I drop to the ground, limp and obviously unconscious. As Gina screams like a monkey on fire and the women in the background also cry out, Dum Dum pulls out his Taser and points it while standing over me, as though daring my battered body to regain consciousness. After taking a few moments to ascertain that two vicious and unprovoked head-first slams into the side of large automobile has, in fact, subdued me, he rolls me over and handcuffs me (which I vaguely remember, being around the time when I regained consciousness). Then Dum Dum jerks me to my feet and half-drags me to his police car.

"Dude, I thought he was gonna tase your ass! That would have been straight fire!" Tyler says excitedly. Rachel fixes him with the same mind-melting stare that I was on the receiving end of moments ago, and he takes a step back. "Sorry, ma'am. I mean, uh, things were not looking too sweet for you there, Gramps dude. I was very concerned about the wellbeing of your fragile old bones. Good thing you didn't get tased, bro."

"Who's this kid, and why's he speaking like an idiot?" Danny mumbles in my ear.

"Because he's an idiot," I mumble back.

Rachel grabs Tyler's phone and watches the video again, her eyes wide. She winces during the part where I'm slammed into the SUV and bites her lip as I'm led to the police car. I have to say, it's not a pretty sight. I don't even remember the second faceplant into the side of the vehicle. The video ends but Rachel continues to stare at the screen. Then she lifts the phone to shoulder height and grips it angrily.

"Was that Dum Dum Dunham?" she hisses, still gazing at the screen.

"Yeah. I think he's still pissed off about high school."

"This dude beat you up in high school? Or you beat him up?"

Rachel glances at Tyler, which shuts him up, at least momentarily.

"The next time I see him, he's going to be sorry," said Rachel.

"Dum Dum," Danny says thoughtfully. "Isn't that the kid you wrote the song about in high school? The guy that wouldn't leave Rachel alone?"

I nod. "He's a cop now." I don't think I've ever seen Rachel this angry, even at me. Somehow, against all common sense, I've become the voice of reason. "You might want to be careful. It's over now, so let's just forget about it and move on."

"I'm going to make sure he loses his job. I know the police chief quite well."

"Ellie's Gram, kicking butt and taking names! Taking on the po-po!"

Rachel hands the phone back to the teenager. "Tyler?"

"Yes?"

"Go find something to do."

"Yes, ma'am. Later, Gramps!"

We watch as Tyler slowly makes his way across the living room dance floor, bumping into people while doing a mix of the robot and flossing, before meeting up with a group of gigging girls on the other side of the room.

"Did he just call you Gramps?" Danny asks.

"Yeah. That's the kid Ellie likes." Tyler takes two Cheese Doodles and sticks one in each nostril, resulting in squeals of disbelief and laughter from those around him. "He's a bit rambunctious."

"Wow. Did we ever act that stupid when we were kids?"

"Probably. But it was okay. We were in a band."

Rachel is watching me closely, the unfamiliar visage of wrath and reprisal having morphed into a more familiar expression of tenderness and concern. Reaching up, she gently touches the swollen and tender bridge of my nose. There's no blood on her hand when she pulls it away, so the cut must be finally clotting. If I were the type to admit it, I'd say my body's healing powers aren't quite what they used to be. But I'm not the type to acknowledge such things.

"Have you been checked out?"

"Looks like you're checking me out right now, baby."

She doesn't smile.

"I mean by a professional."

"Well, there were a couple of hookers in the jail who – " Still no smile. "No, I haven't been checked. But I'm fine. Just a little sore. Nothing to worry about."

A gale of young laughter draws our attention to the other side of the living room, where Tyler has one arm around our granddaughter. In the other hand he holds a tampon by the string against his ear, letting it dangle like an earring. The girls in the area wear horrified expressions, but they're laughing. Ellie covers her face with her hands, but her body is shaking with laughter.

"That's what we should be worried about," I say.

Danny, despite himself, starts laughing. "I don't know whether to smack that kid in the head or shake his hand."

"I'd go with smacking him in the head," Rachel says, but she's wearing a hint of a smile.

A thought occurs to me as I look around the mroom.

"Hey, where's Andrew?"

"He's home with a cold," Danny says. "It's not too bad but he didn't want to spread it to anyone else. Andrew usually gets sick around this time of year. He's a native Floridian and I don't think he'll ever get used to Maine weather."

From where we stand near the foot of the stairway, much of the first floor of the house is visible. Sidney is still in the kitchen, pumping up his ego by slamming kids' hands to the table. Either he's running out of opponents or his obnoxious personality is working its magic, because the crowd around him has shrunk to just a few kids.

Down the hall behind us the door to the game room is open, and a group of gangly teenage boys are leaning on pool cues and talking. In the living room Tyler continues to hold court before an amused and growing group of teens, including Ellie. Some kids are still dancing, but many of them are staring at their phones. Some of the adults are also gazing at their phones, including Megan. She looks up, glances at me, and looks back down at her phone. A minute later, she works her way through the crowd and joins us.

"Have you seen this video of dad getting slammed face-first into a car at Cumberland Farms?" she asks, holding up her phone.

"Yes, I have," Rachel says, her jaw tightening.

"Don't get her started," I say. "Let's just enjoy the party."

"This is why you were late?" Megan asks. "Because you were getting arrested?"

"Yes. Against my will, I might add. If I'd been conscious, I'd have put up more of a fight. Maybe poked him in the eye or given him a noogie."

"Were you drunk?"

"No, honey, I wasn't. Haven't touched a drop of alcohol all day."

"Then why is a cop beating you up like this?" Megan asks accusingly. "Cops don't just beat people up for no reason."

"Ah, we've already forgotten the lessons of Rodney King and the city of Los Angeles."

"The officer doesn't like your father because of a song he wrote in high school," Rachel says.

"He beat him up because of a *song*?"

"You'd be surprised how often things like that happen to me," I say.

"I believe it. You've always had a way of pissing people off," Danny says admiringly.

Rachel describes to Megan how I wrote a deprecating song about Alex Dunham because he wouldn't leave her alone. In the days before the internet, she explains, it took a few days, rather than a few minutes, for the song to make its way around the school. The results were that Alex Dunham was permanently saddled with the derogatory nickname 'Dum Dum' and I was subsequently punched in the face during a rare and obviously inadequate attempt at expressing regret.

"You know," I say, "I just realized that this is the second time Dum Dum has roughed me up because of that stupid song."

Danny laughs. "You've been beaten up twice, over thirty years apart, for the same song. By the same guy!"

"I'd always hoped my songs would have longevity."

"The sad thing is, you were beaten up by Dum Dum. The guy once got a wedgie from a couple of cheerleaders."

"You're not helping me feel better about this. And I wouldn't say I was beaten up."

"You would if you saw yourself in the mirror."

"I think it sounds nice, Daddy defending Mom's honor," Megan says. "Chivalrous."

"It got a little out of hand, but it was chivalrous," Rachel says.

Rachel smiles at me, and Megan smiles at me, and Danny continues to laugh at me. I ignore my former bandmate and focus on the admiration radiating from two of the three people I love most in the world. It's a strange and uncommon sensation, similar to the comforting warmth of a sunny spring morning after a long cold winter. I momentarily bask in that warmth like a pale man tipping his head toward the sun and closing his eyes to soak it in.

Not surprisingly, it's Tyler who puts an end to my basking. He approaches holding Ellie's hand, a reasonably innocent gesture that bothers me perhaps a little more than it should. Rachel and Megan don't appear at all troubled bothered by it, and Danny just looks confused.

"Yo, Mrs. Brennan. Me and the squad are hungry. When are we gonna dig into the birthday cake?"

"I suppose it is time," Rachel says. "Megan, can you help me get the plates ready?"

"Grampy, are you okay to play 'Happy Birthday' on your guitar?" Ellie asks. "Your face is pretty swollen. I saw what that jerk policeman did to you."

"I'm fine. It looks much worse than it feels. And besides, I don't play guitar with my face."

"Dude, this video is lit," says Tyler, looking at his phone. "You'll have over half a million views tonight, maybe more. You're gonna be famous. Well, famouser than you are."

"You mean more famous," I say.

He nods knowingly. "Word, bro."

"My god," Danny mutters.

The plates and utensils are paper and plastic and make little noise, but somehow the teenagers all sense that cake will soon be available. A charge not unlike a herd of wildebeest thrashing across crocodile-infested waters soon commences, and the kitchen is quickly stuffed wall-to-wall with ravenous, hormonal teens. The kitchen counter is packed with the remains of all kinds of dips and sauces and other snacks, so it's difficult to understand why the kids have suddenly become so ravenous. One of the many mysteries of teenagers.

I head upstairs to grab my acoustic guitar, and Danny follows me.

"Has Derek called you?" he asks.

"Yeah, he's left about a dozen messages this week. I started listening to one, deleted the rest."

"I talked to him earlier. He saw the video of us jamming yesterday at Phil's house. Like the rest of the world, I guess. He wants us to do a few shows. Says there's a lot of interest in us and we can make a ton of money. The Tonight Show wants us, so we can kick off the tour doing a song there."

"First of all, who's *us*?"

"The Dropouts, of course. Phil already called me. Sounds like he's in, as long as Cam says yes. Cam will be a hard sell, but if we explain how much money he'll be able to give to the church he might do it."

I sit down on my bed and strum the guitar to make sure it's in tune. "I'm not interested, Danny, for a number of reasons."

"Such as?"

"I don't need money. I don't want to go on the road, I want to stay here and try to be a father and a grandfather for the first time in my life. And I remember what just a taste of fame did to me and the band. You guys were my best friends, but I didn't talk to you for about twenty years and I just saw Phil and Cam for the first time in thirty years. Cam was still so angry, he punched me. I don't think it's healthy for us to go on the road together. I've been in a lot of bands and most of them broke up acrimoniously. Let's work on repairing our friendships instead of going on tour."

"But you felt it when we jammed, didn't you?"

"Of course. That was the most fun I've had playing in years. But you saw Cam. Even if I agree to doing a few shows, Cam never will. And like Led Zeppelin, if one member of the Dropouts is missing, there is no band."

Danny nods in agreement and watches as I continue warming up. I like to warm up for several minutes before playing (another concession to age) but I think just a couple minutes' warmup is enough to play "Happy Birthday" and a couple other songs, if requested.

When I stand up to go back downstairs, guitar in hand, Danny asks, "What about just the two of us?" Seeing the confused look on my face, he continues, "I told Derek that there was a chance Cam won't do it, no matter what. He mentioned an acoustic set, just the two of us. We'd be introduced as 'Danny Crane and Jesse Maze of the Dropouts.'"

"Derek thinks of everything, doesn't he? It's funny, I don't remember him being this good of a manager when the band was actually together."

"It's not a bad idea. We could play small theaters, between a thousand and two thousand seats. Give it an intimate feel."

"When we started out, two thousand people would have seemed like a stadium."

"Neither of us needs the money," Danny says. "But I have to say, I think it would be a lot of fun. I'd love to play our songs in front of people again. Maybe write some new ones as well."

"What about Phil?" I ask.

"Phil has more money than all of us combined, so he's not worried. He could join us on the tour if he wanted. But I don't think he wants to go on the road. I think he just wants to get the band back together to jam and have fun and maybe record a few new songs."

"If he came on the road with us, it'd be back to the Dropouts, minus Cam."

"But you're interested in an acoustic tour, the two of us."

It's tempting. Though playing the music of the Dropouts could be seen as taking a step backward, I might look at it as an opportunity to have fun playing music with the guy who's always been my best friend, even during the years when we didn't talk. I want to tell Danny I'll think about it. But before I can, Ellie's voice calls to me over the dense rumble of teenage noise.

"Grampy! Mom's lighting the candles! Time to sing Happy Birthday!"

Danny gestures for me to lead the way. We go down the stairs and through the crowd until I'm standing in front of the cake beside my family. Then, with three dozen teenagers and adults wildly singing along, I play "Happy Birthday" to the most beautiful fourteen-year-old girl in the world.

18

2005

It was early in the morning when I got the call that Megan was in labor. I wasn't used to seeing this hour of the day and it took me a minute to remember I was in Philadelphia, playing guitar for Alice Cooper on his latest tour. It was the biggest gig I'd had in years and I hated to screw it up, but my daughter was in labor. I left a message with the tour manager, then rented a car and drove straight through to Maine.

I arrived at the hospital in the middle of the afternoon, but Megan hadn't yet given birth. I tried to stay away from hospitals unless there was something good happening, like a baby being born. Going into the delivery room was never an option for me – I felt lightheaded and queasy just watching old episodes of ER. Similar to when Megan was born, I spent the time waiting for Ellie's arrival sitting nervously on a bench outside the hospital. This time I had no bandmates to keep me company, to joke around and keep my mind occupied. In their stead I had a pint of Jack Daniels in the inside pocket of my jacket. I sipped from it intermittently while gazing up at the clear autumn sky like a hobo watching the countryside pass by from the open doorway of a train car.

The father-to-be wasn't in the delivery room either. Sidney waited outside near the front of the hospital with a few of his buddies, smoking cigars and ogling every woman who walked past. I watched him hug a nurse as she left the hospital and then walk her to her car. They obviously knew each other. The lingering kiss they shared in the parking lot was proof of that. His friends greeted him with fist bumps and high-fives when he returned. I thought of my poor daughter going through the agony of childbirth while her husband's friends congratulated him for kissing another woman. Then I took another sip of Jack Daniels.

When Rachel waved to me from the hospital entrance I hurried inside. She'd been in the delivery room and excitedly told me that everything had gone perfectly and Megan and the baby were resting comfortably. She looped her arm through mine as we walked to the maternity wing, and I asked where Harry Ass was.

"We split up," she said, her smile faltering for a moment. "In March. Our divorce was finalized last month."

I nodded and struggled not to do cartwheels down the shiny white hallway.

"We just weren't right together. I believe I was just lonely when I met Harry. My mother had passed away, my father's health was failing, and Megan was getting older and pulling away from me, as it's natural for teenagers to do. When my father went to the nursing home I moved into his house and that triggered a lot of memories, which brought their own problems. Harry could be a nice guy, but I think he was just an anchor to keep me steady for a while."

We stopped before a set of locked double doors. Rachel pressed a button beside the doors, then there was a loud buzz and a click as they were unlocked. We entered the maternity wing and the doors closed and automatically locked behind us.

"I was really sorry to hear about your father passing away," I said. "He was a good family man."

"Thank you. I appreciated your kind email."

As we passed a doorway, I looked inside and saw a mother, bathed in warm sunlight shining through the windows, breastfeeding her newborn. The image struck me as perfect for an album cover.

"You know, my father didn't hate you," Rachel said. "I believe he was hoping you could be like a son to him. I think he was proud of you when the Dropouts hit it big. He just wanted you to be a family man, to take care of his girls."

"I know. Looking back, I don't blame him for anything he ever said to me. He was right. I was never there for you and Megan. It's hard for me to believe I'm saying this, but I wish I would have been more like your father." I paused for a moment. "Or my father."

Rachel squeezed my arm. "You're here with us now. That's what matters."

Standing up on her toes, she kissed me on the cheek, then led me by the hand into Megan's room.

The first time I saw Ellie she was tightly swaddled in a blanket that seemed no bigger than a hand towel. She was small and pink and wrinkly and the most beautiful thing I'd ever laid eyes on. Megan held her close, staring into her face with an expression conveying absolute joy and love. Standing next to the bed, Sidney alternated between staring at his daughter and staring at the attractive young nurse who periodically entered the room.

Rachel waited impatiently for roughly thirty seconds before gently taking the baby from Megan. She gazed at the baby's face with an expression similar to Megan's. I stood with my arm around Rachel, staring down at the tiny sleeping baby. It struck me then that I was a grandfather, that we were grandparents. I smiled at Megan and she smiled back. She looked so tired yet so happy. It seemed like almost no time had passed since she was the little baby that had filled my heart with love.

This time it would be different. I missed most of Megan's life because I was on the road. I said I was doing it for the money but that was bullshit. I sent money to Rachel here and there, but after leaving the Dropouts

I barely made enough money to support myself. Rachel never cashed my checks because her father had enough money to support several generations of descendants.

Gazing into that little scrunched-up face, I vowed to always be there for Ellie, to be a better grandfather than I was a father. It shouldn't be too difficult. If I were to total the days that I was in the same room with Megan after I left Rachel, they would add up to six months, tops. Probably much less. And this was over a period of eighteen years. I wasn't out fighting a war, serving my country and protecting innocent lives. I drank beer and did drugs and screwed around with younger women and played guitar. That's the life I put over my family.

As far as I was concerned, that was over. In this hospital room were the three people I loved most in the world (except Sid). In this room was my family (except Sid). I kissed Rachel on the cheek, and she handed the baby to me. Ellie was warm and light and fragile. I'd never felt so protective in my life. After a minute I handed her back to the waiting arms of her momma.

"Have you held her yet, Sid?" Rachel asked.

"Nah," he said, winking at the nurse who'd come to check on baby and momma. "That's the wife's job. Get back to me when the kid's out of diapers."

Rachel and I glanced at each other. The nurse appeared repulsed. Megan smiled but seemed on the verge of tears. I considered throwing Sid out the window, but they would have just brought him to the emergency room and patched him back up.

"I love her name," the nurse said softly to Megan. "Ellie is so pretty."

"Takes after her dad," Sid chuckled.

The nurse shook her head in disgust and whispered that she'd be back soon to assist in feeding Ellie. I abhorred violence, especially when I was involved, but I loathed Sid even more. I took a step toward him, not sure of exactly what I planned to do, but Rachel grabbed my arm and held tight. I was kind of glad she did. Sid had about fifty pounds on me, most of it muscle.

"Sid, Megan's looking very tired," Rachel said. "Maybe you could join your friends for a cigar so she can rest for a little while."

He looked like a kid being told that he could go play outside after being grounded for a week. Kissing Megan quickly on the forehead, he hurried out of the room without a look back. Megan visibly relaxed, and the air in the room seemed lighter. I wondered if they were having marital problems – being married to Sid, it seemed highly probable – but wisely decided to keep the focus on the bundle of joy sleeping in Megan's arms.

Megan started to nod off, and when the nurse took Ellie to get her shots and physical Rachel decided we'd leave and let the new mother get some sleep. We walked through the maternity ward, my arm around her shoulder and hers around my waist, past Sid and his friends celebrating loudly with champagne and cigars while a stern-looking nurse threatened to have them removed if they didn't quiet down.

We left the wing and walked down the shiny hallways, looking for the cafeteria, clutching each other and smiling without saying a word. When we found it, Rachel grabbed a table while I got us coffee. It was dinnertime and the place was quite crowded. Rachel had gotten us one of the last empty tables and we sat among the aggrieved and the relieved, the healers and the healing. There weren't many smiles or laughs in the large room, and those who did show happiness moderated it out of respect for the families of the sick. The atmosphere reminded me of a wake, not the best place to be when you're practically bursting with joy.

"Are you sure you aren't hungry?" Rachel asked, watching me sip my coffee.

I shook my head. "I'm too excited to eat."

"Me too."

She smiled, and for the first time I noticed tiny lines around her eyes. I'd heard my mother refer to them as crow's feet but on Rachel they looked more like laugh lines and only served to enhance her already extraordinary beauty.

"Can you believe it?" I said. "We're grandparents. I don't know about you, but I certainly don't feel old enough to be a grandparent."

"You don't look old enough, either." She reached across the table and placed her soft hand on mine. "You still look like a rock star."

"And you still look like the beautiful girl I fell in love with. Only prettier, if that's possible." I grinned. "Grandma."

She laughed loudly, then looked around with embarrassment. "Sorry," she said, to nobody in particular.

"Besides the day Megan was born, this is the happiest day of my life."

She nodded. "Same here."

"I'll be honest. I'm glad you split up with Harry Ass and it's just the two of us here, sharing this together."

She smirked, until she saw I was serious. She squeezed my hand.

"I'm glad too."

We sat for a long time in the cafeteria, talking about the future of our granddaughter and touching on only the good parts of our past. By the time we got up to leave, darkness had fallen outside the windows and surly-looking kitchen workers were busy wiping down the tables and mopping the floor.

We arrived back in Megan's room hand-in-hand. Sid was nowhere to be found. Megan was nursing the baby, or trying to, which caused me a great deal of embarrassment. I tried to leave the room but both women insisted I stay. I wound up staring out the window into the darkness, trying to avoid the room's reflection, while Megan and Rachel tried to include me in the conversation. Finally, Rachel had had enough.

"For goodness sake, Jesse. She's feeding the baby. It's the most natural act in the world."

"Uh huh.

"They're just breasts, Dad. What's the big deal?"

"The big deal is that they aren't just breasts. They're *your* breasts, my daughter's breasts. And one of the primary rules of fatherhood is that a man should never see his daughter's breasts."

"I'm feeding the baby, Dad," Megan laughed. "There's nothing sexual about it."

"I can't hear you," I said, covering my ears.

Rachel came up behind me and pulled my hands away from my ears.

"This really bothers you that much?"

"Yes. It's not natural."

"Jesse, there's nothing more natural than a mother feeding her baby." She paused. "How many breasts have you seen in your life?"

"Hundreds. Thousands," I blurted out, before hurriedly adding, "But none as perfect as yours."

Megan laughed and mumbled, "Oh my god" while Rachel patted me on the back, thanked me for the kind words about her perfect breasts, and pushed me to the door.

"Go have a seat," she said. "I'll come get you when the horror of your granddaughter being fed mother's milk is over."

I was in the waiting area, halfway through an article about the top ten places to get lobster in Maine, when Rachel came to get me. We said a quick goodbye to Megan and the baby and then left them alone to sleep, promising to return in the morning.

"We don't want to arrive too early tomorrow," Rachel explained as we passed through the locked doors to the wing. "Maybe mid-morning. Give mother and baby some alone time."

We walked down the bright hallways and out into the dark autumn evening. The air was crisp, the sky clear and loaded with stars. I stopped for a moment to look up and thank whoever was up there for the beautiful family that I didn't deserve. Then I took Rachel's hand and we walked to the parking lot.

Rachel insisted I stay at the house with her, saying the place was too big and lonely and she'd welcome the company. I wondered how lonely she was and if that loneliness, combined with the memory of our long-ago union which served as the starting point to the birth of our beautiful baby granddaughter, might result in us spending the night in her bed going at it like drunken teenagers. Then she pointed to the upstairs guest room, kissed me on the cheek, and disappeared into her bedroom, closing the door behind her. So much for nostalgia.

I woke to the smell of blueberry pancakes, which I believe is the among the best ways to start any day. At around ten we left Lazy Daze to return to the hospital and stayed until late afternoon, when the room became overrun with friends of Megan who wanted to see the baby. Still no sign of Sid.

We returned later that evening to say goodnight to Megan and Ellie. I brought along an acoustic guitar and softly played "Goodnight" by the Beatles before we left. As I sang the last words, I suddenly remembered that I was supposed to be playing guitar onstage with Alice Cooper somewhere. New York, probably. I hadn't even given it a thought until that moment.

Rachel spent the next morning cleaning Megan's already spotless house for the baby's arrival. They were being discharged from the hospital around noon, so Rachel got an early start. I rolled out of bed around ten – no pancakes today, to my disappointment – and after showering I called Alice's tour manager. There was a show that evening at Mohegan Sun Casino in Connecticut and he informed me in no uncertain terms that if I wasn't there for sound check at five, I was off the tour.

I walked the rutted quarter-mile car path from Lazy Daze to Megan's house. It was a beautiful fall day, with a clear blue sky and colorful leaves fluttering lightly to the ground all around me. The air was crisp and sweet, with the gentle background music of water brushing softly against the nearby shoreline. It was the perfect day for Ellie to have her first look at the outside world.

Rachel dusted and vacuumed an already spotless house while I sat on the couch and watched. Megan's house was very comfortable, an open-concept ranch with pine paneling and wooden ceiling beams. I finally convinced Rachel to take a break and told her about the tour with Alice Cooper. She wasn't a fan but was very excited for me and asked why I hadn't mentioned it until now. I thought that was obvious. The attention should be on the happiness surrounding the birth of our first grandchild, not on my job.

After hearing the ultimatum I'd received from the tour manager, Rachel insisted I return to the tour immediately. I didn't want to leave. We felt like a family and I'd missed so much of that over the years. I didn't want to miss a moment because I'd missed almost all of Megan's. But Rachel was right – this tour was the biggest thing I'd done in decades and might lead to something more.

Megan and Ellie arrived home just before 12:30, with Sid driving. At least he'd finally showed up. I hung around as Megan showed the baby her new home and Sid made himself a protein shake. I stared at Ellie and tried to memorize her face, knowing she would change a lot in the days and months ahead.

Half an hour later, I had to leave. Sid had already left to go to the gym, and I can't say I was too broken up about it. I kissed Megan, then Ellie. Staring into my granddaughter's angelic face for a long moment, I decided I was moving back to Apple Brook to be with my family as soon as the tour was over.

Rachel walked me to my rental car. We hugged, and I held onto her for a long time. I told her I'd be back in less than two months, as soon as the tour finished. There were tears in her eyes as I pulled away, and in mine too. I wasn't yet out of the driveway and I already missed them.

I didn't see them again for two years.

19

While the kids stuff themselves with cake and ice cream, Danny and I set up in a corner of the living room. There really isn't much to set up, just a couple of stools, microphones, and amps. Danny brought all the equipment and we have it set up in a few minutes. I lean against one stool while he sits on the other and starts texting.

"Andrew really isn't feeling well," he says a couple of minutes later, stuffing his phone into the front pocket of his jeans. "He's got a hundred-and-two-degree temperature. I may have to bring him to the hospital."

"You can go if you need to," I say. "It's no problem. I can handle this on my own. It's just a couple of songs."

"I'll stay. It'll be fun. Andrew will text if he needs me."

"I'm wondering, are guys the same as women in relationships? I mean, do they say one thing and mean another?"

Danny laughs. "Sometimes, yeah." He shifts on the stool. "Have you given any thought to Derek's offer? You know, doing a tour with the Dropouts, or just the two of us if Cam refuses to get involved."

"Have I thought about it? You mean, in the fifteen minutes that have passed since you originally told me about the offer?"

"Okay, okay. Maybe I'm getting a little ahead of myself. I'm just excited. We had so much fun jamming together yesterday, I think a tour would be a blast."

"I'll consider it, I promise." A few kids begin trickling into the living room. "Let's think of this as the first night of our tour."

"It is a full house," Danny says.

A couple of fortyish moms approach to tell us how much they loved our music growing up. The one with auburn hair smiles brightly and tells Danny that in junior high she cut his picture out of a magazine and taped it on her bedroom wall, next to her George Michael poster. I smile and almost blurt out that a photo of Freddie Mercury would have completed the gay trifecta, but I bite my tongue.

The taller mom seems a little shyer than her friend and speaks with a heavy Maine accent. It'd be a safe bet that she was born and raised here and lives within ten miles of her childhood home. Looking at me nervously, she says, "I had a wicked big crush on you in high school. When I was a freshman, I lost my virginity and pretended the guy was you."

"Glad I could help," I say.

Kids are making their way into the living room, some still eating cake from paper plates. I wonder if any of the boys at this party will someday take a girl's virginity while she fantasizes about someone else. If so, I wonder if they'll care. One thing is probably certain – it won't be me the girl's fantasizing about. That fantasy is reserved for middle-aged soccer moms.

Ellie appears with a couple of her friends. Swinging her arm around my shoulder, she says, "Hi, Mrs. Conrad. Do you know my grandfather?"

"I was just tellin' him what a big fan I was in high school." Mrs. Conrad gives me a look that I don't think

Mr. Conrad would approve of. "I'll leave you alone to get ready. Maybe we can continue this conversation later."

Mrs. Conrad and Auburn Mom walk away slowly, overly swaying their ample hips back and forth for our viewing pleasure.

Ellie giggles. "Was Mrs. Conrad hitting on you?"

"Maybe a little. I'm sure she didn't mean anything by it."

"Oh my god!" Ellie and her friends burst into a fit of rapid-fire giggles.

"Your grampy's still smooth with the ladies," I say.

The giggles rise an octave, nearing a pitch only audible to dogs.

"Go tell your friends to get in here," Danny says. "Every minute counts when you get to be our age."

We chuckle as the girls bounce away to the kitchen. A few kids are glancing in our direction, probably wondering what happened to the hip hop dance music. Across the room, Mrs. Conrad and Auburn Mom are staring at us with the force of a lusty tractor beam. Just another night in the lives of a couple of former rock stars.

We decide to play three songs: "Brand New Rock Star", a Dropouts song that almost reached the Top 20 in the 80's and has shown up recently in a couple of TV shows; "Thoughts of You", the song I recently wrote and played for Rachel; and, of course, "Your Love Line" as the grand finale.

Just as I hit the opening chord to "Brand New Rock Star", I notice someone impatiently trying to force their way through the crowd of people around us. I stop playing and Phil appears with a snare drum in one hand and a cymbal in the other. Hanging from his back pocket is a pair of brushes. Rachel is behind him, carrying his drum stool.

"Hey, you guys in need of a good drummer?"

Danny smiles. "Yeah, man. You know one?"

It only takes Phil a couple of minutes to get set up. While he's lining up his cymbal Danny asks if he's talked to Cam. Phil says yes. I tell Phil the three songs we're playing. He hasn't heard "Thoughts of You" but I tell him to jump in any time he wants. Danny asks if Cam's coming. Phil shakes his head.

When Phil is seated and ready, Danny leans into his mike and says, "You folks are in for a treat tonight. As a surprise guest we have Phil Cabana on drums, meaning you've got three quarters of the Dropouts playing for you tonight." After some clapping and whistles, he says, "We've been on hiatus for about three decades, so excuse us if we sound a little rusty."

"Brand New Rock Star" goes off perfectly. Some of the kids sing along with a look of surprise. They've obviously heard it on TV but didn't realize we were the guys who played it. We sound like an acoustic version of the band thirty years ago. Danny's voice is in fine form, and Phil is as steady as he ever was. The light from at least a dozen cell phones is a little blinding, and I know this set is going out live on Facebook and Twitter and YouTube and Instagram and every other social media site where kids and their phones congregate. Because of the internet I've had more attention in the past two days than I have in my entire life. I don't mind people seeing us tonight, though. Maybe it'll distract them from the video where Officer Dum Dum Dunham assists me in headbutting an automobile.

My new song, "Thoughts of you," is slower. Danny reads the lyrics from a sheet of paper I printed out earlier, and Phil plays a soft steady beat behind us. About halfway through the song he looks down at his pants. The pocket with his phone inside is glowing. Either a text or a phone call. I nod toward it, but he shakes his head and continues singing.

When the song is over there's a healthy round of applause, though noticeably less than what we received after "Brand New Rock Star". Both Ellie and Rachel are wiping away tears, and Megan wears a sad smile and gives me a thumbs-up. I watch as Sid, standing nearby, attempts to put a comforting arm around her shoulders and is rewarded with an elbow to the solar plexus. As Sid doubles over and gasps for air, I nod and return the thumbs-up.

Danny leans over and quietly says, "Andrew just texted me. His temperature is up to a hundred and three, and the dragon he's talking to in the corner of our bedroom is getting hungry." He smiles but looks worried. "I need to leave and get him to the emergency room."

"Yeah, of course," I say, leaning over to avoid being picked up by the mike. "We'll call in a little while to see how he's doing."

"Thanks." He stands and squeezes my shoulder, then nods toward the crowd. "Maybe you shouldn't play "Your Love Line". These nice kids don't deserve to be tortured by your singing."

"Some people would love to have my voice."

"Name one."

"Yoko Ono."

"Have at it, Yoko," Danny says. "Might want to hand out earplugs first."

"Don't worry, buddy. I have a plan. Now go get Andrew to the hospital."

He slaps my shoulder, shakes a bewildered Phil's hand, and disappears through the living room. The crowd looks confused and I see Rachel hurry across the room to catch up to Danny. Phil leans over his drum to ask me what's going on.

"Are we done?"

"Nope," I answer. "Danny has an emergency with Andrew, but you and I still have one more song to do."

"Oh boy, don't tell me you're going to sing." He looks at me closely. "What happened to your face? It looks worse than yesterday. Did Cam hit you again?"

"No, it wasn't Cam. I ran into another acquaintance from high school."

"Still Mr. Popular."

"Yeah. I'll tell you about it later, after we play "Your Love Line"."

"Who's singing?" Phil asks. "Want me to give it a try?"

I shake my head. "I have a better idea."

Ellie is standing by the fireplace, drinking a Pepsi and talking with a couple of friends during our unplanned break. I wave her over and explain that Danny had to leave and now we don't have anyone to sing "Your Love Line".

"It's your party. I was wondering if you might want to sing it."

"No way." She shakes her head vigorously. "I can't sing."

"Must run in the family," Phil mumbles, just loud enough for me to hear.

"Well – I can't believe I'm saying this – but do you think your friend Tyler would want to sing with us?"

Ellie's face brightens.

"Are you serious? He'd love that!"

She turns to go find him, but I grab her hand. "Wait. Can he actually sing or is he full of shit?"

"Oh, no, Grampy, he's a great rapper. The best in our school!"

She runs off to get Tyler. Watching her, Phil says, "A great rapper?"

"I know. Kind of like saying he's mastered the kazoo."

"I'd rather hear the kazoo," Phil says.

Ellie returns with Tyler. A smile is spread across his handsome young face.

"Yo, Gramps. Ellie says you need a singer. I'm your man, bruh! 'I'm the greatest of all time, singin' Your Love Line!'"

Phil's eyebrows shoot up.

"Do you know the words to the song?" I ask. "The actual words, I mean. Not some shit you make up."

"I do, Gramps! I know them all. 'You're lookin' fine and if you've got the time I'd like to be a part of your love line!'" The kid looks proud of himself. "Sweet, right?"

"Can you do it without breaking into some idiotic rap? Because, if you do, I'll have to hit you with my guitar and I'm pretty sure Phil will crash his cymbal onto your head."

Tyler appears to notice Phil for the first time.

"Yo, bro, you're Phil from the Dropouts! Your playing is lit, dude!"

Phil tilts his head and gives the kid a curious stare.

"Okay, you're in."

Ellie claps her hands. "I have to go tell everyone."

"Savage, dude! Singing with the Dropouts in front of my squad. This is straight fire!"

"Yeah." I gesture to Danny's stool. "Have a seat."

"You mind if I stand?" He begins bouncing on his toes and rolling his shoulders. "I'm more comfortable if I stand."

I shrug. "Do whatever you want."

Phil leans in and speaks his first words to Tyler: "Don't fuck this up, kid." Then he goes back to his stool, grabs his brushes, and prepares for whatever is about to happen.

20

There's a lot of excited murmuring from the roomful of teenagers when they see Tyler talking to us, building to loud whoops and shouts when Tyler grabs the microphone. Every cellphone in the place seems to be pointed in our direction.

"We've got a little surprise for you all tonight," I say into my mike. "Danny Crane had an emergency and won't be able to sing our final song. Taking his place, for one night only, is, uh, Tyler." I realize I don't know Tyler's last name.

"Yo, yo, yo, what up, peeps?" Tyler calls into his mike, walking back and forth and waving his free arm in front of him in some ridiculous rapper way. He looks at me with a big smile on his face, which disappears quickly when he sees me glaring at him. "You're gonna love this one!"

Both kids and adults start whooping it up as I hit the first chords to "Your Love Line". Tyler has a surprisingly good voice, and I'm impressed with how restrained he is while singing. He's a natural performer and plays to the crowd without too many rap mannerisms. He's not Danny, but Danny wasn't Danny at fifteen years old. I'm having a good time watching the kid and the small crowd's reaction to him. About halfway through the song I glance back at Phil, and the smile on his face tells me that he's feeling the same way.

When the song is finished the crowd cheers and shouts for what seems like a long time, and then they begin steadily chanting Tyler's name. He doesn't drop the mike to the floor and walk away like I was afraid he would. Instead, he thoroughly enjoys his fifteen minutes of fame, bowing and slapping hands, all the while wearing that handsome smile. Phil and I stand on either side of Tyler to take a bow together, and the kids go nuts.

The next few minutes are a blur as everyone approaches to tell us how great we were. I've always enjoyed meeting with fans, although things have changed a lot from the old days. Back then nobody called me "sir" or "Mr. Maze" or "Gramps". Instead being asked for autographs, I'm now asked to smile for selfies. After more than thirty years on the road I'm used to the changes, even though it's been awhile since I've played anywhere live.

Phil is smiling but seems a little less comfortable with the selfies and hangs back as much as possible. Tyler's taking to the sudden attention like a sponge soaking up water. Ten minutes later most of the teenagers have followed him into the kitchen, leaving Phil and I alone talk for a few minutes. I ask if he's heard from Derek.

"Got a text and a voicemail this morning," he says. "I'm guessing we all got them, except Cam. I don't think Cam has a cellphone."

"What do you think about a tour?" I ask. "I mean, this was fun, and jamming together yesterday was cool."

"It was great. But I don't think Cam will do it, and I'm not doing a tour without him. Plus, I couldn't leave Lynne by herself for weeks at a time, and taking her on the road with us for that long would just be too difficult."

"I understand completely. The wife comes first."

He's sitting on Danny's stool and I'm on mine. In the dim light of the living room he doesn't look that different from how he looked in high school. Better dressed, hair a little thinner and a lot shorter. But still the same Phil.

"Now, if you were to ask me to record a few songs together, I'd be all in because I'm pretty sure we could convince Cam to do it. We could record it in the studio at my house."

I tell him about the offer Derek made to Danny, about Danny and I touring together, doing an acoustic set if it turns out that the other guys reject the offer. His expression doesn't change.

"The thing is," I say, "I love playing live, and I can't remember the last time I had as much playing as I have the past couple of days with you guys."

"So are you and Danny going to do the tour by yourselves?"

"I don't really know what Danny's feeling. But if he wants to, yeah, I'm in." I shrug. "The thing is, with the way our music's coming back, none of us really needs the money. But, like I said, this is the most fun I've had in years. At our age, if the opportunity to have fun comes along we should take advantage of it, right?"

"Hell, yeah." Phil gazes off for a moment, then says, "What about recording an album, or even a couple of songs? Are you interested? I'd like to record that new song we played tonight."

"If Cam and Danny are involved, definitely. But it'll have to wait until after the tour, if Danny and I do it. Sounds like it will last two to three months."

"Perfect. That should give me just enough time to convince Cam to do it."

"Just so you know, a new album wasn't part of Derek's offer. Sounds like he thinks people aren't interested in hearing anything new from the Dropouts.

Nostalgia's what sells, and I can't disagree with him. The Who and KISS tour with only two original members and charge hundreds, even thousands, of dollars per ticket, and the fans buy it. But they don't release new albums. As for us, I don't know if we'd even get a label to release a new album."

"Fuck Derek, and fuck the labels," Phil says, leaning forward. "We'll release music independently. Form our own label, maybe. Do most of it on the internet. We may sell a few less copies but we'll end up making more because we get all the money instead of having the label take most of it. We might not need the money, but a little extra can't hurt. The Dropouts have name recognition so it's not like we're starting from nothing. That's how Prince did it."

Phil has obviously given this a lot of thought. It sounds good, and I tell him so. The idea of playing together sounds great. Earning a few bucks would be cool, too. We're all doing pretty well, but Phil's right - a little extra never hurts. I could put the money from the tour and an album towards Ellie's college tuition. Probably pay for everything in what I'll make from the tour. Cam will give his money to the church, which, unless they are building a ladder to heaven, is a waste, in my opinion. But I'll keep that to myself.

Just as I'm asking him to email me some of the songs he's written, we're approached by Mrs. Conrad and Auburn Mom. I'm beginning to wonder if they even have kids at this party, or if they just showed up because they heard the Dropouts were playing here tonight.

Auburn Mom introduces herself to Phil while Mrs. Conrad gazes at me, as sleek and focused as an English Pointer watching a pheasant. It's a little uncomfortable, leading me to wonder if she's reliving my imaginary role in the loss of her virginity.

"I just wanted to tell you that it was wicked good meetin' you," Mrs. Conrad finally says, still fixing me with that hungry gaze. Nearby, Auburn Mom has somehow worked the fact that she wears lace thong underwear into the first minute of her conversation with Phil. Subtlety is obviously not the strong suit of either of these ladies.

"It was nice meeting you as well," I say. Uncomfortable with the silent, lusty gaze that follows, I continue, "Would you, ah, like an autograph or something?"

"How about a hug and a kiss on the cheek?" she asks.

I look around the room and the kitchen entrance for signs of Rachel, Megan, or Ellie. I'm not sure why, but I feel the guilt of a kid about to take a peek at the Playboy magazines he found hidden in his father's closet.

As soon as I stand up from my stool, Mrs. Conrad wraps herself around me and hangs on like we're Kate and Leo on the Titanic. She smells nice, and admittedly, it's not a bad feeling. Her crotch is pressed so tightly against mine that I can feel the heat radiating through our clothes. From the corner of my eye I watch Auburn Mom slapping her ass with one of Phil's brushes while he looks on, wide-eyed, nodding his head. While the exact wording of their conversation is unknown, the context is pretty clear.

Important parts of this interaction were not fully spelled out beforehand, and I'm not sure if Mrs. Conrad wants to kiss me or wants a kiss *from* me. Taking a gamble, I turn my head to give her a peck on the cheek. My lips never arrive at their scheduled destination, though, because with the swiftness of a snake she turns her head and presses her lips to mine. Like an invading force her tongue thrusts its way into my mouth, and though ninety percent of my being is thoroughly enjoying the sensation and wants it to continue, the ten percent that I usually ignore is insisting that I put a stop to all this depraved pleasure immediately. With a groan of resignation that Mrs. Conrad and her swirling tongue and grinding hips mistake for pleasure, I pull my head back and push her away. It's not easy – she's quite determined, while only ten percent of me is in support of my actions.

"Wow!" she says. "That was amazin'! I'm gonna imagine the rest while I'm with my husband tonight."

"Mr. Conrad's a lucky man," I say, wiping her sticky red gloss off my lips. Still a bit unstable on my feet, I sit back on my stool. "I'm sure the three of us will have a wonderful time together."

She grabs Auburn Mom – who is whispering something into a visibly stunned Phil's ear – by the arm and leads her away. I peel my eyes from their swaying backsides and glance toward the kitchen, where Rachel is watching me with an expression I can't read. How much of what just happened she witnessed, I'm not sure. I smile and nod to her. She smirks and turns away. This doesn't tell me anything, except that she probably saw enough to be pissed off at me. Or, worse yet, disappointed. I want to go to her, tell her it wasn't my fault, because it really wasn't. But it'll have to wait, because I'd rather not stand up at this particular moment.

"Who the hell were those women?" Phil asks hoarsely. His cheeks are bright red and there are small beads of sweat on his upper lip that weren't there before.

"Fans. Very loyal fans."

"Gotta love the fans." Phil says, staring dazed at the brush in his hand. "Do you know what she offered to do with my brushes?"

"I can guess."

"My god. I can't go on the road with you guys. No way. With fans like that I'll be in divorce court within fifteen minutes."

"We loved fans like that in the old days."

"I could handle it back then. I was young and single. Now I'm old and married, proudly faithful for over thirty years. But right now, my pecker and the faithful part of my brain are at war, and my faithful brain is getting the shit kicked out of it." He sighs. "I need to get home. I'm too old to face temptation."

We move the stools and microphones so the DJ can resume pumping out the beats. I set my guitar aside and help Phil carry his stuff out to his SUV. It's parked on the side of the road at the end of the driveway, a quarter mile of cold drizzle and frigid winds with no jacket on. We do the man hug and promise to talk tomorrow about the tour and the album. By the time he drives away I've already jogged halfway back up the driveway. I enter the house feeling as wet and cold as a licked popsicle and I'm craving a warm glass of whiskey. Instead I go upstairs to dry off and change my clothes.

The crowd is thinning by the time I head downstairs and return to the party. It's around ten o'clock, which, according the invitations, is the time the party is supposed to wind down and parents should arrive to pick up their kids. Through the windows shines the glare of many headlights packed together in a traffic jam, and those who were considerate enough to arrive first and pull to the head of the driveway will unfortunately be the last to leave.

Glancing around the crowd, it appears that Mrs. Conrad and Auburn Mom have already left. It's a relief because I'm not used to rejecting an attractive woman so many times in one night, and a mix of common courtesy and hormones (heavy on the hormones) will make it more difficult with each blatantly sexual overture she hurls my way. I gaze around the room, looking for something to distract me from my dangerous thoughts.

Sid is standing at the coat rack, and just the sight of him is enough to drive away any carnal urge. He's making a big deal of putting on his jacket, acting like he's too big to fit into it. And he is, but it has nothing to do with the size of his muscles – the jacket appears to be a size extra small and wouldn't fit Ellie. One thing you can always count on with Sid – he puts on a good show.

Megan and Rachel stand by the door saying goodbye as the guests leave, thanking them for attending the party. I watch Sid approach Megan to ask for help getting into his jacket. She rolls her eyes but otherwise ignores him. I smile. Eventually a couple of teenage girls help him squeeze into the jacket. Then he puffs out his chest until the seams of the jacket are visibly straining and struts around like a curly-haired peacock, causing the girls to giggle. Sid looks pleased, because in his mind it's the shy, admiring giggle of pretty young women. In the real world, the girls are laughing at the old fool and his outdated attempt to flirt with them.

I approach, wearing my biggest smile, and say, "Hey Sid, you look really uncomfortable. Next time, you may want to try shopping for jackets in the adult section."

It's funny, and the girls burst into hysterics. It's also the sort of thing that tends to get me punched in the face. Sid certainly looks like he wants to, but instead he stomps off.

The girls tell me how much they like the Dropouts – "You guys are, like, my favorite old band" – and then we take the obligatory selfie. One of them tells me that her grandmother saw us in concert when she was their age, and I want to ask how Gram's body has held up over the years. I realize they are just being nice, though, so I say I enjoyed meeting them and sign an autograph for sexy old Gram.

I see Sid talking to Ellie. Tyler stands next to Ellie, wearing a hooded sweatshirt that I assume passes for his jacket. Sid hugs Ellie and shakes Tyler's hand before heading for the door. I don't like Sid much but I'm happy to see him at his daughter's birthday party. At least he's trying to be involved in her life. He might not do it often enough, but I'm not one to talk.

At the door he hugs Rachel, who looks as though she'd rather snuggle with a skunk. Then he reaches for Megan and she shakes her head, giving him a look that screams, "Danger Ahead". Taking a step back, Sid mumbles something and then walks out the door.

"Hey, Gramps, that was savage, bro!"

I know who it is without turning my head. "I have no idea what you're saying, Tyler. Speak English, please."

"That song we did, it was sweet, dude!"

"Thanks. I wrote it with you in mind."

"Grampy," says Ellie, who's come up beside him. "Be nice."

"Sorry. Yeah, Tyler, it was great. Thanks for stepping in. You did a really nice job with it. You have a good voice. Shame to waste it rapping when you could be singing in a rock band."

"Maybe we could get together and jam sometime. You can bring that other old guy, Phil, if you want."

"When I said you could sing in a rock band, Tyler, I didn't mean mine."

"Grampy?"

"Sorry. Maybe, Tyler. We'll see. Stranger things have happened. You've got a good voice, and you definitely have charisma."

Tyler grabs my hand and pulls me into a bro hug, banging on my back until I want to tell him my lungs are clear. But, under strict instructions to be nice, I say nothing.

He's on his way to the door, holding Ellie's hand, when he turns back to me. "Yo, Gramps. There're about ten videos of you playing tonight all over social media, with me and the other old guy, Danny. Dropouts Live, they're calling it. That guy's voice is lit, dude. It's getting a ton of hits. You've got a shit ton of videos that have gone viral just this weekend, dude. You're, like, the most famous guy in the world right now!"

When they reach the door, Tyler gives Ellie a hug and a quick kiss on the lips. Megan and Rachel don't seem bothered and I'm not, either. To my surprise, I like the kid.

It's after eleven by the time everyone leaves the party. Megan and Ellie are the last to go. We all hug and promise to see each other before I head back to Miami, and then it's just me, Rachel, and a very messy house.

I help her clean the place up for a few minutes, and then she pours herself a glass of wine while I get a fire going in the fireplace. I sit down on the couch and check my phone. The most recent text is from Danny, saying they are keeping Andrew at the hospital overnight but he should be fine. I text back, tell him that's great news and I'll give him a call in the morning.

There's a text from Kendra, saying she made a mistake by leaving me for the photographer. She realized she was wrong – right around the time she found out the photographer was sleeping with someone else, I'm guessing – and she hopes she can move back into my condo and have a fresh start. Below the text is a photo of her wearing what appears to be the world's smallest white bikini.

It's only been a few days, but I'd almost completely forgotten about Kendra. She's part of a whole other world, another life. I don't want her back in my condo, though I'll admit the bikini picture is a very compelling argument in her favor. But no. I text her back, saying we'll talk when I return. Then I forward the photo to three people – Phil, Danny, and Cam. To Phil I write *The temptations of the road,* hoping that Lynne doesn't see it; to Danny, *This is what you've given up, you stupid bastard;* and to Cam, I write *I hope God was worth it.* I don't know how Cam will react to that. The old Cam would have loved it. Cam now, with all the bad blood between us, may feel differently. I hope not.

There's a text from Derek: *Just watched you guys live on Facebook. Sounded great. Where's Cam? And who's the black kid? Don't do any more shows without letting me know, we should be getting paid for this! Call you tomorrow.* I wonder if Derek spends all his free time online, stalking us. Kind of seems that way.

Rachel sits down beside me on the couch and sips her white wine. I put my arm around her, and she snuggles up against me. For a while we say nothing, content to just stare into the crackling fire and be with each other.

"Some party," I finally say.

"Yes, it was. Ellie's really happy, and that's what it's all about. I think her favorite part of the evening was seeing her grandfather being a rock star."

"Everyone seemed to have a good time," I say. "Hard to believe we have so many fans, having broken up over thirty years ago." I smile at the fire. "Feels good, though, playing with those guys again. I thought we sounded good."

"You did. Too bad Danny had to go, but Tyler did a really good job. The kids loved him."

"Mmm."

Rachel leans her head back to look at me. Shadows from the firelight dance across her lovely face and I want to kiss her, but doing so will almost certainly ruin this perfect moment.

"What do you think of him?" she asks.

"Tyler? I don't understand half of what he's saying, but he's a good kid." I knew it from the first time I drank a beer with him. "I also think he's just a temporary crush, soon to be replaced by another, and another, and another. You know how it is at that age."

"We weren't much older when we met," she says. "And we're still here."

"Together," I say, "but not *together*."

"Maybe not, but we still love each other." She lays her head back against my shoulder.

"That, we do," I say, gently rubbing her arm.

For a long time we sit like that, enjoying the warmth of the firelight and each other. When the fire starts to die down, I get up to throw on more wood while Rachel goes to the kitchen to refill her wineglass. "Sure you don't want a beer?" she asks.

"No thanks. I have everything I want right here."

The truth is, between attending my granddaughter's birthday party, playing live with three members of my former band, and sitting in front of the fire with my arm around Rachel, this is one of the best days of my life. Take away getting faceplanted into my rental car by Dum Dum Dunham and it might rank in the top five.

"Are you saying that Tyler and Ellie could stay together for the long haul?" I ask when she returns.

"I'm saying that you can never be sure what will happen." She throws a blanket over us and again fits herself against me, under my arm. "One thing I do know – the Brennan women aren't exactly known for choosing the right man. Megan's relationship with Sid and mine with Harry are proof of that."

"Don't forget about me."

"Oh, I haven't." We both laugh, and she says, "You were the right man. Maybe just at the wrong time."

I'm not sure how to reply to this, so I do what I always do when faced with a situation that has the possibility of becoming emotionally deep – I deflect. My therapist often says I'm a master deflector. I usually reply by joking that being a master deflector is better than being a masturbater, a comment which my therapist says is another example of deflecting. She isn't much into humor.

I tell Rachel about the text I received from Danny, saying that Andrew is staying overnight in the hospital but is expected to be fine. I mention the texts and voicemails from Derek, though I'm pretty vague about it. She asks about my run-in with Dum Dum Dunham earlier in the day and we spend a long time joking and laughing about old friends and good times from when we were young.

"My goodness, you were so good-looking," she says, with a giggle that tells me she's become tipsy. Women over the age of forty rarely giggle, but I love that Rachel does. "And you were very sweet too. Not much has changed," she says, looking up at me. "You're a very handsome man, and you still have that sweet and vulnerable quality that I love so much. You were definitely the right guy for me."

"And you were the right one for me. I was just too stupid to know it." I pause for a moment, then continue, "You're still the right one."

As soon as the words are out of my mouth, I regret saying them. Not because what I said was untrue; Rachel really was and is the one for me, the only woman I've ever loved past that initial period in a relationship where the line between love and lust is often blurred or ignored. But saying those words leaves me exposed, and though I know that Rachel wouldn't use them against me or to her advantage, it's an uncomfortable feeling. I'm not sure what my therapist would call it. Knowing her, she'd probably think feeling so raw and exposed is a good thing. My therapist may have sadistic tendencies.

For a long time, Rachel says nothing. Of course, I want her to say that I'm still the right one too, after which we'll tear our clothes off and go at it all night in front of the fireplace. But saying nothing at all is worse than her patting me on the knee while saying how fond she is of my sense of humor, or telling me that ship passed a long time ago. Anything would be better than silence. But still it goes on, for what seems like forever, until I can't take it anymore. Like a needy child, I ask, "Am I still the right one for you?"

She giggles, and says, "Fill this glass for me, and you could be the right one for me tonight."

I race to the kitchen and grab the bottle of wine.

21

I open my eyes, blink, and stare at the ceiling. Two things come to mind: I'm not hungover on a Sunday morning, and I'm in Rachel's bed. For a moment I wonder if last night was a dream. Maybe I'm in bed with Kendra, or someone else. Maybe this, right now, is a dream. Or, perhaps, the past thirty-something years of my life have been a dream, and Rachel and I are teenagers waking up from a night of intensely clumsy lovemaking in her parents' bed while they spend the weekend skiing at Sugarloaf.

For a long time, I lay staring at the ceiling, enjoying the ignorance and bliss. I hold up my hand. Unfortunately, it's not the hand of a teenager. There's soft, gentle snoring beside me. Not Kendra's snoring. Kendra doesn't snore. Maybe her sinuses and nasal passages are as perfectly streamlined as the rest of her. I don't know. But she doesn't snore.

I prop myself up on my elbows and take in my surroundings. It's the same bedroom Rachel and I slept in while her parents went to Sugarloaf, but it's no longer her parents' bedroom. Their bedroom was dark and looked like a place you'd expect John Wayne or Ernest Hemingway to sleep, complete with a mounted bear head on the wall. I once asked Rachel how her mother could sleep in that room every night with that hairy bear head staring down at her. When I put forth the idea that the bear was actually better looking than Mr. Brennan and probably helped with her parents' lovemaking, at least from her mother's side of things, Rachel gave me one of those pretending-to-be-angry looks and then started laughing.

The bedroom now is all Rachel, full of light and bright colors, photos of Megan and Ellie, and a set of French doors that let in the sunlight and lead to a small balcony looking over the lake. Chic but not snobby, modern but down-to-earth. Not a bear head in sight.

I finally look over at Rachel. I've been putting this off, wanting to savor it, like saving the piece of cake with the most frosting for the last bite. It's been over thirty years since we last slept together but everything fit together just as well as always. We stayed up most of the night and did it a total of three times. Not to pat myself on the shoulder, but that's an impressive number for a man of my age without the aid of drugs like Viagra. I'm ready to do it again but I don't want to wake her. I sit up and for a while I watch the early morning sun sparkle on the surface of the lake. Then I look at Rachel, hoping the force of my loving and lustful gaze will cause her to awaken and pull me on top of her, but no luck.

I quietly roll out of bed, grab my clothes, and leave the room. I go upstairs, brush my teeth, grab my guitar and go back downstairs. My phone is on the arm of the couch where I left it the previous evening – earlier this morning, actually – when Rachel took my hand and led me to her bedroom. The short walk was pure excitement. I don't remember the last time I've felt so aroused. Maybe never.

It's just after six o'clock. I've seen this time on a Sunday morning a few times before, but only because I'd been up doing drugs all night long. I've slept about two hours and should feel like shit but I'm as full of energy as I've ever felt in the morning. Hungry, I check the refrigerator. Nothing interesting. I could make eggs but I don't want to wake Rachel. Leftover cake would be nice, but there is none; the teenagers went through that like termites devouring an old house. I settle for scooping my hand into a bowl of stale potato chips and chewing slowly and quietly.

Sitting on the couch with my guitar, I begin playing, very softly, Kris Kristofferson's "Sunday Mornin' Comin' Down". I love the song and it normally is an apt description of how I feel on a Sunday morning. Not today, though; today I feel fantastic. But when the choice is between "Sunday Mornin' Comin' Down" or "Sunday Bloody Sunday", you always go with Kristofferson.

For nearly an hour I sit there, playing some of my favorite softer songs and wondering what Rachel will be thinking when she wakes up. For all I know she's lying awake in bed, awash in a rising wave of regret that will only begin to diminish when my taillights turn out of her driveway. Hopefully that's not the case and she feels the same spring in her step that I do.

I'm quietly playing and singing "Don't Go Away", by Oasis, when Rachel sits beside me on the couch. She's wearing a thick green robe with no makeup and her hair is a mess, but she looks beautiful. I stop playing but she shakes her head and smiles.

"Keep going. I like that song."

So I finish the song, lean my guitar against the end table, and ask if my playing woke her up.

"No, but the first thing I heard when I woke up was you playing "Rocky Mountain High". What a wonderful way to start the morning."

She's smiling, and I'm leaving in a few hours, so I ask for her thoughts on what happened between us last night. Her smile grows brighter.

"You mean, do I have any thoughts or critiques for you?"

"No, I mean, I just – " I start, and she starts laughing.

"I'm very happy about last night," Rachel says. "Couldn't be happier. It was wonderful. I suppose the question now is, where do we go from here?"

"Well, I'm not sure," I say, not sure how to put what I'm feeling into words. I could write a song and present it to her, but now is probably not the time. "This is what I want. You are what I want. Maybe we could try to start over where we left off years ago, as a couple."

For a long moment, she stares at me, expressionless. Shaking her head, she gets up and starts walking out of the room. It's obvious I've said the wrong thing, and I feel like slapping myself in the face. Then she turns around and opens her robe. There's nothing on underneath. Smiling at my confused expression, she says, "Come on, babe. We've got to start making up for lost time."

We have sex in the bedroom, take a shower together, and then do it again. I'm proudly performing like an 18-year-old, although I wonder if I should tell her not to expect this every time. This is thirty years' worth of built-up lust and love and guilt being released, and at this point my tank's on reserve. She seems quite satisfied, though, and I keep my worries to myself.

A car pulls into the driveway while Rachel cooks some postcoital breakfast and I stand behind her, nibbling on her neck. There's the hollow thump of a car door slamming shut. I check the clock – it's just after eight – before looking out the kitchen window. A pudgy, bald-headed man in a long coat looks up at the sky, squints in the sunlight, and walks to the front door. When the doorbell rings, I sigh.

"Who is it?" Rachel asks me, without looking up from the stove.

The pudgy man presses his face against the glass of the door, hands cupped around his eyes. When he sees me his face lights up and he waves. For a moment I only stare, until I finally recognize the pudgy man. And I'm instantly annoyed.

"It's fucking Derek," I say, releasing Rachels's hips to unlock the kitchen door.

"Here you are!" he says, pulling me into a tight embrace the instant he steps inside. I don't return the hug. I couldn't even if I wanted to, because my arms are pinned to my sides.

"Hi, Derek," I say, sounding as annoyed as I feel.

"Good morning, Derek," says Rachel, and I can hear the irritation in her voice. She uses a spatula to scrape scrambled eggs onto two plates. "If I'd known you were coming, I could have made you breakfast."

"Thank you, I've already eaten. It's so good to see you guys." He's absolutely beaming. "How long's it been? Twenty, thirty years?" Without waiting for an answer, he says, "So, has my favorite couple finally decided to give it another go?"

"What are you doing here, Derek?"

"Ha, ha. Still the same Jesse. Always ready to get down to business. No small talk for you, my friend. Yes, so, have you received my messages? I'm using the same number as the last time we chatted, a Miami area code. Have you changed numbers?"

"Same number. It's been a busy weekend, Derek. I got your messages. I just haven't had time yet to answer them."

Rachel sets the plates at the kitchen island and takes a seat. I sit down next to her, begin eating, and hope Derek will go away. He moves to the other side of the island, where he can face us.

"Geez, Jesse, your face looks like shit. I watched that video of you getting slammed into the side of a police car. I'm guessing all those cuts and bruises are the result of that."

"Some of them. Get to the point, Derek. I'm leaving in a few hours and I'd like to spend that time with friends and family. You're neither."

"Wow, Jesse, just . . . wow." He paces back and forth, running his hand through what remains of his stringy hair. "That really hurts. Like, ouch, man. Right here." He taps his chest. "I've always considered us to be friends. I was there when you guys were nothing but a cover band, when you were barely scraping by in small clubs in Buxton and Old Orchard. How do you think you became successful?"

"I always attributed it to hard work, good music, and luck," I say, pouring some ketchup on my eggs.

"Luck . . . ha! I'm your luck! It was me who visited all the clubs to beg the asshole club owners for gigs. *I* made all the phone calls, pleading with labels to give your demo a listen or come to one of your shows!"

"And all for free. That was awfully kind of you, Derek."

He waves his hand as though shooing away a pesky fly. "I was at the hospital when your beautiful daughter was born, Jesse! Because I was your friend!"

"The way I remember it, you wanted to check and make sure that I wasn't going to miss the following night's gig."

Derek stops pacing, staggers, and clutches his chest like Redd Foxx in *Sanford & Son* while staring up at the ceiling.

"Help me, Lord. One of my best friends in the world is falsely accusing me of lies and treachery, and my poor old heart can't take any more. This might be it" – he squeezes his chest harder and places his other hand on the counter to steady himself – "I think I'm a goner! Lord, please forgive him. Forgive Jesse, for he's a selfish asshole and knows not what he's done."

"Derek" – he squeezes his eyes shut and nods in acknowledgement – "you're facing the wrong way. No one up there is listening to you. If you truly are dying, the direction you're headed is south. Way, way south."

He shakes his head and groans. "Don't bother calling 9-1-1," he gasps. "I don't want to be revived. I have nothing left to live for. Oh, here it comes!"

"I'm going clean up the bedroom," Rachel says, giving me a wink. "Derek, I only ate half of my eggs and one slice of toast. You can have the rest, if you like."

Derek opens one eye slightly, enough to look at Rachel's plate. Then he coughs, stands up straight, and walks around the island to sit next to me in Rachel's chair and devour the rest of her breakfast. A miraculous recovery.

When he's finished, he looks at me and smiles. There's blueberry jelly in the corner of his mouth. I hand him a napkin, and he blows his nose in it. Same classy Derek.

"You're not really angry with me, right?" he asks, watching me load the dishwasher.

"I'm not angry, no, because I rarely think about you. But I don't like you. You're a big reason the Dropouts broke up."

"Wha . . . puh . . . puh . . ." He looks like a fat fish gasping on a dock.

"You pushed me to leave the band. Said I should go solo. You did the same to Danny. Guess you figured by splitting us up, you'd make twice as much money. Danny was too smart to be fooled by your bullshit. But not me. I was a stupid, egotistical idiot who believed your lies. What kind of manager tries to break up his own band? We were just kids!"

"Now, you can't blame me for your actions, Jesse. And I wasn't much older than you at the time, you know. Live and learn, I say."

I add soap to the dishwasher, close the door, and start it. Rachel hasn't emerged from the bedroom and I'm assuming she's waiting for Derek to go away. She was never a fan of Derek's when we were younger, and her feelings apparently haven't changed.

My phone dings with a text and I grab it from the counter before Derek can get his nosy little eyes on it. It's from Danny – *Spent most of the night at the hospital sleeping on a cot. Very sore. Going back to get Andrew in a couple of hours, he's much better. I saw the video of that kid singing with you guys. Not bad, hope I'm not being replaced.*

I smile and the phone dings with another text from Danny – *Got a text from Derek. Says he can get us on the GNR tour. Let me know what you think.*

I read it twice before looking up at Derek.

"Guns N' Roses?"

He nods excitedly. "That's why I'm here! That must be Danny?" He nods at my phone and, without waiting for an answer, says, "Their people called me late last night. Saw the videos of you guys jamming together, and then playing live last night. They also saw the one of you getting knocked out by the cop. They loved it! Called it very rock and roll. Isn't the internet wonderful? You get your face smashed in by a cop and hours later there's an offer to join the biggest tour in the world!"

"Backing up Guns n' Roses?"

"Well, not headlining over them." Derek chuckles pompously. "We aren't that big yet. But yes, they want us on the road for them for three months next summer, playing stadiums! Isn't that great!"

Several thoughts hurtle through my head. Touring with Guns n' Roses would have been great, years ago, but we can't do it without Cam. But Guns n' Roses! I'm just starting over with Rachel and I can't leave, and I want to be around for Ellie. But stadiums! The road life of sex and drugs and rock n roll offers too much temptation, and I'm too old for this shit. But Guns n' Roses!

"Tell them no. Cam will never do it. I doubt Phil will, either."

Derek looks like someone just stole a puppy right out of his arms. "We don't need Cam. Just get another bass player! Hell, I'll do it! I've played some bass in my time, you know."

"Nice try. Then you'll get paid as a manager *and* as a band member, you sneaky fucker."

Derek huffs and puffs but says nothing.

"Tell you what," I say. "Go see Cam, see what he says. If he agrees to a stadium tour, I'm in. How's that?"

"Uh . . . well, last time I saw Cam we had a bit of a disagreement, and he . . . he punched me in the face."

"He's just doing what we'd all like to do." I get up and walk to the door. "Nice seeing you, Derek. Let's do this again in another thirty years."

"But I'm your manager!" he says indignantly.

"Honestly, man, I didn't even know we still had a manager until the checks started coming in from the TV show. And I'm guessing the only reason we stuck with you is because we're too lazy to bother finding someone else."

Derek's lower lip begins to shake like a worm on a line and his eyes quickly well up with tears. I roll my eyes and wait for the inevitable heart attack, but he surprises me by standing up, clutching his head, and dragging his leg as he moves toward the door.

"Stroke this time, huh?"

"I think I need to get to a hospital," he says, ignoring my sarcasm.

"Well, you know where it is." I hold the door open for him. "Top of the hill overlooking the river, about five miles away."

"You've become a cold person, Jesse."

"Nice seeing you, Derek," I say, as he passes through the doorway.

I begin to close the door, but he sticks his foot – the one not affected by the stroke, I assume – in the door jamb. Wincing at the imaginary pain in his head, he says, "Did you get my messages about you and Danny touring together, a small acoustic thing? That's still an option for you guys."

"I did," I say, smiling. "Danny and I will talk about it and get back to you."

"Really?" His eyes brighten and he removes his hand from his head. "Thank you, Jesse, thank you! It's a great deal, you know. Very little travel, home every other week, great money." He starts down the stairs and throws his arms open wide. "I seem to be feeling better now. It's a miracle! What a great day to be alive!"

"Bye, Derek," I say, closing the door behind him.

22

My plane is scheduled to fly out of Portland at three o'clock and I plan to leave Apple Brook by noon. The Sunday morning sun is bright and warm and the temperature is in the fifties by midmorning, with enough of a breeze to helicopter many of the remaining leaves to the ground. The sweet decaying smell of the autumn air takes me back to days of youth, when we'd cruise around town on days like this, crammed inside Danny's blue Chevette, smoking pot or sipping blackberry brandy and looking for something to do.

I don't want to leave. I'm happy, really happy. Content, a word my therapist would be surprised to hear me say when describing my feelings. Everything I want right now is here. Would I feel the same way in the middle of January, when there's three feet of snow with a temperature in the single digits and frigid wind howling like a wolfpack through the bare naked trees? Probably not. But right now, it sounds a hell of a lot better than stepping off a plane and into the damp blast furnace known as Miami.

Rachel gives me a ride to the lot behind the jail, where she argues with the hungover-looking attendant about the ridiculousness of paying a fee on a car that was towed during a false arrest. He scratches the stubble on his face, adjusts his greasy ballcap, scratches his ass, leans over and spits to the side, and says, "Rules are rules, lady. I don't have nothin' to do with the arrestin'.

Alls I know is, you want your car, you gotta pay me a hunnert dollars."

It's like arguing with a stump, but Rachel appears willing to put in the effort. Not wanting to waste my remaining time in Apple Brook quarrelling with what appeared to be a direct descendent of Gomer Pyle, I pull out a hundred-dollar bill and hand it to him. A long fifteen minutes later my rental pulls up in front of the office. Rachel is already outside, talking on her phone with an angry look on her face.

There's a dent in the driver's door, just about the size of my head. For a moment I stare at it, filled with a sense of pride over the strength and power of my skull. When I glance back at Rachel, she is finishing up her conversation. She walks up beside me with her phone out, takes a few pictures of the dent, and immediately sends them to someone. With a last angry look at the attendant, who is watching from the office steps, she walks around to the passenger side and gets inside. I also shoot the attendant a dirty look. He bends over, spits between his feet, and remains expressionless.

"That was the mayor," she says, obviously still angry. "I donated money to his last campaign and hosted a fundraiser at Lazy Daze, so he's very receptive when I have something to say. I sent him the photos of the dent, which he will be passing along to the police chief. Not that they'll really need them – that video of you being assaulted has over a million views already. Officer Dum Dum's going to lose his job and be charged with assault for this. And the town's going to pay for whatever the rental company charges you for damages. I'll make sure of it."

I don't say anything. I'm quite happy right now, driving with Rachel, holding her hand. I really don't care if Dum Dum Dunham gets fired or not. I wasn't seriously injured, and I have enough money to cover the damages. Not to say I enjoyed being handcuffed and dragged across the gas station parking lot, but fortunately I was quite dazed and remember very little of it. Spending a few hours in jail was less than enjoyable, but I made it home in time for Ellie's party and that's all that matters.

Up ahead, standing clean and tall among the other buildings on Main Street, is the Prince of Peace Church, also known as The House the Dropouts Built. I stare at the high white bell tower as it grows closer, wondering about the Sunday mass schedule.

"You mind if we make a couple of stops?" I say.

Without waiting for an answer, I pull into the half-full church parking lot and drive to the back where Cam's apartment is located. Rachel waits in the SUV while I walk to Cam's door and knock. While waiting I watch well-dressed couples and families cross the parking lot and disappear around the corner where the church entrance is located. Most of the couples and families are young, and I don't see any elderly people. They must be at the Catholic and Protestant and Baptist churches.

I knock again, and it seems like a very long time – though it's likely only half a minute – before the door opens. Cam is dressed nicely in a tie and slacks, and what's left of his once-wild hair is neatly combed. He greets me politely, though he appears impatient.

"Hey, I'm leaving in a couple of hours and I wanted to say goodbye."

He smiles, making his prematurely aging face appear much younger.

"So long, Jesse. I've thought a lot about this, and I'm really glad that you showed up at my door a couple of days ago. It was nice to see you after all these years, and, well, I'm sorry that I punched you in the face. I hope we don't have to wait another thirty years before we all get back together again."

"Funny you should say that, Cam, because Derek stopped over Rachel's house this morning unannounced to inform me that Guns n' Roses wants the Dropouts to join them on a stadium tour next summer."

"Gee. I was thinking maybe we'd just get together for a reunion game of Dungeons and Dragons."

We look at each other for a moment, and then we both start laughing. It's nice to get a glimpse of the old Cam.

"So, I should tell Derek no to G n' R, but yes to D and D."

"Yes, that's exactly what you should say. And tell him he's an asshole."

"Already done." We both laugh, and then I say, "Danny and I might go on tour together next year, just the two of us doing an acoustic thing. That bother you?"

"Not at all. I'm sure you guys will sound great. I'd actually like to see it."

"I'll set aside some tickets for you."

He looks past me, to the parking lot, and waves. I turn around to see Rachel smiling and waving back from the shaded interior of the tinted SUV.

"You two back together?"

"Maybe," I say, shrugging. "I hope so."

"That's good."

We look at each other for a long moment in silence, and in that time I'm back in high school, hanging out with Cam, Danny, and Phil, planning our future as the biggest rock band in the world. In our teenage imaginations, there was no life after thirty. That was too far in the future to even contemplate.

"You ever think we'd end up here?" I say, almost without realizing I'd spoken aloud.

Cam shakes his head. "I don't know what's harder to believe – that I live in a church, or that Danny's a queer."

We look at each other for a moment and nod our heads. "That Danny's a queer," we both say, and burst out laughing.

"How would you feel about jamming sometime, just the four of us? Between games of D and D, of course."

*Dong . . . dong . . . dong.* The church bell in the tower starts ringing. Cam takes a step back, looking worried.

"Shoot, it's eleven. The service is about to start and I'm not there. I'm sorry, Jesse, I need to go." He sticks out his hand. "Thanks for stopping by."

I step past his outstretched hand and into the doorway, where I pull my old friend into a hug. He's caught off guard but then returns the hug. After slapping each other on the back, we pull apart.

"Go make God proud," I say. "I'll be back around some time with my Dungeon Master's Guide and my dice . . . and my guitar."

He smiles, nods, and closes the door. I imagine him running through his apartment to enter through the back door of the church like an altar boy who's slept in and is late for mass. With another look up at the now-silent bell tower, I walk slowly back to the SUV. Rachel is playing the music loud and even with the windows up I can hear the *thump, thump* of the bass from fifty feet away. When I open the driver's door, I'm greeted with "Your Love Line."

"It's playing on WBLM," Rachel says, bobbing her head with the beat.

I smile, wonder if this might be a sign from God, and turn the stereo down.

"How's Cam?"

"Good. He's good. And he and I are good."

Rachel takes my hand. "That's important."

I stare at the massive building. "Your Love Line" fades out on the radio, replaced by Van Halen's "Dance the Night Away."

"Think I should go to church sometime?"

"Kind of late for you now, isn't it?" she says, with a teasing smile.

"It's never too late," I say, and steer the SUV out of the parking lot.


Megan and Ellie were supposed to meet us at Lazy Daze at eleven and we're already late, but I have one more quick stop to make. While Rachel texts Megan from the passenger seat to tell her we'll be a few more minutes, I walk up the cobblestone walkway to Danny's front door and ring the bell. I look around the leaf-strewn front yard and gaze up at the blue sky for about a minute before starting back to the car.

"Hey." I turn around to find Danny standing in the doorway. "We just got home a few minutes ago. What're you doing here, man?"

"I just stopped over to say goodbye," I say, heading back up the walkway. "See how you and Andrew are doing. Face to face is usually better than texting, in my opinion."

"I fucking hate texting, but I guess you gotta do it." He pulls out his phone to show me a list of unopened recent texts. "Yeah, we're okay. I just helped Andrew into bed. He's feeling better, but he's tired. I don't know how anyone gets any sleep in a hospital. I'm going to make him some chicken soup, hopefully it'll help."

"Can't hurt," I say. "Listen, Derek stopped over this morning. He was there when you texted me. He's still an annoying asshole, by the way."

Danny nods. Then he notices Rachel in the SUV. He waves, and she waves back.

"What's going on there?" he asks quietly, as if she may overhear him from inside the car.

"I'm not sure. I think we might be getting back together. We slept together last night." I smile. "And this morning."

"I'm not surprised. She has been looking pretty desperate lately."

"Ha. Funny. So, yeah. It looks like we might be back together, after all these years."

"Good news. For you, anyway. But bad timing, don't you think, with you heading back to Miami? Long distance relationships don't work, no matter what the songs say."

"Yeah, I wanted to talk to you about that, along with a few other things. First the Guns n' Roses tour. It's not happening. No Cam, no band. And being on the road, on a tour that big . . . it's not good for any of us."

Danny nods in agreement.

"We're about thirty years late for that, I think," he says. "Life has taken over."

"Second, I'm thinking of moving back up here, to Apple Brook. Not just thinking about it, actually; I've already made up my mind. I want to be with my family."

"About friggin' time," Danny says. "Gets pretty cold up here in the winter, though, in case you've forgotten."

"Oh, I remember. That's why I'm keeping the condo in Miami. I'm not a total idiot."

"Hey, if you need a place to stay for a while, Phil's got a really big house."

"That's very generous of you," I say, laughing. "So, about the acoustic tour. Phil doesn't want to tour but he does want to get together to jam, maybe record a few songs. Cam definitely doesn't want to tour, but Phil thinks he can talk him into jamming with us."

"That could be fun."

"I agree. But for now, what do you think about doing the acoustic tour? Sounds like Derek can get it all set up to start whenever we're ready. I think it sounds good – we'll be home every other week."

"The Danny and Jesse show," he muses. "I just don't want to be away from Andrew that long. Even a week is too long."

"I agree. Take him on the road with us, if that makes it easier."

Danny thinks about it and then nods. "Sounds like a good idea. You gonna take Rachel?"

"If she wants to go on the road with us, sure. Probably what I should have done thirty years ago."

"Tough to make good decisions as a young man." Danny squints up toward the treetops for a moment. "Let me talk it over with Andrew. If he's okay with it, I'm in."

We shake hands, and then I pull him into a hug.

"Who'd have ever thought it," Danny says when we separate. "Jesse Maze, hugging men of his own free will."

"You're the second guy I've hugged today," I say. "But don't go getting any ideas. I'm not ready to join your team."

"Don't worry about that," Danny says, laughing. "We don't want you."

I promise to get in touch within a few days to bang out the details of the acoustic tour, and then turn to go. Halfway down the walkway, I turn around to ask about something that's been bothering me.

"It's been a long time, man. You think anyone will still want to see us play together?"

"I don't know." He shrugs. "But I know I want to see it."

We smile at each other, and with a last wave Danny steps back inside and closes the front door.

A couple minutes later we pull into Rachel's driveway. Ellie comes to the window and waves to us. We smile and wave back. When Rachel reaches for the door handle, I stop her.

"I need to talk to you for a minute."

She nods, looking a bit apprehensive. I'm reminded of when we were teenagers, boyfriend and girlfriend in the throes of first love and still living with our parents. On our first dates I used my father's car, a 1980 Pontiac Grand Prix, with plenty of room in the back seat. Unfortunately for me, Rachel was a good girl and made me wait what seemed like an eternity and we never made that short, thrilling leap into the back seat of the Grand Prix. After a few months I was able to purchase my own car, a 1973 Pinto wagon. I told my parents that I'd bought a wagon because we needed something to haul around the band's gear, but really I'd purchased it because of what I saw as the carnal advantages of a roomier back seat. I'd come to find out that it didn't serve either purpose very well, though at seventeen years old it didn't really matter. I'd have been happy doing it in a dusty broom closet.

Most of the important things that occurred between us in those exciting early years, when just hearing the other's name would set our hearts pounding wildly, happened in that Pinto. Not losing our virginity – that happened in the Brennan's fishing camp, which I can see on my left, across the cove. But the countless other sexual encounters – we were like experimental rabbits, it was all so new and wonderful – along with the first time we said we loved each other, the long talks about our future together, even the emotional night when Rachel told me she was pregnant – all took place in that rusty old car. And here we are again.

"So, this morning . . . we never really answered the question of where we go from here."

"I guess we got a little distracted."

She flashes the same wicked smile I remember so well from high school, and I'm ready to jump into the back seat. She'll be impressed – I've finally learned how to unhook a bra. But, first things first.

"I've decided to move back to Apple Brook, to be close to you and Megan and Ellie. I'm going to look for a house nearby. Something to rent or buy on the lake, hopefully, so I'll be close by." I hesitate, then say, "I hope you don't have a problem with that."

"Actually, I do," she says, and my stomach drops.

"You do? I was, well, hoping you might be happy about it. After last night, you know. And this morning."

"My problem is, why would you live somewhere else? Why not just move in here, with me?"

I stare at her for a long moment, not sure how to reply.

"I realize it's moving fast," Rachel says. "But we're so comfortable together, it sometimes seems like all the years apart was just a long weekend. Like John Lennon's Lost Weekend."

"Much longer, though. But just as wild."

"For one of us, anyway." She smiles. "The way I see it, we're meant to be together. I've fought it for a long time because I don't want to be hurt like that again."

"I wouldn't do that —" I begin, but she holds her hand in air like a crossing guard, cutting me off.

"I don't think you meant to do it the last time, Jesse. You're not a mean or vindictive person. In fact, you're very kind and good-hearted. But you are also quite self-destructive. And, when you were younger, you were selfish. I'm not blaming you," she adds, seeing the look of protest on my face. "I did then, but I've had a long time to think about it. You got a taste of success — and all the benefits that come with it — at a young age. Sex, drugs, and rock and roll. There aren't many young men who'd have behaved differently in your situation.

"I believe you are still the same person. Still kind, and still self-destructive. It's not all your fault — bad luck sometimes seems to follow you around like a sad little puppy. But you have changed, it seems, in one important way."

"I'm rich?"

Rachel smirks and slaps my forearm.

"No, wise ass. You put me and Megan and Ellie first, even above yourself."

From the corner of my eye I see movement. I look away from Rachel, to the house, where Ellie is back in the window. Her eyes are wide and she's holding her palms up in front of her, as if to say, "What the fuck?" Only my sweet little granddaughter would never say such a thing. That's just my own vulgar interpretation.

I hold up my index finger – "Just another minute." She shakes her head and frowns, and then disappears from the window. I wonder if she's actually angry, or just playing. Either way, it's good to know she's growing impatient, because that means she really wants to see me.

I look back at Rachel. Her eyes are a little wider than usual, her expression a little apprehensive. I agree with everything she's said, as I usually do. She's very intuitive when it comes to me, and the fact that she's nearly always right doesn't really surprise me anymore. I don't know about being kind and good-hearted – Dum Dum Dunham certainly doesn't share that opinion. But I am self-destructive, and only a very selfish person would give up his best friends, his daughter, and the love of his life because he believed he deserved more. I was younger then, that's true, but I don't know if that's much of an excuse.

A leopard can't change its spots, the saying goes. And here's where Rachel may be wrong, because in a way I haven't changed. I'm still selfish. I still want what's best for me. The difference between the young and the old Jesse Maze – well, middle-aged; certainly not old – is that now I know what's best for me. And what's best for me, at this stage of the game, is to be around friends and family. To be with a beautiful, intelligent, secure woman, not a bikini model who considers Paris Hilton to be a classic television star. What I need, in a sense, is a do-over.

I used to believe, if given the choice, I wouldn't change what I did when I was younger. I regret cheating on Rachel and walking out on her and Megan. I regret walking out on my three best friends at a high point in our career. But . . . if I hadn't cheated on Rachel, with all the temptation that comes the way of a young man with a guitar and growing fame, I'd have always wondered what I was missing. And that curiosity may have eventually overwhelmed me into cheating on her later, when I was married, with more children. Not to say what I did was right, but the possible alternative would have caused even more pain.

And while the band was at a high point professionally, the guys in the band were scraping bottom, all fucked up on drugs and ego. We didn't write together anymore. Our next album would have been terrible because we were too messed up to write good music. And our friendships had eroded to the point where we barely spoke to each other. If I hadn't left the band, we'd have smashed into that wall we were hurtling toward at a hundred miles an hour, and sooner rather than later.

That's what I believed for a long time. It helped me deal with all the pain I'd caused to myself as well as others. My shrink encouraged me dig into that. It helped. I am different now. I want what's best for my girls. And I'm also the same. I still want what's best for me.

"What are you thinking?" Rachel asks. "Are you wondering whether or not you should move in here?"

I wasn't, not specifically, but now I am. I've lived with a lot of women; that's not the issue. What's different here is that I want this relationship to work out, to be the 'happily ever after' that most humans are in search of. The other women I've lived with over the years, while all wonderful and unique and beautiful, were like the disposable paper plates you use at a picnic.

Rachel is that good china that you cherish and only bring out on the most special occasions.

"Are you sure about this?" I say. "Don't you think there should be a trial period, or something like that?"

"The last thirty-five years have been our trial period, Jesse," she says, laughing softly. "I think that's long enough. We're in our fifties now. Time's getting short. At our age, if you want to do something, it's best to not sit around thinking about it."

"Some people might call that a negative, defeatist attitude."

"Those people didn't watch their parents die not much older than I am now." She smiles grimly. "And I see it as having a very positive attitude. None of us knows how much time we have on our little adventure here on earth, but we do know that the end is growing closer every day. Instead of moping around and worrying about it, I'm going to do what I want, what's right for me. What's right for me is love. I love you, and you love me. It's time we finally act like it."

"Well, gee. After a speech like that, I can't really say no, can I?" I lean over to kiss her. "Want to try out the back seat?"

Gently, Rachel takes my face in both hands and turns it toward the house, where our granddaughter is standing in the open doorway, glaring at us with her hands on her hips and her mouth tight.

"I remember your mother giving us that same look," I say.

"Me too," she sighs. "We'd better get inside, before we're grounded."

23

Megan and I walk across the yard down to the lake. The dock is out of the water and stacked in several pieces next to a massive oak tree to our left. The lake is flat and quiet, peaceful yet lonely, and rimmed with the bright reflection of fall foliage.

I pick up a small gray, flat rock and try to skim it across the water's flat surface. The rock skips five times before disappearing with one last feeble plunk.

"Ellie's glad you came up for her birthday," Megan says. "You definitely made her weekend."

"How about you? Are you glad I'm here?"

"Uh, yeah, I suppose I am," she says carefully. "Most anything that makes Ellie happy makes me happy as well."

"I understand that." I crouch to grab another flat rock from the wet sand at the water's edge. "But that's not really what I was asking."

"I know." She sighs. "It was surprisingly nice having you home." After pausing for a moment, she says, "Really, it's not all that surprising. It was usually nice having you around when I was growing up. The problem was, it hardly ever happened, and when you left, I never knew when or if I'd see you again."

"I really am sorry about that."

Leaning sideways, I toss the rock from around waist height, using mostly my wrist. My angle is off and instead of skipping across the surface, there's a thick *plunk* and the rock sinks to the bottom like a torpedoed ship.

"I've learned to deal with it," she says, gazing across the lake. "But I don't want Ellie to go through what I did. I want you to promise that you won't do that to her. If you want to redeem yourself for your actions during my childhood, be the grandfather Ellie deserves and keep in touch with her regularly. Text. Email. Use Skype or Facetime. It doesn't matter to me how you do it."

"I can do even better than that," I say, and then I tell her about my plans to move back to Apple Brook. "Mom has asked me to move in with her. We've been talking a lot over the past few days, and we've decided that there are feelings between us that neither one of us wants to ignore any longer. We want to start over together." I've been staring at the water as I talk, and when I look at Megan, I see that she's staring at me with an expression I can't read. "So, what do you think?"

Her stare is a bit unnerving – she doesn't seem to blink – and in it I see a strong resemblance to her grandfather. He'd fixed me with that same stare many times and I never knew if I was about to be shot or welcomed to the family. His gaze, like Megan's, took in everything while giving away nothing. From what I understand, Mr. Brennan was an excellent poker player. I have no doubt that Megan could be as well.

"I don't know, Dad. Mom is level-headed and intelligent and knows what she wants, but this seems a little fast."

"I agree. I'd planned to just move up here for a little bit, rent a house, see how it goes. But your mother said we're old and have to move quickly before we die."

Megan smiles. "I doubt that's how she phrased it, but I can hear her saying something along those lines."

She turns back to the lake and stares off, deep in thought. I bend over, find a rock about the size and weight of a golf ball, and throw it as far as I can into the lake. It doesn't go very far but causes a good splash and ripples on the surface of the still water. It also causes a slight pain in my shoulder. Yet another small but significant sign that I'm aging. I roll my shoulder in a circle, trying to work out the kink.

"And you," she says. "How do you feel about moving in with Mom after all these years? Can you do it without hurting her, and us?"

*That, my dear, is the million-dollar question.* I've never had a relationship that didn't end. Technically, I don't even know if I might still be in a relationship. Kendra broke up with me to move in with the photographer, but it sounds like she didn't even have time to move in with him before discovering his other affairs. For all I know, she may have moved right back into the condo in Miami. I hope not. But that's the sort of relationship I'm used to, one based on confusion and chaos.

"Yeah, I think so," I say at last. "I'm going to do my best. Your mom's the only woman I've ever truly loved, and I love the three of you more than anything in the world."

"Think that's enough?'

"I don't know. I'm not a perfect man." Megan makes a sound like a horse blowing, and I smile. "Yeah, you know that. But I want to be with my family. I want some sort of stability. I want . . . this." I gesture to the lake, the trees, the peace and quiet and beauty of our surroundings. "And I promise, no matter what, to always be honest with all of you. I may fuck up at times, but I'll be honest about it."

For a long time, Megan stares silently across the lake. I don't say anything – I've learned that my talking rarely makes a situation better. I continue to search for rocks along the shoreline and toss them into the lake, enjoying the tranquility of such a simple act.

"When are you planning to do this?" she finally asks, still staring into the distance.

"I'll stay in Miami for a couple of weeks, I figure. Get things sorted out. I'm going to keep the condo down there because I don't know how I'll feel in the middle of a Maine winter. I may need to take us all down there for a break. You'll love it."

She glances at me, her eyebrows raised, but says nothing.

"I haven't had much time to think about this or talk it over with your mother, but I'd like to be back here before Thanksgiving. I may go on tour with Danny for a couple of months – we're planning an acoustic tour – but that won't be until next year. Spring, probably."

"Wait." Now she looks at me. "You're going to leave Mom and go back on tour, right after moving in with her?"

"I'm planning to take her with me, if she wants to. I hope she does. Danny's probably going to take Andrew too. And it's going to be a week on, week off type gig. We won't be away for long, and your mom will hopefully be with me."

This seems to satisfy her. She nods, then looks back at the house.

"I don't want you to say anything to Ellie about moving here. Not yet."

"Okay, but why?"

"I want to make sure you do what you say you'll do. Many times, when I was a kid, you said you'd visit again soon, and I wouldn't see you for two or three years. Doesn't do much for developing a kid's sense of trust."

"No, I don't imagine it would," I mumble. "That's fine. I understand. I won't say anything to her until I come back next month." I smile. "Maybe we can surprise her with it on Thanksgiving."

Megan nods, but does not smile. "Maybe."

"So, what are your feelings about having me around all the time?"

She shrugs, and I can almost hear the clang as the walls go up.

"No feelings at all?"

"For so long, I've tried to have no feelings at all regarding you. Sometimes bitterness and anger seep through." She watches a flock of birds fly over the house and sighs. "I always wondered what it would be like to have you around, like a real dad, like all my friends' dads. I guess it might be nice to see you, go to lunch or for walks, to talk to you reg –"

Her voice catches in her throat and she turns away from me. Instinctively, I put my arm around her. She pushes against me but then relents, leaning her head against my shoulder and wrapping her arms around me. I feel myself getting choked up again, but this time I'm not embarrassed.

When Megan pulls back to wipe her eyes, she appears disconcerted by the tears running down my cheeks.

"Are you . . . are you crying?" she asks.

"I am," I say, wiping the tears on the back of my hand. "This was a touching moment. My daughter loves me."

I choke up again, and this time I am a little embarrassed.

"But –" she shakes her head in confusion "– you never cry. Do you?"

"Sure. I cried when you married Sid."

She half-laughs, half-cries. "Well, that's understandable." She wraps her arms around my waist and squeezes. "I do love you, Dad," she says into my chest.

If there was any doubt about whether or not I was making the right decision by moving back to Apple Brook, it has disappeared. I feel like the Grinch when his heart grows three sizes.

A door slams. Megan and I, still locked in an embrace, both turn our heads toward the house, where Ellie is standing on the top step outside the porch.

"You need to leave soon, Grampy, or you'll miss your plane. It's twelve-thirty."

"We'll be inside in a minute, honey," Megan says.

After a long, quizzical look, Ellie waves and disappears inside. I kiss Megan on the forehead before we separate to wipe our faces, both of us softly laughing with embarrassment. A couple of minutes later we're red-eyed but otherwise back to normal.

"Remember," Megan says, as we walk toward the house, "don't say anything to Ellie. Not that I don't believe you're coming back, but . . ."

"Yeah, I understand. No problem."

With one last look back at the lake, I follow her up the back steps and into the house.

You'd think I would have packed, knowing I was leaving this afternoon. But the unexpected conjugal change in my sleeping arrangements over the past few hours has left me pleasantly disconcerted. Luckily for me, Rachel already packed my bag and placed it at the bottom of the stairway, along with my guitar.

"I wish you didn't have to leave," says Ellie, with a sad little pout.

"Me too. But I'll see you again soon, I promise."

I ignore the sharp stare I feel coming from Megan, but I don't say anything more. I see her whispering to Rachel and assume she's relaying her wish that we say nothing to Ellie until I actually come back and move in.

"Are you going to come to my birthday party next year?"

"Yeah, I think I can arrange that."

I pull her into a tight hug and hold on for a long moment. She doesn't cry and neither do I. Must have drained my tear ducts in the backyard. When we separate, I pick up my guitar and hand it to her.

"Give this to your friend Tyler."

"Really?"

"Tell him it's a musical instrument, a guitar. People used to play them, back when music was great and came from the heart and soul. Before untalented morons started buying computer-generated beats and pushing a button to create plastic, soulless music with lyrics that a vulgar five-year-old could have come up with."

"Whoa, Grampy." Ellie takes an exaggerated step backward. "Tell us how you really feel."

I laugh. "You're right, sorry. Just an old man complaining about kids today, I guess. Tell him it's a thank you gift for helping us out the other night. He might want to try to learn how to play it, because I think the kid's got talent and might find it more fulfilling to actually create music."

"That's better."

She holds the guitar awkwardly, cradling it in both arms like she's carrying a load of firewood. At this moment I can see both the gangly, awkward girl of early adolescence and the beautiful young woman she will soon become.

"Oh, and tell him that guitar once belonged to Glenn Frey, of the Eagles. It's worth quite a bit of money. Have Tyler look him up, it'll help expand his limited knowledge of music."

"I've heard of the Eagles, Grampy."

"I know you have, sweetie, but has Mr. "Yo Lit Fire Sweet Bro"?"

With a smirk, Ellie stands on her toes, kisses me on the cheek, and carries the guitar into the game room, where, I assume, she'll call Tyler. Or text. I don't think kids call each other anymore.

"That guitar was once owned by Glenn Frey?" Rachel whispers in amazement.

"Nah. I just want to mess with the kid a little."

Megan snorts, and Rachel slaps me on the arm.

"That's not very nice at all! What if he tries to sell the guitar and finds out that Glenn Frey never owned it and it's only worth fifty dollars?"

"Well, maybe he should play the guitar instead of selling it. And it's not a fifty-dollar guitar – I paid about a thousand for it. Plus," I add, with a cocky smile, "it might not have belonged to Glenn Frey, but it was owned and played by Jesse Maze of the Dropouts. That should affect the value some."

"So, we're back down to fifty dollars," says Megan, causing us all to laugh.

After glancing at the clock on the wall, I say, "I'd better get going." I pick my bag up from the floor. "My plane takes off in two hours, and I still have to return my rental car and listen to their shit about damaging the merchandise."

"I promise, that will be taken care of soon enough," Rachel says, an irritated gleam in her eyes. "And if they give you a hassle, just show them the video of you having your head run into the door. Maybe they've seen it already. Seems like everyone else has."

"If they give me a hassle, I'm just walking out. I have a plane to catch."

I pull Megan into a one-armed hug, give her a quick peck on the cheek, and tell her that I'll see her on Thanksgiving. She gives a short nod, making it clear that she'll believe it when she sees it. Then she gives me a tight smile and goes into the game room to check on Ellie.

Rachel looks up at me, tears in her eyes, and hugs me tightly. Just when I'm about to mention that I have a plane to catch, she loosens her hold.

"I'm going to miss you," she says.

"I should be back in a couple of weeks. I'll call you tonight when I get in, and we can talk about our future. We never really did talk about it."

"Not much to talk about, I don't think. You, me, together . . . and they lived happily ever after."

I smile and kiss her. She holds my hand as we move to the front door. I look outside at the SUV, black and shiny in the high autumn sun.

"Last chance to try out the backseat," I say. "I promise, I'll be quick."

"Just what every woman loves to hear."

"I'll take that as a no?"

"No. But don't worry – they'll be plenty of opportunities in the future."

I nod, kiss her again, and open the door. As I'm crossing the driveway, she calls my name.

"How about if we Facetime tonight, instead of just talking on the phone? Then we can see each other. You can show me around your condo in Miami."

"It's a date," I say, praying that Kendra hasn't decided to move back in.

The afternoon sun on her face in the open doorway shows her age, and at that moment I find her more beautiful than I ever have. I gaze at her, at the house, at the surrounding cornucopia of bright fall colors fluttering from the trees, at the calming stillness of the lake. They say you can't come home again, but I have.

Megan and Ellie join Rachel in the doorway and wave goodbye as I turn the SUV around. With a final wave, I head down the driveway, on the road to the airport and back to Miami. I'm sad, but it's easier knowing that I'll be back soon.

I've said it before, but this time things are different. This time, I mean it.